SUMMER FLING

Praise for Jean Copeland

The Revelation of Beatice Darby

"Debut author Jean Copeland has come out with a debut novel that is abnormally superb."—*Curve Magazine*

"…filled with emotion and the understanding of what it feels like for a girl to discover that she likes girls and what it will do to her life."—*The Lesbian Review*

"Uplifting and an amazing first novel for Jean Copeland." —*Inked Rainbow Reads*

The Second Wave

"This is a must-read for anyone who enjoys romances and for those who like stories with a bit of a nostalgic or historic theme."—*The Lesbian Review*

"Copeland shines a light on characters rarely depicted in romance, or in pop culture in general."—*The Lesbrary*

By the Author

The Revelation of Beatrice Darby

The Second Wave

Summer Fling

SUMMER FLING

by

Jean Copeland

2017

This Trade Paperback Original Is Published By
Bold Strokes Books, Inc.
P.O. Box 249
Valley Falls, NY 12185

First Edition: September 2017

CREDITS
EDITOR: SHELLEY THRASHER
PRODUCTION DESIGN: STACIA SEAMAN
COVER DESIGN BY MELODY POND

Acknowledgments

Writing is a solitary process for sure, but sharing it with the world is anything but. That's why I have so many people to thank for their contributions during every step of my novel-writing journey. I'll start with the readers who buy my books and motivate me to write with steadfast discipline. To my lifelong friends, proofreader Anne Santello and photographer Denise Spallone, for their eagerness to assist me in any capacity needed. To all my other friends, near and far, who faithfully buy my books, retweet my tweets, and share Facebook posts promoting my work. I'm also thankful for the professional support I receive from the ladies at Bold Strokes Books, my tireless editor, Shelley Thrasher, and the sister BSB authors whom I also call friends. Of course, I'd be remiss if didn't thank my father, James, for his endless support of everything I've ever done, and my girlfriend, Jen, for her patience and willingness to schlep all over with me to signing events.

In memory of Sandy "Sondy" Choronzy Borchert
You'll always be part of our cocktail parties.

Chapter One

The Intervention

Kate Randall knelt in the cemetery and ran her fingers over the grass under which lay buried memories of the woman she was supposed to spend her life with. She'd lost Lydia exactly four years ago and was grateful that her best friend, Didi Huston, had decided it was too hot to hike across the grounds with her. She needed a moment to reflect.

"Kate," Didi shouted. She trudged up the embankment, fanning her ample cleavage and glistening olive skin with a handful of paper napkins. "What the hell are you doing up here?"

"What do you mean?" Kate asked, playing innocent. "I'm visiting my father's grave."

"Your father's grave is over..." Didi's red, overheated face blanched. "For the love of Edith Windsor, Kate," she roared. "Seriously?"

"What? It was hot over there. I needed some shade." She stood quickly and brushed grass clippings from her knees.

Didi glared at her. "You're looking for that urn of card and photo ashes, aren't you?"

Kate wilted in shame. "Today's the anniversary of when I lost Lydia."

"Yeah. You lost her all right—to the skank she cheated on you with. Viv and I didn't come over that night with a bottle of vodka and an acetylene torch so I could find you meditating over her burnt-up crap four years later. It's sick."

"Okay, Didi," Kate said calmly. "Point taken."

"We buried it here for you to symbolically lay that bitter part of your past to rest—not to rehash it every year."

"I'm aware of that," Kate said.

"How are you supposed to move on with someone new if you're still hanging on to that baggage?"

"I said all right. I had a little slipup. In retrospect, we probably should've buried it on the other side of the cemetery, not so close to my dad."

"Um, okay, fine, but I'm not helping you exhume anything today. It's too friggin' hot. Now let's go." Didi looped her arm through Kate's. "Viv is waiting for us. We have to get to the train station. Hi, Mr. Randall," she said as they passed Kate's father's headstone. "I'm only glad Viv wasn't here to witness this."

Kate rolled her eyes as Didi led her from the cemetery like a teacher dragging her to the principal's office.

On the train ride into New York City, Didi and Kate sat quietly, each scrolling her cell phone. Suddenly, Kate's dinged with an email notification.

"What the hell?" Her jaw nearly unhinged as she read the email.

Didi glanced out the window.

"Dee, why am I getting a notification from a woman on a dating site that I never signed up for?"

Didi eluded Kate's eyes by checking her phone. "How do you know you didn't sign up for it? Maybe you forgot."

"I've never signed up for a dating site in my life. Please tell me this isn't your handiwork."

"No, honest," Didi said. "But it's a brilliant idea, nonetheless."

"No, it isn't." Kate planted her elbows on her knees and frantically composed a text. "Fucking Viv. Wait till I get my hands around her skinny brown neck."

"Kate, don't blast her a new one."

"Don't blast her a new one? She'll be lucky if that's all I do to her."

"Keep it down," Didi said out of the corner of her mouth. "We're in the quiet car. They're gonna escort you off at the next stop like they do the crazies."

"You two have pulled a lot of stunts with me over the last year, but this has gone too far."

"Just tell her to deactivate the account. No biggie."

"You're missing the point again, Didi. I'm single because I want to be. I don't need you guys meddling in my personal life like there's something wrong with it. It doesn't need fixing."

"Kate, Lydia left four years ago. You say you're over her, but you make no effort to get out and meet anyone. And then I catch you being all weird and morose over her in a cemetery."

"I am over her," Kate said. "If you want the truth, that moment wasn't about her at all. It was about me honoring how strong I've become since she left."

Didi squeezed her hand. "You have. You're a different person now, a much better one. You dealt with your codependency issues in therapy, and I've never seen you more confident and content in the thirty-plus years I've known you."

Kate smiled and held her hand in return. "Aww, thanks, Didi."

"Now don't you think it's time you find someone to share all this fabulousness with?"

Kate groaned in defeat. "I will someday, when the right woman comes along. And not through the devious, half-assed schemes you and Viv keep plotting."

"I beg your pardon. Devious? Half-assed?"

"Come on. Look what I've had to endure over the last year. On three separate occasions, I think we're going to happy hour only to have a random single woman you know happen to show up. I almost wouldn't have minded the scam if they were even remotely right for me."

"They were lovely ladies. You're too picky."

"Let's not forget when we went to dinner, and you failed to mention the lesbian speed-dating event at the restaurant. That you signed me up for. And now this?"

Kate's email dinged again.

"Oh, look." She handed her phone to Didi. "She's seventy-three and from North Dakota. She wants to chat with me. Am I being too picky if I decline?"

"She's attractive for her age, and she's well-educated," Didi said meekly.

"That's great, except I'm forty-seven and live in Connecticut."

Didi glanced at the screen. "But it says she's willing to relocate for the right woman."

"You can't be serious."

"Well, you can't expect to hit the jackpot on every spin."

"Do you know how to get me off this site?" Kate shoved her phone at her. "Viv isn't answering my text."

"She probably went into hiding," Didi mumbled as she poked at the account deactivation screen.

Kate slumped down in the seat, closed her eyes, and sighed.

"C'mon. Don't be mad at us, Katie. Yes, our efforts have been somewhat unorthodox at times, but we love you and just want you to be happy."

"Then leave me alone."

"Kate, are you really mad at us?"

She let Didi stew for a while.

"Kate?" Didi elbowed her in the side.

"Not mad, frustrated. I'm fine being single, and I don't want you and Viv to pressure me anymore." Her tone softened. "Just because you're both pussy hounds."

"Pussy hound?" Didi said. "I'll take that to mean I have to make up for a lot of lost time."

"What's Viv's excuse?"

"She's, um, how shall I put this? She's, uh…strong-minded. Once she finds the woman she wants, she doesn't give up without a fight."

"Yeah," Kate said. "Her stalking case was the most challenging of my legal career. It nearly precipitated an early retirement." She chuckled.

"I can't believe her father didn't know any judges he could've thrown money at."

"He didn't need to," Kate said. "I did a fine job on her defense. She doesn't have a record, thanks to my legal expertise."

"I hope you've calmed down enough that when you see her in fifteen minutes, you don't end up with a record of your own."

"Am I off that site?"

"Yes," Didi said. "And I promise not to meddle any more."

"Good." Kate smiled and patted her hand.

Didi smiled back. "As far as I'm concerned, you can die a reclusive old woman surrounded by your thirty-seven loving felines."

Kate glared at her. "When you commit to something, you don't screw around."

"Damn right. This actually works out better for me. One less beautiful, successful blonde to compete with. It's bad enough all I have to do is glance in the direction of an attractive woman, and Viv appears like cockroaches in the kitchen of a Times Square theme restaurant."

"I can't tell you how much I'm looking forward to watching two middle-aged lesbians battle for the same woman at an overcrowded bar."

"You'll be sorry you're not in the game. Tonight's the Pride Week kickoff at Moxy's. It's going to be epic."

"I don't know how I let you convince me to come."

Didi smiled. "Like Bobby Darin sings, there's nothing like Sundays in New York."

"Maybe I'll go home after dinner," Kate said.

"No way," Didi said as the train screeched into the station. "You're always working or making up excuses why you can't go out with us. You owe your two best friends a girls' day in the City."

"Fine."

They bumped shoulders as the train lurched to a halt.

"You can run interference for me with Viv when I spot the woman of my dreams," Didi said. "I need all the help I can get."

"Don't be ridiculous. You have so much to offer a woman."

Didi pursed her lips. "Her father's a millionaire and her mother's a former supermodel. She's got it all. What do I have going for me? I'm a middle-class legal secretary with minimal experience with women and a big Italian ass. No contest."

"Yes, she's got all that, but she's also a stage-five clinger. She may get the ladies, but she has a worse track record with long-term relationships than Taylor Swift."

Didi shook her head. "I'd love to have her problems for a day."

"Hey," Kate said, patting Didi's shoulder. "Where's all this self-doubt coming from? You're adorable, funny, and you'll make some woman a wonderful wife someday—when you finally outgrow your lesbian puberty."

Didi leaned her head against Kate's. "Thanks, Katie. And don't worry. My future wife and I won't let you spend holidays alone having 9-Lives casserole for dinner."

"Thanks."

"Hey, mamas," Viv yelled as they walked out of Grand Central Station into the blistering heat of Forty-second Street.

"Our chariot," Kate said, indicating the open limousine door.

The girls crawled into the Chanel No. 5–scented car, and Vivienne swept them up in a group hug as the chauffeur drove off.

"Damn," Didi said. "I'm glad your daddy's rich and your mama's good-looking. It's hot as Hades out there."

Viv sucked her teeth. "Girl, whatchu mean about my parents? I'm rich, and I'm good-looking. But don't get any ideas."

"Yeah, right," Didi said. "You're not my type."

"Why? Because I'm biracial?"

"No, because you're an a-hole."

The ladies roared with laughter.

"How I've missed my girls," Viv said. "I'm honored you could finally carve some time out of your busy schedule, Kate."

"Don't push it, Viv," Kate said. "I only got over being violently pissed at you fifteen minutes ago."

Vivienne threw her arm around Kate. "Look. I'm sorry about that dating site. It wasn't meant as a prank or anything. I sincerely thought it might be the push you needed to put yourself out there."

"What's so great about being 'out there'?" she asked. "You two are out there. How's that been working out for you?"

Didi and Viv exchanged helpless glances.

"Can't we just have a genuine girls' night out? A nice dinner and some drinks after at the club?"

"Of course," Viv said.

Didi nodded. "Absolutely."

"No skirt-chasing," Viv said.

Didi confirmed the promise. "Just the three of us."

"You guys are so full of it," Kate said.

They cackled at Kate as Viv popped the cork on a bottle of Dom Perignon.

Chapter Two

The Setup

The bass of Moxy's house music thrummed through Kate's lungs. She scanned the eclectic crowd of women as she sipped a cosmo. Never a fan of the bar scene, she'd found it particularly disheartening to be tossed back into the tempest in her forties. But since she was there with her friends, she figured she might as well seize the moment—after she stifled a yawn.

Didi and Viv, on the other hand, were like college students on dollar draft night.

"One night at Moxy's is all it takes," Didi said, her eyes ravaging the pages of *Girl Talk*.

"For what?" Viv sipped from a flute of Cristal.

"I don't know," Didi said. "That's what this tourist magazine says."

"Maybe tonight is the night I'll meet the one." Viv's eyes were wide with possibility. "Peace out, Maia."

Kate and Didi exchanged looks.

"I hope so," Kate said. "But do yourself a favor and wait until you've had at least two dates before you move her in."

"I don't do that," Viv said.

Kate arched an eyebrow.

Didi jumped in. "Name one girl in the last twenty years you dated without moving her in."

Viv scoured her memory for several moments. "I can't help that I'm a romantic. Some women actually find that appealing."

"There's a fine line between hopeless romantic and having a Lifetime movie made about your relationship," Kate said.

Viv wielded her manicured finger between them. "Don't be hatin' on me because I get more play than both of you."

"You also get more restraining orders than we do," Didi said.

"One. I've had one restraining order in my life." Viv sipped her drink. "We've all had that one girl we got a little Glenn Close over. That hardly makes me a stalker."

"Right," Didi said. "The good news is your attorney is right here in case you get a little too *Glenn Close* again tonight."

"This attorney is off the clock, so you both better behave," Kate said. "Besides, I'm not staying all night."

"What do you mean?" Didi said. "You can't leave early. Look, this hot singer is performing at ten." She fanned the advertisement in the magazine in Kate's face.

"And this concerns me how?" Kate said.

"Damn, girl," Viv said. "This doesn't do anything for you? You must be dead inside."

Kate grabbed the magazine. Jordan Squire. She had to admit the girl was hot—wild brown curls, ripped jeans revealing the right amount of thigh, and a guitar. Again, so what? She looked really young and, if she was true to her profession, probably had a girl in every dive she headlined.

"Of course she does something for me," Kate admitted. "Look at her. I'm sure she does something for everyone in here. But do you think I want to stick around and climb over you two and everyone else like bridesmaids diving for the wedding bouquet?"

Didi scoffed. "Kate, don't be ridiculous. You have just as much of a chance with her as anyone else in this joint."

"Yeah," Viv said. "Don't worry about me. I don't want her. I'm tired of white girls."

Kate chuckled at her friends. They were a handful, but luckily the size of their hearts eclipsed the collective mass of their insanity.

"Okay. I'll stay. I can't in good conscience bail on a girls' night out."

"That's the spirit," Didi said. She sipped her martini as she glanced around. "What a treat to be in a club and not be the oldest one in it for once." She indicated a trio of silver-haired sisters holding court at the enormous circular bar in the middle of the club. "I feel like we should be carded or something."

Kate agreed with a giggle.

"Hmm, I wonder if Maia will show up," Viv said. "I'm thinking about asking her to Aruba next month."

Kate jerked her head toward her. "Maia. As in Maia, the complainant on the aforementioned restraining order?"

Didi shot Kate a look and then, "Unless you have a chloroform rag in your purse, how do you propose to convince her to go?"

Viv rolled her eyes. "It's all good. I'm seeing a counselor."

"Another one?" Didi said.

"Yes. One more in tune to the needs of lesbian relationships. We're working on my narcissism issues. I'm quite motivated this time."

"That's great," Kate said, trying to be supportive. "But maybe you ought to cut your losses with Maia and start fresh with someone new."

"That's a defeatist attitude, Kate," Viv said. "Nobody ever got anywhere in life by giving up. Where would aviation be without Howard Hughes's *Spruce Goose*?"

Kate pondered that for a moment. "Einstein didn't give up either, and he ended up with the formula for the nuclear bomb."

"Serial killers," Didi said. "Serial killers don't give up either."

Viv and Kate glared at Didi.

They had migrated toward the stage for a prime position in the crowd for the evening's featured event, Jordan Squire and her acoustic guitar. Caught up in their conversation, Kate hadn't realized she was right in front of the stage until the lights went out and Jordan leaped out with a hard strum of her guitar.

It took Kate's eyes about a day to climb Jordan's long legs to her muscled forearm to her luscious lips pressing against the mic. Jordan had the audience mesmerized through her opening song as she whipped her tresses around and belted out a husky rendition of Dusty Springfield's "Son of a Preacher Man."

As hardened as she thought she was, Kate was by no means immune to her allure.

"She's amazing," Didi shouted to Kate over the cheers. "What a voice."

"Yeah," Kate said, still staring at Jordan.

"Thank you, ladies," Jordan said, flipping her hair off her face. "Welcome to Moxy's Pride Week dance. How y'all feeling tonight?"

Cheers thundered through the music hall.

"You mind if I do an original for you?"

The crowd again cheered their approval. As Jordan strummed the intro to the song, Kate did a double take. Was she making eye contact with her? No, of course not. It was so hard to tell under the flickering lights. She could be looking at anyone or no one at all in the sea of faces. Whatever. She was adorable to stare at regardless.

A few more songs into the set, Didi turned to Kate. "Is Jordan looking at you?"

"I don't know," Kate said. "I thought she was at one point."

"Oh my God," Didi said, clutching Kate's shoulders. "She's flirting with you."

"Shut up. No, she's not."

"Yes, she is," Didi insisted.

"No, she isn't."

Jordan finished her song and flung her guitar pick at Kate, settling the dispute once and for all. Kate smiled a *thank you*, Jordan winked a *you're welcome*, and off into her next original she went.

"You lucky bitch," Didi said. "Where did Viv disappear to? She's missing this. Kate, you're finally going to get laid."

Appalled at the suggestion, Kate shoved Didi away from her and inadvertently into a cluster of women next to them.

"I'm sorry," she mouthed to them as they helped Didi regain her balance.

Toward the end of Jordan's first set, Kate needed space and air. She swam through the undulating bodies toward the ladies' room, hoping to find Viv along the way. What was happening to her? A sexy young woman flirted a little, and suddenly, she was falling apart. Where the hell was Viv?

She shouldered open the bathroom door, slammed the stall door behind her, and sucked in stagnant air. Maybe the girls were right. Maybe she needed to get back out onto the dating scene—if for no other reason, to get reacquainted with the custom of meeting and interacting with another female. She sat on the toilet and texted Viv. No response.

As she left the ladies' room, she contemplated texting them both and sneaking home to New Haven on her own. She veered down an unfamiliar hall and nearly physically ran into Jordan Squire as she was exiting the backstage area.

"Oh, I'm sorry," Kate said, her eyes locking with Jordan's.

"No, that's okay. My bad," Jordan said. "Hey, I saw you in the audience before. I hope my singing didn't drive you away." Her face broke into the most alarmingly cute smile.

"Not at all," Kate said. "You're fantastic, actually, especially your originals."

"Thanks. Well, I'll be selling copies of my debut CD after my second set. Hang around if you can."

"Okay, sure," Kate said. "I'd love to get a copy."

They held each other in a lingering glance before parting ways. As Kate searched for Didi in the dispersing crowd, she caught herself smiling and promptly relaxed her facial muscles. Then she smiled at having done that.

"Where have you been," Didi asked when Kate found her at the bar. "I thought you ditched us."

"Believe me, I thought about it. Where's Viv?"

"She's down at the Starbucks two blocks over. She met someone."

"Better at Starbucks than a hotel." Kate pondered the notion for a moment. "Are you sure the Starbucks isn't in a hotel?"

Didi shrugged. "Listen. Don't disappear again. Jordan's going back on in a few minutes. Maybe we can hang around after the show and you can talk to her."

"I just talked to her."

"What? What are you saying?"

"I got lost coming out of the bathroom and ran into her coming off stage. She told me to stick around and buy a CD after."

Didi's eyes bugged with possibilities. "We'll both get her CD, and you'll get her number."

"No. We'll get her CD and that's that."

"Kate, ask her for her number. What do you have to lose?"

"I don't want her number. She's clearly too young for me, and I'm not schlepping all the way down to the city to date someone."

"Are you kidding? Long-distance relationships are the best. Think of all the me-time you'll have. You can do whatever you want but still have someone to have sex and dinner with. It's brill."

"It's not brill. All that back-and-forth is a pain in the ass."

"You're a pain in the ass."

"There it is." Kate rolled her eyes. "Real mature."

Didi grabbed her by the arm. "C'mon. Let's go elbow our way back to our spot near the stage. Jordan'll be looking for you."

As strong as Kate's outward protests were, she was actually amused by Didi's throwback to high school chase games. It had been decades since Kate had embraced such innocent fun. Not that she was going to admit that to Didi.

After the show, Jordan might not have been looking for Kate, but she certainly seemed pleased when Kate's and Didi's turn in line came up. Her sage eyes flowered with apparent delight.

"Hi again. I'm glad you could stay," she said. "Would you like me to sign it?"

"Of course," Kate said.

"You can sign mine, too," Didi said. When Jordan finally peeled her eyes away from Kate, Didi gave her a petit wave.

"Thank you again," Jordan said to Kate. "I hope you can check out another show sometime."

Another lingering glance, this one awkward.

Kate exhaled. "Sure, I'll definitely try. But I live in Connecticut and don't make it into the City too often."

"She will," Didi said. "We'll check out your website for dates and stuff."

"Connecticut?" Jordan said to Kate. "I do a lot of shows there. That's because I live there, too." That smile again.

Women grumbled behind them, waiting for their chance at Jordan.

"Okay, well, uh, like she said, we'll watch your website for upcoming shows," Kate stammered.

"How about I let you know when I'm in the New Haven area," Jordan replied. "Got a card?"

Kate's lips parted but nothing came out.

"Yes, she does." Didi sprang into action, digging in her purse until she unearthed one at the bottom. "She'd love to hear from you," she said, handing her the crinkled card. "My cell's on there, too, just in case I can help you with anything."

Jordan smiled uncomfortably at Didi and then flashed Kate a wildly flirtatious grin that turned her to mush.

"Pleasure to meet you," Kate said. "See you around."

She grabbed Didi's sleeve and dragged her away. "We have to find Viv before she ends up engaged," she said.

Didi stopped before they reached the exit. "Kate, hang on. Don't you think you should wait until she's done?"

"No. Why would I do that?"

"You can't be that dense. She's totally into you."

"Didi, it was a little flirting. That's what she does. She's a lesbian singer trying to build a following. She's friendly with everyone."

"Yes, she was friendly with everyone, but she was into you. She wasn't looking at anyone else the way she was gazing into your gorgeous baby blues."

"Forget it," Kate said. "She's gotta be twenty years younger than me. I'm a stable, mature attorney. She's a kid who travels around singing at nightclubs. I like to be in bed by the time she takes the stage. Not exactly the ingredients for a successful match."

Didi scoffed. "Is there no end to your excuse-making? Let's go find Viv."

They walked the two city blocks to the location of Viv's last known whereabouts, the Village still vibrant and sweaty with Pride revelers after one a.m.

"I just found Jordan's artist page on Facebook," Didi said. "Wow. She's got a lot of followers. Go on it and like it."

"I will." Kate stared ahead pensively as Didi strolled beside her, preoccupied with her phone.

"It says she's from Westport."

"Yeah?"

"What's that, like a forty-minute ride for you," Didi said, her voice climbing a few octaves. "You guys are practically neighbors."

"Didi, I don't want to talk about her anymore." Kate's thoughts were still spinning from her interaction with Jordan. "Hey, is that Viv?" she said.

Viv was perched on a cement wall a block down from Starbucks, looking quite unlike an exotic, sophisticated cosmetics company heiress-slash-executive.

"What's the matter?" Kate said.

"Why are you sitting here alone?" Didi said.

Viv sighed. "Tonight was a disaster. Maia didn't show up at the club like I'd hoped, and this lovely young woman, Greta, I met at the bar turned out to be a straight woman scouting a third party for her husband's fiftieth birthday."

Kate called up patience from her dwindling reserve. "Viv, you need to reevaluate your criteria for what constitutes a disaster."

"And in all likelihood, Maia did show up tonight," Didi said. "But she saw you first."

Didi and Kate stifled a duet of giggles out of respect.

"Listen, it's late." Kate held out her hand to Viv. "Let's go to your place. We'll stay over. You'll feel better in the morning after a sleepover with your besties."

Viv slid off the wall, still pouty. "I'd feel better after a sleepover with Halle Berry and Charlize Theron."

"You're not exactly my first choice for a pajama party either," Didi said.

"Well, we're all we've got tonight," Kate said. "It'll have to be enough."

Viv melted into a smile. "It is."

They all looped arms together and walked to the corner to wait for Viv's driver to whisk them off to her posh apartment on the Upper West Side.

"Which rooms do you want us in?" Kate yawned as they walked into Viv's apartment.

"Can we all sleep in my bed tonight?" Viv said.

"Come on. Really?" Kate glanced around, still awed by the lavish digs overlooking Central Park she'd seen a hundred times before. "You have four bedrooms, and we all have to cram into your bed?"

"What you mean, cram? I've got a California king. Please?" She pouted. "I don't want to be alone."

"I'm not sleeping in the middle," Didi said. "I don't trust Viv. She's been single for like six months now."

Viv raised an eyebrow at her. "Bitch, please. You wish you could have a taste of this dulce de leche."

Kate stopped at the bedroom door and glanced back and forth between them. "I think I'll go sleep on the couch in the living room."

"No way," Viv said. "You're not leaving me in here with this thirsty old bag."

Kate rolled her eyes. "Why don't you two just do each other and get it over with?"

"Ewww," Viv and Didi yelled in unison.

"That'll never happen," Didi said. "We know too much about each other."

"Word," Viv said. "She's practically a virgin. I ain't got time for that."

"I am not a virgin," Didi said. "I've had steamy romances with women."

"Girl, you still got your training wheels on."

"No. I've slept with a whole slew of women," Didi said.

"I wouldn't go around advertising that," Viv said.

Kate watched them, fighting a smile. "I'm serious. I'll sleep down the hall. You two just get in bed and let it happen."

"Eh, why not?" Didi said to Kate. "You slept with her. Viv, we can complete the circle jerk."

Kate stared at Viv in horror. "You told her?"

With no defense, all Viv could do was shrug.

"I thought we'd agreed long ago to pretend that drunken college cliché never happened."

"I'm the one who should be offended, not you," Didi said. "I've known you since high school, and I had to hear it from Viv."

"Didi, take this as a lesson being that you've come late to the lesbian party," Kate said. "Don't sleep with your friends. And don't kiss and tell, especially if you sleep with your friends."

Viv raised her palms toward the vaulted ceiling. "Amen."

"Look, I'm really tired," Kate said. "I need some sleep."

"Okay," Viv said. "We're tired, too. Let's just all go to sleep. Kate, you're in the middle."

After their nightly beauty regimens, they got into bed in the agreed-upon order, and Viv shut off the light. After some throat-clearing and sheet-rustling, they settled into their positions. A dainty fart broke the silence. Didi and Viv giggled.

"Come on," Kate said. "Not while we're in the same bed. We're forty-seven years old, for God's sake."

Viv giggled louder. "We checked our maturity at the door when we all put on jammies and piled into one bed."

Kate threw the covers off her. "I'm going to sleep in the lobby."

She tried to get up, but Viv and Didi grabbed her arms and yanked her down.

"No, no. I swear we'll shut up now," Didi said.

"Yeah, yeah. Look. I'm going to sleep." Viv rolled over on her side facing the window.

After a few muffled snorts and giggles, the room finally fell quiet.

"I love you lunatics," Kate whispered.

Didi and Viv rolled on their sides toward Kate and cuddled up to her.

Chapter Three

Jaded, Party of One

The next day, Kate and Didi had an early lunch with Viv at the Four Seasons before heading back to Connecticut. Kate glanced out over Fifty-second Street, recalling the strange and surprising dream she'd had about Jordan Squire. In the dream, Jordan had signed the CD like she had in the club the night before, but she'd kissed Kate after handing it to her. It was a nice kiss—sweet and sensual—the kind that made Kate wish she could've slept a little longer.

"So what do you think about that, Kate?" Didi asked.

"Huh?"

"Exactly," Didi said. "I'm trying to have an intervention with Viv here about leaving Maia alone. Would you like to weigh in?"

"Right," Kate said. "Viv, don't text her anymore."

"I haven't texted her." Viv seemed proud of herself as she sipped her Bloody Mary.

"She sent a dozen roses to her work, anonymously," Didi said.

Kate nodded. "How did that work out?"

Viv stalled with another, longer sip. "She texted me and said she'd call the cops if anything else shows up for her anywhere or from anyone."

"Okay. Well, I think she's conveyed her position quite clearly. So that takes care of that," Kate said. Then, after a moment of no response, "Doesn't it?"

"One would hope," Didi said.

"Girls, she's still hurt right now. I need to give her more time."

Didi bit her fist and turned to Kate. "I could make the best joke about her getting time, but I won't do it. I'm trying too hard to be a better human being."

"Look, Maia's very special to me," Viv went on. "She's the one who inspired me to make a real change. I just want her to give me the chance to show her."

"Look, honey," Kate said, patting the top of Viv's hand. "It's great that you've gone back to therapy and finally recognize your problem with egocentrism and possessiveness. It's a huge step. But refusing to leave Maia alone after she broke up with you for being too selfish and possessive is showing her you're exactly the same person you were when she left you."

Viv seemed confused as her eyes appealed to Didi.

"Get over it and move on," Didi said and licked a drop of martini that spilled on her finger as she raised the glass.

"But Maia loved me," Viv said. "I know she did. She didn't want to break up."

"I know that but—" Kate said.

"If she sees I'm finally working through my issues, she'll want to give us another shot."

"Viv." Kate grasped her hand. "I understand how you feel, but I can tell you from experience that just because someone loved you once, that doesn't mean they'll fight for your relationship, no matter how long you've been together. Three months, eight months, or seventeen years—when it's over, it's over."

"She's right, Viv," Didi said. "She gave Lydia the seventeen best years of her life, and look where it's gotten her? She's a forty-seven-year-old shell of a woman, alone and bitter, petrified to let down her guard and love again. Don't be her, Viv. Don't be Kate. Free your soul for better things."

"I'm not bitter or petrified," Kate said. "Unlike the rest of you, I've learned from my mistakes."

"If you walked away from that sexy girl at Moxy's, you're petrified," Viv said.

"Why do these conversations always revert back to me?" Kate said. "I'm the most well-adjusted one in this trio. I'm perfectly satisfied with my life."

As if on cue, Didi slapped her hands on her thighs and used the chewed straw clenched in her teeth as a pointer. "Don't you see what's going on here, girls? We've reached a pivotal juncture in our lives. It's time we start living by our own rules. We may be older than we've ever been before, but we're also wiser and reeking with life experience."

"I attended a lecture similar to that idea last year." Kate tilted her head skeptically. "I paid eight hundred and fifty bucks for a weekend retreat in the Adirondacks called 'The Locus of Aging: Setting Your Own Place at Life's Banquet Table,' and I have to say, I'm not so convinced."

Didi huffed. "I'm trying to make an important point here."

"Sorry."

"Okay, so those self-help retreats are kind of hokey," Didi said, "but this is absolutely not the time to surrender to a fate of pre-menopausal night sweats and Maalox moments. This is our shining moment, ladies." Her voice reached a crescendo as she brought the theme home. "It's our last ticket to ride, our final opportunity to be everything we've ever dreamed of before we drop dead. So let's claim our destinies."

She leaned back in her seat and waited for the deluge of applause.

Kate smiled, and Viv offered a delicate hand clap.

"You overachievers are so irritating." Deflated, Didi wiped sweat from her forehead. "Man, it must be a hundred degrees in here. Don't they have any a/c in this place?"

"It's on," Kate said. "You're getting yourself overheated in your fervor."

"Girlfriend can sell it though," Viv said.

Kate nodded. "Yes, your spiel was very inspirational. You should package it for that retreat in the Adirondacks."

"Thanks." Didi smiled as she chewed the ice cubes in her water.

"You know, I think we need to defer to an important albeit overused maxim: everything happens for a reason. Lydia left me because our relationship ran its course. Didi, you haven't met the right woman yet because you still have some self-reflection to do, and Viv, well, all your relationships end because…"

Didi stepped up with the assist. "Because, uh, um, like me, you still have some self-reflection to do."

Kate nodded her gratitude. "It all comes down to serendipity. What we need will come to us in the right moment. In the meantime, we have to stay in the present to find our joy."

"If that's true, why are you pretending you didn't meet an amazing girl last night?" Didi said.

"I'm not pretending anything. Yes, she was amazing, but she's not for me. Here's something else to consider: evolved adults don't act on impulse and rush into things."

"Then you wouldn't mind if I went for her?" Didi asked.

Kate's head snapped up from her plate. "You?"

Didi nodded.

"Go right ahead," Kate said, straining to sound cool. "Be my guest—even though she's way too young for you."

"I don't care how old she is," Didi said. "She's beautiful, talented, and seems like a very sincere person."

"Good luck with that," Viv said, rolling her eyes as she signaled for the check.

"I don't need luck," Didi said. "I'm gonna set my place at life's buffet table, damn it."

"It's life's banquet table," Kate said.

"Whatever," Didi snapped. "I like buffet better—you know, all you can eat." She ended with a low, dirty laugh.

Viv challenged her with a look. "How the hell can you come out the closet a few years ago and act like you got it all together, when Kate and I have been gay all our lives and still haven't figured women out?"

"Speaking as a recovering repressed lesbian, I am intimately acquainted with self-doubt and confusion. If you two want to waste your time chasing women who don't want you or chasing no women at all, have at it. But I'm not wasting anything anymore. I'm gonna live it up, bitches." Didi concluded her speech with a flourish of her arm.

"Good for you," Kate said flatly. "We have to get to the train station."

"And I can't wait to see the look on your face when I parade that hot dish, Jordan Squire, in front of you and make you wish you'd got off your ass and gone for her yourself."

Kate humored Didi with a smile as they headed out of the restaurant. "And, Viv, if you decide to keep chasing Maia even after she's asked you not to, you should know that my retainer is triple what it is for clients who aren't morons."

"I'll make a note of it," Viv said.

❖

A few days later Kate returned to her office after spending much of the afternoon in probate court on behalf of an elderly lesbian widow. She dropped on the leather sofa in the reception area, lobbed her valise onto a nearby chair, and propped her feet up on the coffee table.

"Tough day?" Didi asked from her desk.

"I just hate seeing some of the old-school folks lose so much money because they didn't have wills or, in Margaret's case, a marriage license. Thankfully, these kinds of cases are phasing out with the younger generation."

Didi rose from her desk with a stretch and joined Kate on the couch. "Have you heard from Jordan?"

"Jordan? No. Why would I hear from her?"

"She asked for your business card days ago. Did you go on Facebook and like her page? Follow her on Twitter and Instagram?"

"I don't have Twit-agram, and I barely remember I have Facebook, so the answer is no."

"That's probably why she hasn't texted or called. Where's your phone? Let's go on and do it right now." She snatched the phone out of Kate's hand.

Kate dropped her head against the couch. "Didi, this is so stupid. Honestly, I have no interest in this girl, *girl* being the operative word."

"She's interested in you, and if, I mean when, she calls, I hope you'll have the sense to at least meet her one-on-one for a drink or something."

Kate exhaled, exasperated.

"Promise me if she asks you out, you'll go? You have absolutely nothing to lose—except another night home alone with your cat. And really, how many of those in one week can you take before you start preferring the company of her over humans."

"What do you mean *start* preferring?" Kate said with a wry smile.

"This is what scares me about you. C'mon. Promise me."

Kate chuckled and felt confident in humoring Didi. "All right, all right. If she asks me out, I'll go."

"Aces." Didi smiled with satisfaction as she ambled back to her desk. "Then you can introduce me to all her hot friends."

"Ah yes, the all-you-can-eat buffet you mentioned the other day." Kate strolled toward her office. "What's on the agenda for tomorrow?"

"You're busy." Didi flipped through the appointment book. "The Ulman-Gravino adoption at nine a.m., that closing at eleven, and then the graphic designer to update the website at two."

"I thought he wasn't available until next month?"

"He's not. But I took the liberty of making an appointment with another highly sought-after designer whose body of work is quite impressive."

"Who is it?"

"Innovative Designs."

"Okay, thanks. I'll check out their website later," Kate said and headed into her office.

"Why? Don't you trust me?"

She popped her head around the door frame, surprised by Didi's pouty tone. "With my life. Why are you asking?"

"It's just that you're so busy, I figured I could handle this for you, and all you'd have to do is show up for the meeting tomorrow. I mean, jeez, I can handle some things on my own, you know."

"I didn't mean to imply…You know what, you're right. I have a bunch of stuff to finish tonight. Thanks for taking the initiative on this."

"Glad to be of service, Boss," Didi replied with a two-finger salute.

The next day, Kate took advantage of the low humidity and light June breeze by venturing out to a food truck parked along the New Haven green for a quick lunch. She sat on a bench across from the fountain with her gyro and iced green tea, and indulged in the silent intrigue of people-watching downtown. The sun warmed her face, and as soon as she closed her squinted eyes, images of Jordan Squire rushed against her eyelids. Her sultry voice belting out Dusty Springfield, her toned body swaying against her guitar, those piercing green eyes sending her messages she was convinced she was misinterpreting. She'd never admit it to Didi or Viv, but Jordan Squire had been occupying a lot of space in her mind since Sunday, and it was kind of nice to feel jazzed about something, someone, even if it was just a fleeting moment of flirtation.

Still smiling at her thoughts, she checked the time on her phone and decided to head back to the office and freshen up for her meeting with the graphic designer. As she walked down Church Street, she hoped Didi's guy was as creative and reputable as the one Viv had recommended from New York City.

"I was about to text you," Didi said, harried, when Kate walked in. "Go fix your hair and brush your teeth. Your appointment is arriving any minute."

"I have fifteen minutes," Kate said, puzzled by her urgency.

Didi looked her over. "And you're gonna need every second of it. Now go." She shoved her into her office.

Kate stood in front of the mirror in her private bathroom, brushing her teeth with one hand and raking her fingers through her wind-blown hair with the other. Wiping her mouth on the hand towel, she scrutinized her reflection after Didi's comment. *Some fine lines around the eyes and mouth, but the skin's still pretty tight and smooth, with a golden hue from a day at the beach last week. "Late forties" sounds worse than it is.*

"Attorney Randall?" Didi's voice rang out through the intercom. "Your appointment is here."

Kate walked into the reception area and skidded to a halt when she saw Jordan Squire standing at Didi's desk.

"This is Ms. Squire from Innovative Designs."

Jordan approached Kate with an extended hand. "Hi. It's nice to see you again."

Kate grasped Jordan's hand and nearly melted into it. "Yes, this is certainly a pleasant, strange surprise. Uh, would you like to make yourself comfortable in my office for a minute while I consult briefly with my secretary?"

"Sure."

"Great." Kate smiled and made sure Jordan was safely inside before she laced into Didi. "What do you think you're doing?"

Didi tightened her mouth in an attempt not to laugh while being chastised, a feat she'd perfected as a hyper kid in Catholic grammar school.

"That child is probably half your age," Kate said. "You've got furniture older than she is. And I'd rather you didn't use the practice as a pawn in your lurid bid to seduce her." She folded her arms across her chest. "You've put me in a terribly uncomfortable position. What if her work sucks? Am I supposed to hire her anyway so you can get laid? You need to get ahold of yourself. You're out of control."

Didi looked at her patiently. "Are you through?"

"It depends. Are you?"

"Before you get your panty liner all up in a bunch," Didi said, leading her away from the open office door, "I didn't do this so I can get laid…" She bobbed her eyebrows up and down.

"What? Me?" Kate boomed and then dialed it down to a whisper. "That's even worse. I don't want her. I already told you that. Why don't you ever listen to me?"

"Can we argue about this later? She's in there waiting for you."

Kate glared at her. "Oh, we're gonna argue about this later. Don't you worry."

Didi turned Kate around and nudged her toward the office. "That's it, girl. Go get her."

Kate stopped at the door and whispered through gritted teeth, "I cannot believe I didn't smell this coming a mile away. I should have known something was desperately wrong when you refused my offer to buy you lunch today."

Didi winked and sashayed back to her desk like a Disney princess.

Kate entered her office pawing at her neck, as it suddenly felt sweaty. "Sorry to keep you waiting, Jordan. Why don't we set up on this table over here?"

"Sure." She grabbed her laptop case and arranged it on the small, round conference table across the room.

"How do you find the time to be a graphic designer and have a music career?" Kate tried out a few casual poses before Jordan turned around.

Jordan chuckled. "The question is more like how do I find the time to have a music career while I'm running a graphic design company to pay the bills."

"After seeing you perform, I'm sure that won't be a problem for long. You're really in your element up there."

"Thanks, Kate. That's so nice of you to say." Jordan's smile and stare shot a current of nerves through Kate. "I'm ready if you'd like to get started."

Kate couldn't slide into the chair next to her fast enough. Damn, she smelled good.

"Okay, so did Didi give you the links I sent her so you could see my work?"

"Um, I'll be honest. I haven't had time to look."

"Okay, no problem. Let's take a look at what I did for Schick Corporation." She punched away at the keys until the site popped up. "Can you see it okay?"

"Uh, yeah," Kate said, craning her neck.

"Here. You can move closer." Jordan's voice was drenched in sex appeal. "Or I can just hand you the computer." She giggled, seeming a little embarrassed.

"Either works for me. I mean you need to see the screen too, right?"

"Right." Jordan smiled and moved closer to Kate. "I like this layout. It's really user-friendly, and I've gotten the most positive feedback from my clients on it."

Kate tried to focus on the screen, but the proximity of this gorgeous, sexy, delicious-smelling woman sapped her powers of concentration like kryptonite.

"Yeah. I like the logo placement and access to the navigation bar." Kate sneaked a whiff of Jordan's hair dangling near her face.

"It's eye-catching and tastefully understated at the same time. I also did the design for a winery in Stonington. Want to see?"

They locked eyes for a moment, and Kate couldn't help smiling. Jordan smiled back, and suddenly their business meeting felt as awkward as a first good-night kiss.

"I, uh, I was about to say something else," Jordan stammered. "Sorry, I…"

Kate smiled wider as their professionalism spiraled into blatant flirtation. "The winery in Stonington?"

"Oh, yeah, duh," Jordan said. "Now I'm thinking my presentation would've been far more professional if we were Skyping."

Their laughter reduced the boiling sexual tension to a simmer.

"No worries, Jordan. I'm impressed with your work and the delivery of your sales pitch."

"Thank you." She pulled a flyer out of her bag. "Here's the list of links to my other clients' sites. In the meantime, do you have any questions for me?"

Kate arched an eyebrow. *You mean like where have you been all my life?* "Uh, no. I'm good right now. I'll review those sites, and when I choose one I like, then we can talk pricing."

"Great. Thanks for your time. I look forward to hearing from you."

They stood at the same time, and Jordan shook her hand again. As they walked to the door, Kate stopped her.

"Say, I do have one question, a personal one, if you don't mind."

"Sure." She dazzled Kate again with those eyes.

"How old are you?"

She hesitated like a suspect hedging how much the cops already knew. "Thirty."

That's exactly what Kate was afraid she'd say. "All right then. I'll be in touch."

"I hope so." The lilt of temptation in Jordan's voice told Kate she wasn't talking business anymore.

Kate swallowed hard and extended her arm for Jordan to go ahead of her into the reception area.

"So," Didi said, startling them both. "Do we have a partnership here or what?"

Kate scowled at her as she passed her desk and walked Jordan out. After closing the door, she leaned against it and exhaled.

"Well?" Didi asked.

"She's thirty years old," Kate finally said.

"You have an age requirement to have a website designed?"

Kate dropped on the couch and ran her hands through her hair. "Didi, I can't hire her to do the website. I'm attracted to her."

"What does one have to do with the other if you like her work? Besides, if you end up going out with her, that's just a bonus."

"No, no, no." Kate flailed her hand back and forth. "There will be no dating involved in this."

"What's wrong with you? She's smart, sexy, and artistic. And she's obviously smitten with you. You can see it when she lets her gaze linger on you. It's so adorbs."

"Didi, she was born the year I graduated high school."

"Really? That's kind of creepy."

"Thank you."

"Kate, I'm just kidding. I think she's great for you. Age shouldn't matter. It's not like she's twenty. She's established and seems very mature."

"I don't want to talk about this anymore." Kate leapt up from the couch and headed into her office.

Didi appeared in the doorway. "Kate, just go out on one date with her. Not for nothing, but you need the practice. You literally haven't been out with someone new in over twenty years."

"Really?" Kate said. "Seventeen years with Lydia, four years single. Yeah. You're right."

"Which means you haven't been laid in four years." She sucked her teeth. "Pathetic. I'm surprised you let her out of your office without a struggle," she said with a giggle.

"I believe the estimate is closer to six years, but who's counting?"

"Oh-em-gee. Then just sleep with her. Come on. Pretty soon it's gonna pucker shut on you."

Kate laughed. "I'm not going to sleep with her. You know I don't do that."

"You must be exhausted constantly trying to cover all that moral high ground."

"It's not about morality. With the exception of one drunken night with Viv when I was barely out of my teens, I've never been into sex without some type of emotional connection. And right now, I'm not into pursuing an emotional connection either. I'm quite content with my emotionally uncomplicated life, thank you."

"Boy, did we end up in opposite places in our lives. I'd take her into the supply closet right now if she wanted."

Kate scratched her head. "You were friends with two out lesbians for decades. Why did it take you till you were forty to realize you're one, too?"

"Hmm, let's see." She counted off on her fingers. "Catholic. Italian. A son. A mortgage. Xanax."

"Fair enough." Kate headed back to her office.

"What about the website? Are you going to hire Jordan?"

Kate stopped at the door and thought for a moment. "Only if you'll handle it. I don't want to have any more interaction with her. It's not wise to mix business with pleasure. But more importantly, I'm not a fan of cold showers," she added with a grin.

"Fair enough," Didi said and smiled.

CHAPTER FOUR

Indecent Proposal

Her eyes weak from what seemed like hours playing game apps and trolling photos and comment posts on Jordan's Facebook page, Kate curled up in silky sheets, bargaining with herself to shut down her brain and go to sleep. It was after one a.m., but no matter how many times she covered and uncovered her head with the pillow, she could not chase Jordan out of her mind. The whole thing defied explanation. Why was she being taunted with visions of that girl's rich olive skin, juicy caramel lips, and tall, slender figure every time she closed her eyes? Cosmic retribution, that's what it was—the ultimate payback for every judgment she'd ever passed on Viv's dubious romantic dalliances and dig she'd ever made to Didi for drooling over some girl young enough to be her daughter. Karma. 'Tis indeed a bitch.

Now that she'd wrung out every ounce of romanticism from the Jordan situation, how long was this foolishness supposed to last? A woman in her early-late forties had no business lying wide-awake while her emotions surged like they had as a teenager when she'd discovered her first Kathleen Turner movie. And over who? Some kid who'd probably have nothing more than a brief fascination with a woman creeping up on the half-century mark.

Regardless of her momentary lapse, Kate Randall was no teenager, and she resolved to purge these unwelcome feelings from her decommissioned heart if she had to lie there and count sheep until the entire flock stampeded her.

❖

The next day, Kate stood at the water cooler in the reception area of her office sipping water from a cone-shaped paper cup. She eyed Didi, who was engrossed in the Request for Disclosure document she was preparing.

"Do you know what I dislike most about you?"

Didi looked up from her keyboard. "I beg your pardon?"

"When you gloat," Kate said, staring her down. "All week long, every time I've walked past you, I've had to look at your smug face."

"What am I gloating over?"

"You know."

"What? Jordan?"

Kate glared at her with disgust. "Look at you, acting all innocent. Yes, Jordan."

"Kate, I don't know what you're getting so indignant over. I haven't bothered you about her since you told me to handle the website design myself. I even had her come into the office while you were at court, so you wouldn't run into her."

"She came here again? Why?"

"I had a couple of questions, and she said she'd rather show me in person than try to explain it over the phone. I thought it was very sweet of her and a testament to her professionalism toward her clients."

"And I'm sure you didn't mind her near you, leaning over you either."

Didi smirked. "I said it was a testament to her professionalism, not mine. Besides, something tells me her service-oriented attitude had more to do with hoping she'd run into you again. She seemed bummed when I said you were in court."

"Is that right?" Kate tried to tame her elation. "Well, I'm sorry for accusing you of gloating."

"You said she's too young and you're not interested in her. I'm respecting that."

"Thank you, Didi." Kate smiled sincerely. "I appreciate your consideration."

"Even if I do think you're stupid for not exploring the possibilities."

"Thanks, Didi." Kate rolled her eyes and headed back to her desk.

Why was she feeling disappointed? For once, Didi had done exactly what she'd requested of her. She hadn't meddled. Anyway, even if Jordan had considered pursuing more than a business relationship, Kate sent a clear message that she wasn't when she'd left Didi in charge of the website development. Not that it mattered. Summer had just begun, and Kate and her friends were looking forward to a full social calendar of get-togethers, charity events, and fund-raising work for various LGBT causes in Connecticut.

"She asked about you." Didi posed against the door frame with arms folded.

The smile spread across Kate's mouth before she had a chance to contain it, but she remained tight-lipped.

"You know you're dying to know what she said," Didi said. "Even you're not that cool."

Kate reclined in her leather chair. "But you have to admit, I fake it pretty well."

"Too well." Didi sat in a chair in front of Kate's desk. "After the initial 'where were you, how are you' foreplay questions, by the end of the appointment she was gushing about how attractive and smart you are and how curious she was as to how you didn't have a wife, a girlfriend, or a mistress. I said you're waiting for the right one to come along, like the rest of us."

"Good answer," Kate said. "You didn't reveal anything else, did you?"

Didi shook her head. "All other information is on a need-to-know basis, as in maybe you can tell her yourself sometime."

"Or she can meet someone her own age, and you can leave me alone about this."

"But this is so much more fun. She made a point to mention that she performs at a winery. We should go sometime."

Kate offered a noncommittal nod despite the tingles that fanned across her body at the thought of Jordan cavorting around onstage.

"Come on, Kate. We'll get a few people to join us so it won't look so obvious."

"There's no need for subterfuge, Didi. That implies I've something to hide, and I don't."

"Not even the fact that you're crushing on someone for the first time in decades?"

Kate scoffed. "A crush? Oh, please." She began pecking away on her laptop keyboard.

"What would you call it then? You and I both know it's something. Otherwise, we wouldn't be having this conversation."

Kate mulled it over for a moment, staring out at the turret on the old Victorian across from her office building. "A passing interest," she concluded.

Didi laughed. "That's funny. Don't passing interests usually pass?" She stretched out her legs and kicked off her sequined mules.

"It will. It's a slow-moving one."

"It's not a weather front. I hate to break this to you, honey, but you've got a thing for her. Surely you have some recollection of what it feels like."

"I remember having a thing for someone," Kate said, and suddenly all humor vanished into the atmosphere. "If Lydia's leaving taught me anything, it's that those feelings are misleading and fleeting. And once they're gone, it's work to keep a relationship going, hard work that requires two people equally committed to the cause, which rarely happens. Frankly, I'd rather devote my energy to causes that won't ultimately blow up in my face."

"It's good to know you're not bitter or anything."

Kate arched an eyebrow. "Who, me?"

"Look. Romance is a dirty business," Didi said. "But lucky for me, crawling around in the mud's my thing."

"Crawl away," Kate said. She tapped a stack of papers on her desk and placed them in an accordion file.

Didi ran her hand through her dark, purple-tinted hair. "You know, it's quite possible that Jordan coming into the picture is a sign from the universe that you're ready to date again."

Kate scoffed. "Yeah. That's it. If the universe thinks that sending me a hot, thirty-year-old musician who probably gets more ass than a Pride festival Porta-Potty is the way to get me back into the game, then it's as misguided as you and Viv."

"Let's not resort to character assassination here. I thought Viv's idea to put you on a dating site was a brilliant stroke of innovation. It's an ideal way for you to get your feet wet again. You didn't even give it a chance."

"Who wants wet feet? And if it's so brilliant, why aren't you two online?"

"I am. The only reason I went off was because I had to temporarily remove myself to give the slip to this creeper who wouldn't leave me alone. Since then I've met some intriguing women. Forget about Viv. She's pathologically obsessed with the notion that she's going to win Maia back."

Kate studied her for a moment. "How publishers aren't clamoring for you two to collaborate on a dating-advice book is beyond me."

Didi rose from the chair with her chin in the air. "Fine, Kate. Make all the jokes you want, but while you're floundering around in self-imposed social exile protecting your battered heart, I'm living my life, however dubious it may seem at times. My son's in college in Miami, and I'm finally doing what I want, on my own terms, and I'm not ashamed of it."

"That's good. You shouldn't be. What's it got to do with me?"

"Let yourself feel something for someone again," Didi said, sounding exasperated. "Get back in the driver's seat, throw caution to the wind. C'mon, grow a set."

Kate rolled her chair away from her desk. "I stand corrected. It's not your gloating that I dislike the most," she said, wiggling a finger at her whole aura. "It's that."

"What?" Didi sounded offended at the vague insult.

"Whenever you finally find your way out of the dark, you insist on dragging everyone else into the light with you. Except not everyone's fumbling around in the dark," she said, heading toward her private bathroom. "Some of us have already evolved and are perfectly fine the way we are, thank you very much."

Didi chased her around the desk, but Kate slammed the door before Didi could get at her. "It's okay, Kate." She teased her through the door. "Even evolved people can have the hots for someone, even someone as snobbish as you."

Kate whipped open the door. "Snob? Really?"

"Listen, if you think you're too good for a kid who sings in nightclubs, I get it," Didi said as she sauntered back into the reception area. "You have to keep up professional appearances. Now that I think of it, she's a little too rough around the edges for your image anyway."

Kate bent forward menacingly and propped her hands on Didi's desk. "What is this? You're really using reverse psychology on me right now?"

"I'm being a supportive friend. If you're so dead against talking to the girl that you've pawned off something as important as your website design on me, then I'm sure you have your reasons—whether they're logical or not," she said under her breath.

"I'd talk to her," Kate said, then lowered her voice. "I just won't go out of my way to pursue her. If I ever run into her again, of course I'd talk to her."

"Fine. Fabulous," Didi said, busying herself at her desk. "I won't say another word on the subject."

"If only." Kate smiled and headed back into her office.

That evening at the Oceanview, the sun hovered over New Haven Harbor as revelers at the LGBTQ Resource Center fund-raiser cramming the restaurant spilled over to the back patio to admire the views. Kate had evaded the bustle momentarily and was standing at the railing as a light sea breeze caressed her arms.

"There you are," Didi said, handing her a flute of champagne. "I noticed a few new faces. Why aren't you in there getting your mingle on?"

"I'm trying to steer clear of the pasta station. Besides, you know how I am on Friday nights." She muffled a yawn.

"Sadly, we do." Vivienne scanned the crowd. "Listen. While we're here together, I'd like to raise my bubbly to Kate, the best lawyer money can buy and the most loyal friend a girl could ever find."

They all clinked glasses and sipped their champagne.

"That was quite a toast, Viv," Kate said. "Thank you."

"It's nothing, girl. You're my hero." She kissed Kate on the cheek, leaving a sparkly mulberry lip print on her.

Didi smirked. "This may be a bad time to point this out, but you didn't actually win your case."

"Yeah," Kate said. "I mean I was able to plea you down from the violation of the restraining order and disorderly conduct charges, but you still have two years of probation."

"You also have to do community service," Didi said.

"I know all that. But you saved my ass from the joint," Viv said. "Unless prison really is like *Orange Is the New Black*," she said with a flourish across her body, "this ain't cut out for hard time."

"You weren't ever going to jail, Viv. It was your first offense. But if you don't leave Maia alone, that's exactly where you'll end up."

"It's hard, Kate. She's the love of my life, and I ruined everything with my selfishness and hotheaded attitude. We were together five years. That's the longest relationship I've ever had."

"Makes sense," Didi said. "Maia's just as crazy as she is. They really are the perfect couple."

Kate glared at her. "You're not helping."

"I'm having a private conversation with my attorney," Viv said. "Do you mind?"

"Excuse you," Didi said. "We're not friends anymore? I might have some helpful insight to share with you, too."

"Your answer to everything is 'Sleep with her,'" Viv said. "Unfortunately, that doesn't solve every problem."

"I'm sorry I'm so flippant about Maia," Didi said. "But she moved out five months ago. You're on probation. You guys are done. She wanted you to grow up and start a family with her, but you weren't having any of it. Accept it and move on."

"Wouldn't it be convenient if I could just switch teams mid-game like you did?"

Didi looked genuinely hurt. "That's not fair."

"Simmer down, ladies," Kate said. "For as close as the three of us are, it's obvious we have very different viewpoints on things. Viv understands now that she has to accept that Maia is gone and get on with her life. And, Viv, you know Didi's coming-out process wasn't easy."

"I know. I'm sorry, girl. I'm just so lost without Maia. I don't know what to do with myself."

"You need to find a purpose," Kate said in an uplifting tone. "Something that'll make you feel good about getting out of bed each day, something with more impact than liquidating your father's ethnic-skin-products fortune on shoes and cocktail parties."

Viv sipped her drink and nodded. "You girls are right. Losing Maia has finally helped me see it." She raised her glass. "Here's to a new beginning. That nasty little court matter is over, and I'm ready to start living again—with purpose."

Kate and Didi raised their glasses.

"Here's to a new beginning for all of us," Didi said.

"Thanks, girls. I'm gonna go make a lap around the room." Viv glanced at an assembly of women nearby. "Who needs Maia anyway?"

"That's the spirit." Kate patted her shoulder.

"You go, girl," Didi said with enthusiasm.

Viv smiled and swaggered off.

"She'll be drunk-texting Maia within the hour," Kate mumbled.

Didi nodded. "Did you ever hear from Jordan this week?"

Kate regarded her quizzically. "No. Why would I? You handled the website thing, didn't you?"

"Yes, but I really thought she'd call and ask you out." Didi scratched through her hair. "I was so sure of myself."

"You always are," Kate said and returned her gaze to the sun dipping into the horizon.

Didi leaned against the railing next to her. Then, after a moment, "Well, hello, gorgeous…"

Kate swung around, and the vision of Jordan waving to them from the open doors apprehended her as a breeze caught her curls and swept them across her face. Kate sighed heavily as she waved back.

"I told you there were new faces inside," Didi said out of the side of her mouth.

"Dear God, she's coming over here," Kate said through teeth still clenched in a smile.

Jordan's beaming face had both Kate and Didi mesmerized as she made her way toward them, parting clusters of people like she was a celebrity.

After they exchanged air kisses and pleasant greetings, Kate and Didi traded looks of wonder.

"So, I'm gonna give you gals a chance to get reacquainted," Didi said. "I have to visit the powder room anyway. At our age one good sneeze or joke could trigger a small tsunami down there. Am I right or what, Kate?" She chuckled.

Kate glared at her, mortified.

"Right," Didi said, soberly. "I'll be running along now."

After Didi rushed off, Kate and Jordan flailed momentarily in the hellish silence occurring before someone at last initiated dialogue.

"You look beautiful," Jordan said. "If a date with you is one of the silent-auction items, where do I place my bid?"

Kate grinned bashfully. "That's cute, really cute," she said. "But I don't think your date would appreciate that."

"I'm flying solo tonight. Still in the process of making new friends and cocktail connections. It's been so long since I've lived in Connecticut."

"I'm sure it won't take you long, especially with your music. There are also online lesbian social groups you can join. Didi and I go to some of the events. Maybe you can join us sometime, and we can introduce you to some of our acquaintances."

"I'd love that—I mean if you wouldn't mind me tagging along. I'm pretty easy. Anything goes."

Either Kate shouldn't have drunk that champagne on an empty stomach, or Jordan's gaze was stirring up something inside her in places that hadn't been stirred in ages. She trembled from the ambush of Jordan's unrelenting sex appeal and the insane romantic glow of the setting sun across her face. When their eyes locked, the rush of intensity was too much.

"Can I get you a drink?" Kate asked, feeling claustrophobic.

"Uh, sure. A glass of white wine would be great."

"Great. Be right back."

Like an escaped hostage, Kate scurried back inside the restaurant searching for Didi or Viv, anyone who could talk her off the ledge Jordan had her dangling from.

"You have to come back out there with me," Kate said, broadsiding Didi at the bar.

"What's wrong?"

"Jordan. I'm freaking out."

"I can see that, but what I don't get is why."

"We made eye contact," she said, wringing her hands. "Deep, soul-penetrating eye contact."

"Kate, I'm not following you. You're in this frenzied state because you and Jordan made eye contact?"

"Yes. And I feel bad leaving her alone out there. She came by herself."

"She's alone?" Didi propped her hands on her hips. "Kate, this is the dumbest thing I've ever heard. Go out there and talk to her. Or go find Viv. I'm having a lovely conversation with…" She swiveled toward the empty space beside her. "Thanks a lot, ass-hat. You chased her away."

"Didi, we came here together. You have to come back outside with me."

"And pull chaperone duty for you? Fuck that. I want to have my own good time."

"How can you ditch me at a time like this? What kind of friend are you?"

"Woman, you need to snap out of this. What are you afraid of? She's a doll."

"I don't know what I'm doing." Kate clawed at the front of her neck. "You wouldn't believe the butterflies I have right now."

Didi slapped her hand away. "Stop it. You're making your neck all red."

"I think I'm breaking out in hives."

"Kate, listen to me," Didi said in a soothing voice. "You're working yourself up for nothing here. It's okay if you're a little nervous, have a few butterflies. That's normal. Take a deep breath and do a shot."

Kate waved away the shot Didi offered, opting for deep breathing. She did it several more times and felt herself calming. "Okay, you're right, you're right. I'm overreacting."

"Just a little," Didi said, pinching her thumb and forefinger together.

"I told her I'd get her a drink."

"Good. Get her one. And make sure you also get her number so you can ask her to lunch."

"What? Are you crazy?"

"Kate, obviously something is brewing between you two. The chemistry is palpable. And you'd never be getting so worked up if you didn't feel something. Have lunch with her and see what's there."

Kate swallowed, considering Didi's suggestion.

"Look," Didi said. "Here's what I propose: If you go out with her, I solemnly promise to stop nagging you about dating."

"About dating her or dating in general?"

"Dating in general."

"All I have to do it go out with her once?" Kate narrowed her eyes, skeptical.

Didi grinned. "That's the deal."

"You swear?" She searched for confirmation in Didi's eyes.

"Witch's honor." Didi held two fingers under her eyes like Samantha from *Bewitched*.

With a simultaneous nod, they solidified their accord.

After pausing a second to imbibe the view from behind, Kate approached Jordan and tapped her on the shoulder as she took in the purple sky.

"Hi again," Jordan said.

"Sorry I took so long." Kate handed her a glass of wine. "The lines at the bar are so long."

"That's great. It's a fund-raiser, right?"

"Good point." She smiled and joined Jordan, resting her elbows on the railing, studying the speckles of faint stars dotting the heavens.

"It's funny how we keep running into each other," Jordan said after a brief silence.

"Yeah, it is. What brought you here tonight?"

"Besides the hope that you'd ask me out?" Jordan flashed a sassy grin.

Kate chuckled at the finesse with which she could deliver a cheesy pick-up line.

Suddenly, Viv sidled up behind them. Kate wheeled around when she brushed her breast against her back. "What's up, Viv?"

"Didi said you needed help out here," Viv said through lips pursed in a frozen smile. "Introduce me to your new friend." She extended her hand to Jordan.

"Uh, Jordan, this is my other oldest and dearest friend, Viv."

The two women shook hands.

"Vivienne Wilmington, President of Wilmington Cosmetics."

"President?" Kate mumbled to herself.

"I've heard of your company." Jordan smiled. "How do you do?"

"I do quite well," she said with a wink. "And what do you do? Or should I say are there any more like you at home?"

"Viv." Kate admonished her.

Viv chuckled and slapped Jordan on the arm. "Girlfriend knows I'm just playing."

Jordan smiled as she subtly wiped on her pants the white wine Viv had just spilled on her hand.

"So, do you two have something cooking?" Viv said, a French-manicured finger waving back and forth between them.

Kate felt her cheeks blaze traffic-light red. "Viv, isn't there some tanking cosmetics company you could be raiding right now?"

"That answers my question," Viv said with a grin. She grabbed Jordan's hand. "Lovely meeting you, darling."

"Same here," Jordan said.

Kate grinned as she watched her leave. "Yet another friend I always feel the need to apologize for."

"Not at all. They're great—ballsy, and they totally own it. It's awesome."

"I'm glad I ran into you tonight," Kate said, surprising herself. "Some coincidence."

"I'd like to call it a coincidence, but it's time I confess. Didi texted me and said you guys would be here."

"Okay," Kate said. She soon realized Didi would not be relenting on this Jordan thing anytime soon so she might as well get it over with. "So, I'm sure your schedule is pretty hectic these days, but would you like to maybe have lunch sometime?"

Jordan's face bloomed into a garden of delight. "How about tomorrow?"

Kate giggled. "Uh, okay. How about that sushi place on Elm Street? You know it?"

"Better than I know your personal cell number." Jordan's attempt at flirting was precious.

"Then let's take care of that right now." Kate took her phone out of her pocket, and they exchanged numbers. "There. Now we can remove Didi from the equation."

"Deal," Jordan said as her eyes seemed to read everything Kate was trying to hide.

Kate consulted her watch. "I better get in there. They're going to start announcing the raffle winners, and I have to help pass out the prizes."

"Can you pull one of my tickets for the spa-day gift certificate?" Jordan said as they headed inside.

Kate giggled. "Sure. Why not? I'm giving myself the wine-of-the-month-club prize."

Jordan absently bumped into Kate as she laughed.

❖

After the raffle prizes were handed out, Kate rounded up Vivienne and Didi, who were at the bar chatting it up with some younger bois who were plying them with glasses of wine.

"Are you ready?" Kate said in Didi's ear.

"Ready for what?" she said. "It's nine forty-five."

"Hey, ladies," Viv said, her arm snaking around Kate. "This here's Kate, our token blond. She's single, too."

The bois greeted her, one with a howl of approval and one with an offer to buy her a shot.

"No, thank you. I have to get going now. Ready, ladies?"

"You don't mean ready as in go home, do you?" Viv asked discreetly.

Kate nodded. "I'm tired, and since I'm going to lunch with Jordan tomorrow, I need a good night's sleep so I don't go looking like one of those puffer fish."

"Tomorrow?" Viv said. "Are you meeting her there or picking her up in your U-Haul?"

Kate rolled her eyes. "You better call an Uber if you guys get hammered."

"I'm sure we won't have any trouble finding a ride," Didi said, glancing flirtatiously at the bois.

"Just be careful about getting in a car with strange women."

"We don't have anything to worry about with this well-mannered group," Didi said, directing her drink glass at them.

"I was talking to them," Kate said, and everyone whooped and hollered as she sauntered away.

She then assumed the gait of a CIA operative, hoping to sneak out to the parking lot without saying good night to Jordan. She'd already had too much to drink so she could speak to Jordan all evening without tripping and stumbling over her words. One more shot or glass of wine and she might've stumbled into Jordan in a way that would've been impossible to recover from.

"Kate." Jordan called her name just as she was about to clear the front door. "You're leaving?"

"Oh, hey, uh, yeah, my Uber's here so I'm heading out."

"I'd be happy to drive you home," Jordan said, her eyes gleaming with hope.

For a nanosecond, Kate actually entertained the idea of accepting her offer until a car horn startled her back to reality. "I uh, um, my driver's already…"

"Oh. Oh, yeah, of course." Jordan stammered. "Okay, well, I just wanted to…" She hesitated a moment, then kissed Kate on the cheek.

Kate melted in a smile. "What was that for?"

"Just a thank you for being so nice to me while I get resettled here. You're seriously cool."

"Thanks. It's nothing," Kate said. "I'll see you tomorrow."

With a coy smile, Jordan scuttled back inside. Kate climbed into the waiting car and glanced out at the starry sky, her tension released through an extended sigh.

CHAPTER FIVE

Biting Off More Than You Can Chew

Jordan looked sexy as hell as she wiggled a chopstick back and forth between her thumb and middle finger. That's when Kate realized she needed to lay off the sake that early in the day. This young woman seemed to have possessed certain superpowers that could easily weaken her steely reserve.

"Okay, now that lunch is over," Jordan said with a flirty smile, "you can give me the ugly truth."

Kate smirked. "You're going to have to be more specific."

The auburn light from the lamp suspended between them emphasized their decimated wooden sushi boat—and Jordan's strong fingers laced together in front of her.

"You weren't going to ask me out if I hadn't coerced you into it last night."

"Uh, you know, the jury's still out on that one, but I'd hardly say you coerced me." Kate recalled her agreement with Didi and felt like a bit of a heel.

Jordan frowned. "I knew it. At first I thought Didi was trying to pick me up when she cornered me in the toilet stall earlier in the night."

"She what?"

"Well, not that she cornered me. I mean, I could've gotten out if I really tried."

"I have to apologize for Didi. Sometimes her joie de vivre leaves a trail of destruction in its wake."

"There's nothing wrong with her—I just noticed you first at Moxy's." Jordan's eyes cascaded into her plate in the most delectable way.

Kate couldn't help but smile. Jordan's look completely contradicted her personality. By appearance, she was a seductress of biblical proportion, sexuality emanating from every sleek inch of her, yet here was this lovely, gentle creature sitting across from her. How captivating it was learning more about her, unraveling the contrast.

"You're very humble for a woman of your beauty. I pictured you being an entirely different person when I saw you at Moxy's."

Jordan grinned and looked down again. "It's the guitar. It does kooky things to people's imaginations."

"Ugh. Am I being a total cliché?" Kate said. "You must hear this kind of thing from the women you meet at shows all the time. Honestly, I've never been a groupie."

Jordan giggled. "I don't really hear it that much, and believe me, you're not like anyone I've ever met at a show."

"I wouldn't think so. I don't imagine your fan base includes many women old enough to be your mother."

"Don't count on it. Last month I had a woman carrying an oxygen tank come to a show. She cheered louder than anyone. For real." Jordan grinned. "And I don't believe that for one minute."

"What? That I'm old enough to be your mother?"

Jordan leaned back and challenged her with a doubtful gaze.

"I most certainly am…If I'd got knocked up in high school."

Jordan laughed. "You don't look it, and to be honest, I haven't given your age any thought. I just liked what I saw and wanted to know more about you."

"Forty-seven," Kate announced, bracing for Jordan to recoil in horror. "I'm forty-seven. That's a seventeen-year age difference."

"Kate, this is just lunch," she said with a giggle.

"Of course. Jeez. Why would I bring that up? I mean we may never even see each other again after this."

"That's not what I meant." She leaned into the table. "Kate, is age a problem for you?"

"Me? A problem? Pffft. No." Kate grinned despite feeling herself sinking into a pit of quicksand of her own making.

"Good. Because I like your company." She shot her an inviting look that nearly made Kate slide out of the booth. "Regardless of whether you could've got knocked up with me in your prom date's backseat."

Kate relaxed into a hearty laugh. "I like yours, too—company, that is."

"I knew what you meant." Jordan batted her long lashes. "Although I do like where this conversation appears to be headed."

"If it gets there, I'm afraid it'll be more from my lack of grace. I'm still more comfortable trying to sway a bored jury or crotchety judge than I am talking to a beautiful woman."

"If I were a judge, the opposing side would never stand a chance against you."

Kate grinned and glanced across the restaurant to mask her blush. Either this girl was a major player, or she knew exactly how to pursue what she wanted. The only trick was how to figure it out.

"So what's Didi's story anyway? Is she your ex?"

"Noooo," Kate sang. "We've been friends since high school. She was a late bloomer, if you know what I mean. Now that she's out and living the dream, she's appointed herself my life coach and social director. She can't fathom how someone can be single and happy, as if the two can't possibly occur simultaneously."

"No, they can. I've proven that." Jordan leaned onto her forearms and gazed at Kate. "But sometimes our closest friends can see things in us that we can't."

Kate nibbled the lemon slice from her club soda as she pondered that thought.

"Although I frequently dismiss her as a head case, I suppose she has some insights about me after thirty years of friendship. She calls me jaded."

"Are you?"

Kate poked her chopstick at the untouched blob of ginger in the wooden boat. "I don't know. I guess it's kind of hard not to be when one minute your life is all mapped out in front of you, and the next, you're packing half of it away in storage."

She cringed at Jordan's sympathetic eyes. What was wrong with her? She'd just broken the cardinal rule of the first date: Never talk about your ex. Not unless you don't want a second date. But was this an actual, official first date? Had Kate even wanted a second one?

"I think it's hard for anyone to spring back from a serious breakup without feeling some type of way about relationships for a while," Jordan said. "I've never been in a relationship with someone I considered 'the one' before, but it still sucked when it ended, so I can only imagine how it would feel after something long-term."

Kate smiled. Who knew thirty-year-olds were so deep? "Anyway, I don't think I'm too far gone to believe that life can still offer a pleasant surprise now and then, especially when you least expect it."

Jordan gazed at Kate for a moment. "When you smile, you light up everything around you. I think because it starts in your eyes."

"Thank you," Kate said, feeling the blush set on her cheeks.

The waiter arrived to clear the table. "Can I get you anything else?"

Kate's smile faded as his eyes seemed to dart curiously between them. "No, thanks. Just the check."

He placed it on the table, and Kate grabbed it before Jordan could lift one of her folded hands. She offered her credit card, but Kate refused, at the same time realizing she'd been staring at Jordan's cleavage. In all fairness, it was right there right in front of her in that tight black scoop-neck shirt. When Jordan smiled in apparent recognition, Kate dropped her eyes into the leather binder containing the check.

"At least let me pay half since I finagled you into asking me to lunch," Jordan said as she fingered the pewter star attached to her necklace. Her eyes danced with Kate's in a waltz of shy uncertainty and passionate possibility.

In spite of herself, Kate wanted to know more. "Don't be silly." She politely nudged Jordan's card back toward her.

"Then next time's on me." There was that unnerving, penetrating gaze again. "Okay?"

"Okay." Kate forced herself to break eye contact.

"Would you like to take a walk?" Jordan asked. "Unless you have somewhere to be…"

As she twirled the charm over her delicious décolletage, Kate began to entertain the notion she was doing it on purpose.

"I'd like that."

On their way out, the chemistry between them unequivocally satisfied their nosy waiter's curiosity.

❖

A dry breeze sailed through the New Haven green, a welcome reprieve after the last few days of humidity that spawned a massive city-wide outbreak of frizzy hair. Jordan and Kate strolled along on their quest for the ideal, pigeon-poop-free bench near the fountain.

"Didi said you're going to be playing at a winery. You must be excited about that."

"Yeah. They've turned out to be great venues. I'd love for you to stop by if you can." Jordan licked a dollop of mango gelato off her lip. How could Kate possibly say no after that?

"I know Didi wants to, so maybe I'll join her. I'll hang back so I don't rile up your rabid admirers," she added with a wink.

Jordan giggled. "Not to worry. They just show up for the wine."

"Really?" Kate said, doubtful. "Do you ever read what they post about you on your page?" *Damn, Kate. Why don't you just admit you've been stalking her online since the day you met?*

Jordan played along. "No. What do they post?"

"I'm too much of a lady to repeat any of it," Kate said.

Jordan chuckled and almost spit out a spoonful of her gelato.

"Suffice it to say, you've got fans."

"I bet you do, too. How does a gorgeous, successful, community activist like you not have a wife?"

Kate groaned softly. "Jaded, remember?"

"Oh," Jordan said. "I thought that was a joke."

When Jordan went quiet, Kate switched into damage-control mode. "It is…you know. That was in another life."

"Then I'm glad I met you in this one."

"I am, too. You probably wouldn't recognize me in the other one."

"That's intriguing—unless I've inadvertently opened up old wounds you're trying to forget. In that case, how 'bout those Red Sox?"

Kate chuckled. "The old wounds have healed, but isn't this conversation too deep for this situation? I'm painfully out of practice in this arena."

"What arena is that, Kate?" she asked slyly.

"You know…where we had a delicious lunch, and now we're talking, having gelato."

"It's called a date. Boy, you are out of practice."

Kate elbowed her playfully as she spooned in some gelato. "I remember what it's called. I just thought we live in a world now where labeling people and things is passé."

"Unless you come from a world other than Earth, I might have to disagree with you. But if you don't care to call this a date, yeah, no problem. It's whatever."

You sound like a fool, Kate thought. "No big deal. I have nothing against the word." She paused and sighed. "How about you start answering some of my questions now?"

"I've got nothing to hide. My life's an open songbook."

Kate grinned, loving their banter. "Is that so? Then how come I haven't seen you around the Connecticut scene before? It's so small you usually can't hide from anyone if you tried."

"I moved back here about five months ago from Cambridge. I went to BC to put some space between my parents and me, but then I got a job in Boston with a graphic-design company and met a girl. Or three. You know how that goes."

Kate nodded. "Where's the girl or three now?"

"Where I left them in Boston. New stage in my life, fresh start."

"Why did you need space from your parents, if you don't mind me asking?"

"Mostly rigid expectations. I was tired of hearing comparisons to my older sister. Elizabeth is a hedge fund manager in Greenwich with two kids, and a state senator and circuit-court judge for neighbors. My dad is annoyed that I'm a musician. A traveling minstrel for a daughter doesn't quite meet the bar of Squire family success."

"You own your own business. That's a huge measure of success, if that's how you're defining it."

"That's how he defines it." Jordan looked pensive as she glanced away.

Another great first-date topic, Kate. "Jordan, your songs are fantastic. So are your style and stage presence. You're magnetic. I don't know how any parent wouldn't be supportive of a child with so much talent."

"Unless you're getting rich off it, it's just a pipe dream."

"Every great success story started with a dream. I'm certain everything's going to fall into place for you."

"It feels like it's already starting to," Jordan said with a shy smile.

"Excuse me for a second." Kate wrapped a napkin around her finger and dabbed at a tiny smear of gelato near the corner of Jordan's mouth.

In the closeness, their eyes collided. Jordan's natural scent wafted over Kate in the breeze, trapping her in its lure. She stared at Jordan's inviting mouth, absently licking her lips as she imagined their fruity taste. Wait. Was Jordan about to kiss her right there on the Green?

Kate backed away. "I'm sorry I interrupted you. Go on."

"No, that's uh...I was just...What was I saying?" Jordan seemed to be having difficulty shaking off her embarrassment. And it was adorable. "How long have I been sitting here with gelato all over my face like a three-year-old?" she asked.

"Just for a second." Kate tried not to smile. "And it wasn't all over your face. Just in the corner there." She brushed her lips with the napkin again. "I'm sorry. I should've kept my hands to myself."

"No, no, that's okay. Feel free to put them wherever you want."

Kate nearly swallowed her plastic spoon on that one.

"Uh, I mean, that's not what I meant," Jordan said. "Not in a pervey way."

"Yeah, I got it." Kate managed to keep a straight face. "You were saying before I rudely interrupted?"

"Uh, you know what? I don't remember. Wait. I think you said something about how things will fall into place."

Kate nodded, still amused as Jordan clearly scrambled to gather her wits. "I've found that they usually do. It's cut down on my stress levels telling myself that anyway."

Jordan smiled. "I like talking with you. You're a great listener."

"Thanks. It's sort of essential to what I do for a living."

"I thought you're a lawyer."

"We do more than talk, you know," Kate said. "Listening is half the battle in negotiations."

"Do your girlfriends ever stand a chance in an argument?"

"No." Kate grinned.

"Welp, nice meeting you." Jordan rose from the bench and pretended to run away.

Kate giggled and grabbed her shirt. "All right. You can sit down now."

She jerked her down onto the bench. Jordan lost her balance and landed in Kate's lap. Their eyes settled on each other before she slid back to a proper distance.

Kate's mind grew cluttered with intimate curiosities. What would Jordan's lips feel like on her neck? Were they as silky as they looked? And her skin. How would it feel against hers in a set of cool bedsheets?

"Fate's a funny thing," Jordan said. "I've been back for five months, but it took my first performance in New York City for me to meet the most amazing woman in Connecticut."

Kate smiled at the flattery and the novelty of her youthful optimism. "Are you one of those people who think everything is part of a bigger picture, like there's some master plan?"

Jordan was silent for a moment. "I've never framed it that way before, but yeah, I suppose I am. I find the notion kind of romantic."

"I find it kind of depressing. It negates our sense of control, like we're all pawns in some higher power's game."

"It feels that way sometimes," Jordan said. "But when it works in our favor, it's positively magical."

Kate smiled but couldn't help remembering how helpless she'd felt when Lydia announced she was moving out. One person's decision had completely changed the course of her life, and she'd felt powerless to redirect it on her own. Ironically, though, she loved the person she'd grown into after the breakup had torn her down.

"You have wicked eyes," Jordan blurted. "I've never seen that shade of blue before."

"Wicked is good, right?"

"Very good." Jordan flaunted an enticing smile.

"Should we take a walk?" Kate rose from the bench to save her lips from doing something reckless. She stomped out the tingles in her partially asleep leg as she offered Jordan her hand.

"We can head over to my apartment if you want," Jordan said as they walked across the Green. "It's down on Olive Street."

Her apartment? What? Why was she inviting her to her apartment? It was still daylight. Maybe an innocent drink to keep their conversation going? But what if she was secretly planning to seduce her? No. Nobody did that in real life, only in low-budget lesbian movies.

"Sure. I'll walk you home," Kate said. "Chivalry is not dead."

"I don't need an escort, Kate," Jordan said with a giggle. "I'm a big girl. Besides, it's only four o'clock in the afternoon. Too early for gangs of rogue hipsters terrorizing the neighborhood in their man buns and bowties."

Kate's nerves slowed her roll. "Then why are we going to your place?"

Smooth, Kate. Real smooth.

Jordan seemed to study the sky for a minute. "I guess I don't want our date to end." She sighed and gazed deeply into Kate's eyes. "And I feel like once we say good-bye I'll never see you again."

"That's uh, that won't happen. The lesbian scene is a microcosm. We'll definitely see each other around."

"That's not what I meant."

Kate exhaled. "Right. I had a feeling it wasn't."

The dimly lit hallway leading to Jordan's apartment door was an alternate universe compared with the late-afternoon sun peering between office and apartment buildings outside. Kate wondered how her legs had managed to transport her up to Jordan's place without first running the decision past her brain, which surely would've stopped them on the sidewalk. Alternate universe indeed.

"This is me," Jordan announced as they approached the last apartment at the end of the hall. She tilted her head against the door, her face glistening under a thin film of sweat. "I can't believe how this afternoon flew by."

Kate nodded with a curious grin. Where had the afternoon gone? She'd spent a jittery morning wearing a path in her carpet, quietly cursing Didi for manipulating her into doing something so out of character. She'd even contemplated calling Jordan and canceling, but with the promise of finally getting Didi off her back, the risk seemed well worth the reward.

"I have a confession," Kate said as Jordan's rich, martini-olive eyes made explicit suggestions to other parts of her body. "Didi more or less bribed me into having lunch with you. I didn't think we'd have a single thing to talk about."

"I see my first impression really bowled you over."

"It wasn't you. Trust me. I was referring to the twenty-year gap in our ages," she noted, wincing.

"Not twenty. Seventeen."

"Phew! That's a relief. I thought it was something huge." Kate rolled her eyes.

Jordan groaned. "Kate, all that matters is if you had a nice time today. Did you?"

Kate nodded and smiled. "I'd never want any of my colleagues to hear this, but I'm glad I'm so easily bribed."

"I am, too." Jordan slowly moved toward her.

Their lips touched, the soft sensuality instantly reviving Kate's long-dormant sexuality. Each kiss resonated throughout her entire body, the once-distant memory of raw desire stealing its way back into her consciousness.

Jordan pressed her body against Kate's, holding her face as her kisses grew more familiar, more urgent. But her hunger for Jordan overwhelmed her. She brushed her hands from her face, panic demanding immediate action. Flushed and breathless, she needed to get out of there—fast.

"I have to go," Kate blurted and dashed off down the hall, allowing no time for good-byes. One more word, one more touch would've sent her spinning out on a ride she couldn't jump off.

On the street below, the hot sun and fresh air swathed her in a feeling of safety. With Jordan out of sight, she reclaimed some of the emotional control that had deserted her moments earlier. Her heart pounding, she steadied herself against the building's brick façade until she felt grounded.

A sudden avalanche of doubt proved as effective as a cold shower. Had her hasty exit made Jordan feel rejected? Had she just made a complete ass out of herself? What else was she supposed to do? Too many questions, too many emotions. It was time to go home.

❖

The television in Kate's living room blared. She was oblivious to what program she had on as she lowered the volume on the remote with her left hand and clutched the cordless telephone in her right. She retreated to the sanctuary of her plush sofa, her worn New York Yankees batting T-shirt, and some cotton sweatpants she wouldn't be caught dead answering the door in. Her recent experience definitely called for comfortable loungewear as she distracted her racing mind with every portable electronic device she could surround herself with.

An iPad balanced perilously against her thighs as she reviewed the upcoming week's appointments. She picked up her cordless phone and called Didi's cell again. She still wasn't answering, and she hadn't returned the message Kate had left her more than an hour ago despite its rather imperative tone.

Actually, it was a good thing Didi wasn't answering her cell. Who needed another one of her interminable, "I only say this because I care" lectures she was famous for? Kate was plenty busy stewing in her own confusion without Didi lacing into her about how she was an emotional cripple or how appalling it was to witness her shriveling up in the seclusion of her quaint beach house. It was time Kate reclaimed control of her own affairs. No more meddling from Didi or Viv, no more forced encounters with girls half her age. She'd upheld her end of the bargain and now resolved to put this whirlwind week behind her and get back to her orderly, uncomplicated life.

If anything, the experience only reinforced Kate's belief in the old cliché: everything happens for a reason. Didi not calling back allowed her a much-needed period of reflection. The fact that she hadn't heard from Jordan since bolting out on her only served to support Kate's initial argument that a relationship between them was overreaching at best, but more like impossible.

Chapter Six

Throwing Down the Gauntlet

Kate checked her cell phone as the elevator delivered her to her office floor. Nothing. Exactly what she'd found each of the forty-eight or so times she'd checked it in the forty-eight hours since she'd abandoned Jordan outside her apartment door. Shouldn't Jordan have at least texted to see if she was okay? For all she knew, Kate's unceremonious exit could've been precipitated by a rancid piece of yellowtail, and thanks to Jordan's lack of follow-up date etiquette, she wouldn't have found out until she'd read Kate's obituary.

Well, good riddance.

"Hey," Kate said as she strolled into the office.

Didi, munching baby carrots at her desk, speared Kate with a nasty look. "Where in God's name have you been? I was this close to calling the police and having them dredge the Quinnipiac River for your body."

"I was in court. You know how Mondays go. Didn't you check my calendar?" Kate tossed her leather valise on a chair.

"No. I was too distraught by the idea of having to identify your dead, bloated corpse."

"If you had answered one of my numerous calls to your cell phone Saturday night, you would've known where I was."

"I was on a date, like I assumed you were, you know, since they call it date night. Why didn't you return my calls or texts yesterday?"

"I needed to unplug for a while," Kate said, unpacking folders. "Gather my thoughts. I took my mother to the casino for the day. Who were you on a date with?"

"Rhea Marquez, my high-speed-internet connection," Didi said coyly, twirling her chunky bracelet.

"The name sounds familiar," she said, half-distracted.

"It should. I've only told you about her and our amazing chats like five times this week. I met her in person for dinner, and she actually looks like her pictures. But don't change the subject. I'm still peeved. I've been dying to know how it went with Jordan."

"Would lunch help my case? My treat," she said with a grin.

Didi huffed. "How am I supposed to keep being your keeper if you don't keep me abreast of where you're keeping yourself?"

Kate gave her a helpful shove out the door. "Here's an idea—don't."

❖

Carrying two panini from the gourmet-grilled-cheese truck, Kate found Didi under a dome of elm trees in the southeast corner of the bustling New Haven green. Her arms were folded across her chest, a scowl decorating her normally spry countenance.

"Hope you're hungry."

"This is your idea of a peace offering?" Didi said. Disapproval notwithstanding, she took a wolfish bite.

"Come on, Didi. I know you're still new to this scene, relatively speaking, but lesbians are supposed to love being outdoors. I can't remember the last time we've had so many continuous days of glorious sunshine."

"If I'm not mistaken, there are several classy sit-down joints around here with outdoor dining," she mumbled, still chewing. "Anyway, what happened with Jordan?"

Kate sighed as she examined her three-cheese, tomato, and avocado sandwich. "It doesn't happen very often, but I'm woman enough to admit when you're right."

Didi's eyes sparkled. "I knew it. You had a good time, didn't you?"

"For ninety-five percent of the date." She smiled as she watched a young couple play-wrestling in the grass.

"And they said it couldn't be done." Didi mimicked the fervor of an old-time TV announcer. "Kate Randall confounds the experts by actually having a good time." Her eyebrows suddenly bunched. "Wait. What happened during the other five percent?"

"Let's begin on a positive note, shall we?" She took a sip of flavored seltzer. "It was fun. Jordan was terrific company, a refreshing combination of maturity, wit, and youthful enthusiasm."

"She has a smokin' hot bod, too, huh?"

Kate smirked, trying not to encourage Didi's crassness. "Yes. Let's just say nature has endowed Jordan with some noteworthy attributes."

"I'll make a mental note to check out her ass better next time I see her."

"You've become quite the pervert in your old age," Kate observed, primly blotting her lips with a napkin.

"It's retroactive," Didi said and vanquished the first half of her grilled cheese.

"I'll tell you what. It's been a long time since I felt that way with someone." She absently caressed her drink bottle. "She's so easygoing. She has the most endearing laugh, and when we kissed…oh, my."

The strawberry Didi plucked from a container of fresh fruit fell out of her mouth and rolled into her lap. "You kissed?"

Kate glanced away bashfully.

"Come on, Randall. Spill it."

Kate smiled. "I'm sure your imagination can do a far better job than I ever could."

"Stop being evasive."

"Actually, that's the dubious five percent. I mean as first dates go, it ranks right up there with the best of them, but just as we started coasting toward the finish line, the wheels fell off." She quivered as she recalled the mortification.

"What do you mean?"

"The kiss was amazing at first, very sensual." She lowered her voice with discretion. "And tingly in all the right places, if you catch my drift."

"Yes, yes, I know what you mean." Didi gestured for her to continue with the details.

Kate's normal volume returned. "And then I just—I don't know. The kiss started getting passionate, and I think I had a panic attack."

"Kate, I'm sure it wasn't as bad as you perceived it."

"No? I may have broken the sound barrier, taking off so fast. I didn't even say good-bye." She fluttered her eyelids to blot out the horrid image. "She must think I'm one crazy bitch."

Didi studied her in disbelief. "You just ran off?"

"No. I mean I probably said good-bye. Or made some noise."

"Who kissed who first?"

"She did."

"She wanted to have sex with you."

"No, she didn't," Kate stammered, increasingly agitated. "She only invited me back to her apartment for a drink."

"She invited you to her place?" Didi shouted.

"Keep your voice down," Kate said through clenched teeth.

Didi flung her napkin into her paper plate. "Unbelievable. Six years without sex is a remarkable feat in itself, but then you bolt away from an opportunity to have it again with only the sexiest woman in the tristate area. That's a personal best."

Kate bit her lip in annoyance. She calmly collected the lunch trash and proceeded toward the nearest receptacle.

"Where are you going? We're not done eating. Wait for me."

"This is why I didn't call you back yesterday." Kate started power-walking away, forcing Didi into a trot to keep up. "It's more complicated than you can possibly understand, Didi. And I'd like to remind you, we had a deal. All I had to do was take her to lunch, and you'd be satisfied, regardless of the outcome. There was no codicil stipulating that if the opportunity for sex presented itself, I had to take it."

"I never said you had to," Didi said, "but I just can't for the life of me imagine why you'd refuse."

"Because I'm not a slut," Kate snapped, then remembered her audience. "No offense."

"You are so lame."

Kate played innocent. "What?"

"Slut-shaming? Really? You reject that patriarchal nonsense more than any of us. But how convenient it suddenly becomes when you don't want to admit you pussied out on the pussy."

"Your case is dismissed, madam," Kate said and quickened her stride to the office.

"Okay, okay. I'm sorry for being so hard on you." Didi sped up and cut in front of Kate. "But couldn't you have just taken one for the team?"

Kate lightly pinched the skin on Didi's upper arm. "You really need to get yourself laid."

Didi shoved an elbow at her. "I'm working on it, but that's a separate conversation. So, what did Sylvia, the gabardine-clad Oracle of Morris Cove, have to say about all this?"

"Nothing. I haven't told my mother because there's nothing to tell. Anyhow, I spent the day with her so I could forget the madness of this week, expunge it from the record. I want things back to normal again."

They entered the office building and headed for the elevator.

"So you didn't like Jordan? Didn't have anything to talk about? Weren't attracted to her?"

"No."

"No to which question?"

"All three."

"I see."

Kate sighed, irritated with Didi's cross-examination. "Ever think of becoming a prosecutor?"

"Let me see if I have this right. You liked Jordan, liked talking with her, and found her attractive, so the next logical statement out of your mouth is that you want to forget you ever met her."

"Are you going to keep this up all afternoon?"

"I'm just trying to sort out the holes in your story. You're saying that even though you had a mostly positive first date, you have absolutely no desire to see Jordan again?"

Kate stopped at the office door. "No, smart-ass. I'm not saying that. I wouldn't mind seeing her again, but I'm quite certain that after the fool I made of myself on Saturday, Jordan wants nothing further to do with me or my overhead compartment full of emotional baggage. So there."

"That's a relief. Now I don't feel so intrusive telling you that you're having dinner with her tomorrow night at her place. Eight o'clock."

"What?" Kate dropped her keychain on the floor.

"I texted her while we were heading to lunch to ask if she had a nice time on your date." Didi unlocked the office door. "She said yes and then asked me if she should thank you by cooking for you at her place. Assuming you didn't have anything better to do, I took the liberty of accepting on your behalf."

Kate followed Didi to her desk. "Why would you do this to me?" she whispered in desperation.

"Stop it. It's just dinner."

Kate clasped her hands behind her back and faced Didi with the determination of Atticus Finch as she contemplated how to counter such a traitorous move.

"You can always cancel," Didi said, her voice issuing a challenge.

"I can handle dinner," Kate said defiantly. She sauntered into her office and collapsed into the chair behind her desk. *You can handle dinner? You barely survived lunch.*

Kate tapped a pen on the arm of her chair. Why shouldn't she accept Jordan's invitation? She tried a pros-and-cons list. The pros list was easy enough: smart, kind, artistic, beautiful, and sexy. Extremely sexy. Hell, some lesbian couples would be sampling wedding cakes by now, and she was stressing over dinner? Sadly, the cons list weighed more. That enormous age difference and serious ambitions for a music career. Together, they would inevitably lead to a host of problems.

In any event, their afternoon together reminded Kate what she'd been missing all these years: the energy of conversation with an attractive, fascinating woman; the buzz of being pursued; the thrill of a smoldering kiss. Not that she anticipated anything meaningful with Jordan, but it felt good to entertain the possibility again—albeit briefly.

❖

That evening after work, Kate and Didi walked over to Zen in downtown New Haven for an alfresco happy hour.

"Hey, ladies," Viv called as she swept into the outdoor bar and made her way to their table. "Where's your lady, Kate? Thought we were all getting together to make it official."

"Not yet," Didi said, as if delivering top-secret information. "Our girl is still shy about being in love."

"Great. A tag team," Kate muttered and signaled for the waitress. "Look, let's get two things straight: she's not my lady." Glaring at Viv. "And I'm not in love." Glaring at Didi. "It was just frickin' lunch."

Viv and Didi exchanged knowing glances as Viv slid onto a stool at their high table.

"Whatever, Kate," Didi said. "Look, we haven't cocktailed together in weeks. An exchange of information needs to happen here."

"Well, while you bitches were out getting your freaks on—finally, I might add—I got started on my community-service hours."

"I wasn't getting my freak on," Kate said. "It was lunch."

"Chill out," Didi said. "What are you, running for office?"

"Okay, while half of you was getting her freak on," Viv said.

Kate looked at Didi. "You slept with Rhea?"

"Yes." Didi shrank in her chair like a naughty child.

Kate's mouth puckered in reproach. "Then you whine about how you can't find a meaningful relationship."

"I don't whine about that. Viv does."

"That was the old Viv. I got new plans."

Red alerts seemed be blaring in Kate's and Didi's heads as the next round of drinks arrived.

"Don't be looking at each other like that," Viv said. "You have no idea the epiphany I had this weekend."

"What's your community-service assignment?" Didi asked. "Shaking martinis for white-collar criminals at Danbury Correctional?"

Kate laughed and Didi joined in.

"Go ahead and laugh," Viv said, "but I've discovered the true meaning of love."

"You fell for an inmate," Kate said. "One of those tax-evading housewives."

"Shut your fool mouth. You know I'm volunteering at New York Presbyterian. You arranged it."

"I know. I'm just teasing you," Kate said. "Believe me, getting them to agree to you being a volunteer baby hugger was no small accomplishment."

"Aww, you're hugging babies?" Didi asked.

Viv leapt up. "Yes, and it was most magical experience I've ever had. I've finally discovered what matters in life. Maia was right all along. Family, children, that's my true purpose in life. I want to be a mother," she said, her eyes bulging.

Kate's jaw dropped.

"If I'd taken a sip of my drink, you'd totally be wearing it right now," Didi said.

"Uh, Vivienne," Kate said. "You haven't been in contact with Maia, have you?"

"Seriously?" Viv huffed. "I make the most significant announcement of my life, and this is what I get from my two best friends?"

"You have, haven't you?" Kate said. "Forget it. I shouldn't know this." She plugged one finger into her ear and retreated to her cosmo.

Viv took out her phone. "That's it. I'm done. You bitches are gonna be so jealous when I'm having play dates with hot actresses and their kids."

"Viv, you know we're just messing with you." Kate squeezed her knee. "We love you and will support you any way we can. And since Didi's already had a kid, she'll raise yours while you're serving out your previously suspended sentence for stalking Maia."

Didi snorted into her drink.

Viv rested her head on Kate's shoulder. "Thanks. You guys are the best. Oh, listen, Kate. I can't make it to the AIDS benefit with you Friday. I'll be at the hospital."

"Viv," Kate whined. "This community service of yours couldn't have come at a more inconvenient time." She whipped her neck toward Didi. "Please come with me?"

"Hell, no. But I know someone who'd probably love to accompany you. And she'd make a stunning accessory."

"Uh, no. I'll go stag again. She'd be bored out of her mind."

"So would we," Didi said. "But that wouldn't stop you from subjecting one of us to it. This doesn't happen to have anything to do with her age, does it?"

"Is that another thinly veiled suggestion that I'm a snob?"

"No," Viv chimed in. "You're just scared. A scaredy Kate."

"And if I wanted to call you a snob, I'd call you one. Come to think of it, yeah, I am calling you one."

"Gee, this has been fun," Kate said. "Check, please."

Didi giggled. "You know you can't live without us. We're taunting you for your own good."

They waited, silently daring Kate to respond. She gave them nothing.

"What's the matter? Hot, young kitty cat got your tongue?" Viv said.

"I can't hear you," Kate said, scrolling through her phone. "I'm busy working. Work emails."

"Yeah. You're working all right," Didi mumbled. "Working yourself into a froth over which one of your hang-ups will doom this thing with Jordan."

"There is no thing," Kate shouted, winning the attention of everyone at the patio bar.

"But there is dinner," Didi said. "Then we'll see."

Kate glared at her. "Yeah, we'll see."

"Winner buys the entire next happy hour," Viv said with a smirk.

"Deal," Didi said.

"I'll be happy to drink on your money next time." Kate smugly pointed at them. "What are the rules of the bet?"

"That you're gonna sleep with her next weekend," Viv said.

"Ooh. I'll take the over-under by a week," Didi said.

Kate chuckled heartily. "Yeah, right. I just met her, and I'm going to sleep with her next weekend?" she asked Viv. "Or this weekend?" she asked Didi, more incredulous. "I'm gonna eat and drink like a Roman emperor after I prove you both wrong."

"Do we have a bet?" Viv asked.

Kate placed her hand between them, and they piled theirs on top.

CHAPTER SEVEN

The Payoff

Unlike lunch on Saturday when Kate and Jordan crunched along on eggshells of nerves and self-consciousness, this time something was different. They watched each other's eyes through the glimmer of candles in the center of the table as they ate and floated along a current of easy conversation. Kate recalled the bet she'd made with the girls the night before and tried not to let her amusement show on her face. Or was the impetuous smile threatening to break out and betray her secrets the result of good wine, good company, and a connection that seemed unnaturally natural?

"Your scampi was scrumptious." Kate dabbed her mouth while savoring the last bite of buttery garlic-and-herb shrimp.

"Thank you." Jordan smiled. "Cooking is a relatively new endeavor for me. I used to have more take-out numbers in my phone than friends."

"I don't believe that for a minute. You're obviously a closet gourmet."

"Well, now that the secret's out...I didn't want to reveal all my mysteries on the first date. It would've spoiled the intrigue."

"Yeah, about that first date." Kate squirmed as the vivid recollection returned like a relapse of bronchitis. "I wanted to apologize for my rather swift departure. I uh, I'm not quite sure what that was all about."

"No need to apologize. You're not the first woman who ran out on me after the first kiss," Jordan said with a grin.

"That's such a lie. But I do appreciate your diplomacy."

"It was my fault anyway. I should've kept my lips to myself."

Kate sighed as she tugged at the ends of her cloth napkin.

"Unfortunately, the onus of that debacle belongs to me. Being out of the dating loop for ages, I realized last Saturday that regardless of what they say, it's not just like riding a bike, not for me anyway."

"As far as I'm concerned, that was just lunch and this is just dinner with a friend," Jordan said. "But if you insist on taking the blame for that kiss, then it was your fault for being adorable."

When Jordan whisked the dirty dishes to the sink, Kate exhaled in the heat of either a hot flash or a blush in full bloom. It had to be the latter since she'd had to rummage through her mind to recall the last time anyone called her that. It never seemed to apply. She smiled. Considering what a lawyer was accustomed to being called, she'd take adorable.

"Really, you haven't dated much since Lydia?" Jordan asked from the galley kitchen.

"Um, let's see…" Kate fondled the stem of her wineglass as she pretended to search for the answer. "Three dates, and two of them were with you."

"No way. That means you haven't had sex in like *years*." She stated it as though Kate was being informed of it for the first time.

Kate arched an eyebrow. "That sounds about right."

Jordan returned to the table, wringing her hands. "Wow, that was rude. I totally wish I'd run that through my head before saying it."

Kate giggled. "It's a lot less clichéd than favorite films and authors. Besides, it's refreshing not being the one putting her foot in her mouth."

"I'm happy to oblige," Jordan said.

"I like the ambience." Kate picked at the wax hardening on the tablecloth, suddenly not so self-conscious.

"Thanks. More wine?"

As Jordan reached over the kitchen counter to get a new bottle of white, Kate furtively admired the grace of her form. "Yes, please," she said, lifting her glass.

"Isn't this body incredible?"

"I beg your pardon?" Kate fumbled her glass as Jordan poured, sending a dribble of chardonnay onto the tablecloth.

"The wine," Jordan said. "I love the oaky finish. Normally, when I buy a bottle, I get change back from a ten, so this is a real treat. Here. Let me get that."

As she stretched across the table to blot the wet spots with her napkin, Kate inhaled deeply. Jordan smelled like she'd just run through a waterfall, fresh and outdoorsy.

"Still wet?"

This girl was killing her.

"Uh…" Kate felt another flare of embarrassment engulf her face. "No. It's fine. Thanks."

Jordan glided into the chair next to Kate instead of across from her. "So what does Kate Randall do for fun?"

"Hmm." Kate hesitated. A response that didn't sound pathetic didn't exactly roll off the tongue. "Well, I love my job, so that's kind of fun. Also, Didi and Viv and I attend and host fund-raisers for several LGBTQ organizations. They're pretty fun, too, as you may have already gathered."

Jordan nodded, then tilted her head to the side as though in awe of Kate. "You help people in everything you do."

"It's not that altruistic. We drink at these events. A lot. Cash bar, of course."

"Oh, of course. But it's still so awesome that's how you spend your free time. Your clients and the people who benefit from the money raised are lucky to have you on their side. You know, I might be able to volunteer my musical services at a future event if you think you could use them."

This girl was amazing.

"Really? That's great. If you're free, there's a cocktail party at the Oceanview next month for True Colors."

"I'll check my schedule, but it shouldn't be a problem. I'd love to help."

Jordan returned Kate's smile with one full of invitation. And innuendo.

"I bet you could use some dessert." She flitted over to the refrigerator and pulled out two flute glasses filled with tiramisu.

"That looks lethal. Don't tell me you made that, too?"

"I might have." She winked at Kate as she handed her a spoon.

"Isn't there anything you don't do well?"

Jordan tapped her finger over her lips, pretending to think. "First kisses." Then, in a sexy drawl, "But if you let me have a do-over, I guarantee you won't run away this time."

"I have no doubt," Kate said, testing a flirty lilt of her own. *Not bad, Randall.*

Leaning on her elbow, Jordan stretched toward Kate and gave her a soft, cinnamon kiss.

Kate opened her eyes and stared at Jordan's mouth as it retreated from hers. "Mmm, flavored kisses. That'll definitely keep a girl from running."

"That and the bolt I put on the outside of the door."

Kate laughed and kissed her back.

"Would you like to watch a movie or step out onto the deck?" Jordan asked.

"Let's clean this up first." Kate carried the dessert dishes into the kitchen.

"Kate, I can do this later."

But she was already at the sink. In the less-romantic fluorescent lighting of the kitchen, Jordan leaned into her shoulder as they rinsed the dishes and loaded them into the dishwasher.

"Thanks for helping," Jordan said.

The closeness electrified her even if she couldn't tell whether Jordan's nearness was intentional. "You went to such lengths to prepare this incredible meal," she said. "How could I in good conscience not help?"

"Okay. Since you're practically begging me to take advantage of you, far be it from me to refuse."

"We're still talking about the pots and pans, right?"

Jordan giggled. "Why? Do I have another option?"

"I don't know. It's been so long, I kind of feel like a virgin again."

"Don't take this the wrong way, but I think I'd have an easier time courting a virgin."

Kate scrunched up her face. "You mean people don't usually welcome the challenge of cracking down the walls of a woman scorned?"

Jordan laughed. "I'll take the virgin any day. The degree of difficulty involved in seducing one of them can't be as high as a scorned woman."

"You know, when someone says they'd prefer wooing a virgin over me, I think it's time I start cultivating a new image."

Jordan stopped scrubbing. "I'm only teasing, Kate. Honestly, I have no agenda. I just enjoy being with you."

"Me, too," Kate said with a smile.

Smiling back, Jordan absently grabbed the hose to rinse the sauté pan and accidentally sprayed Kate in the face. "Oh, jeez, I'm sorry," she gasped and seemed desperate to suppress a smirk.

"It's okay," Kate said calmly. She wiped her face with the top of her forearm.

Jordan continued choking back giggles as they resumed their assembly line of dishwashing, but alas, a few gurgles escaped.

"The least you can do is not laugh," Kate said, further fueling Jordan's fit.

"I'm sorry," Jordan pleaded. Kate could hear a low rumble of laughter bubble in her throat. "You're making it worse telling me not to."

"It's my fault again, huh?" Kate wiggled her fingers under the faucet and flicked a spray of droplets into Jordan's face.

"Hey," Jordan cried. "I said I was sorry." Laughter now pouring out, she wiped off the smattering of water with her palm.

"There," Kate said smugly. "Now we're even."

Glaring at Kate, Jordan began whistling the theme from the climactic gun-fight scene in *The Good, the Bad, and the Ugly*.

"What are you doing?" Kate asked, alarmed.

"There are two of us but only one weapon." She nodded toward the hose attachment. "On the count of three, we draw for it. One…"

"Jordan, let's not get carried away."

"Two…"

"Come on. We're going to get soaked," Kate said, getting silly.

"Three," Jordan shouted.

Four hands descended on the hose, pressing the lever and shooting a fountain of water into the air that rained down on their heads.

After the screaming and shrieks of laughter died down, Jordan licked a splash of water that landed on her lip. Kate suffered the most damage, her splattered face and forearms itchy with droplets. She blinked the wetness out of her eyelashes and then kissed water off Jordan's lips.

"So much for the water-conservation effort," Jordan said, panting.

"Some environmentalists we are."

Kate cleared her throat nervously as another one of those fight-or-flight impulses threatened to crash their party. But this time she decided to ride it out even though the desire in Jordan's eyes had her trembling inside. She wanted to kiss her again, but each one they shared seemed to be ushering them closer and closer to the point of no return.

"Did you know this building used to be an old bra factory?" Jordan said, suddenly seeming nervous.

Kate chuckled. "How rich with symbolism."

When Jordan licked her lips, Kate almost felt them graze hers.

"You want to see the rest of the place?"

"Sure. It'll give me a chance to air-dry."

"Follow me."

Kate trailed Jordan down the narrow hallway, eyeing her curves in those jeans. The bedroom was only feet away.

"Here's the bathroom," Jordan said. "This is an original glass doorknob. I found it at a consignment shop. Isn't it wild?"

"It sure is," Kate said. "Oooh. A claw-foot bathtub." She brushed past Jordan to get a closer look. "I love these."

"Me, too. My grandmother had one."

"Mine, too. I loved taking bubble baths in them."

Kate turned around, not expecting Jordan to be standing so close. She stepped back and almost tumbled over the side into the tub. Jordan grabbed hold of her shirt to steady her, accidentally pulling it out of the waistband of her pants.

"I'm sorry," Jordan said, releasing her grip. "I didn't mean to do that."

"What? Save me from a concussion?" Kate smiled as she straightened out her top.

"No. I just didn't want you to think…"

Kate nodded. "You can relax, Jordan. I think I'm past the point of taking off on you—I think." She spread her lips into a smile.

"After-dinner mint?" Jordan displayed a small tin of mints she'd dug out of her front pocket.

"Sure." Kate's heart thundered at the implication. She plucked two out of the open box, tossed them into her mouth, and crunched them between her molars.

"And the last stop on our tour…the bedroom." Jordan extended her arm in a flourish like a game-show hostess.

Kate brushed past her in the hall but stopped short of entering the bedroom. What was she thinking, about to just stroll right in? The way Jordan had revved her up, if she had, chances were she wouldn't be coming out of there any time soon. Was she ready for that? This felt more and more like a game of seduction, and Kate had better keep her wits in check so she'd be ready for Jordan's next move.

Jordan flicked the switch, and a small lamp on her nightstand went on. As she whirled around to face Kate, she absently raked her hair back with her fingers. Kate measured every inch of the supple contour of Jordan's torso and firm breasts as they expanded the cotton of her black tank top. After that, rational thought no longer guided Kate's actions as she glided into the bedroom as though on a moving walkway between airport terminals.

"This is it." Jordan sighed wistfully as she backed into position in the doorway, making a panicked escape virtually impossible. "It looked a lot bigger before I moved my ginormous furniture in."

The queen-size bed swallowed the space, leaving a narrow perimeter to accommodate two dressers, two guitar stands, and a computer station with a microphone and recording devices.

Kate thought for a moment. "You manage the space well. It's an artful experiment in conservation."

"I like that," Jordan said. "Makes what I'm paying a month in rent sound less ridiculous."

Kate smiled as the back of her legs grazed the poofy bed skirt, warning her of the bed's proximity.

"I'm sorry if I keep staring at you," Jordan said softly. "You're just so beautiful." She lowered her eyes as though the compliment might have offended Kate. "If you have somewhere else you need to be, I'll understand."

Posed against the door frame, Jordan presented an impenetrable force field of sex appeal. Kate could feel her body heat radiating toward her as the distance between them slowly disappeared.

They stood nose to nose, fingers entwined in front of them, giggling softly as their lips grazed back and forth slightly in a tantalizing duet that drove Kate out of her mind. She wanted so badly for Jordan to shove her down on the mattress, pin her there, and drive the fear from her heart. But Jordan wasn't impolite like that. Kate grabbed Jordan's face in her hands and kissed her harder, her frustration pulsating throughout her as they'd raced well past the point of manners.

Jordan whimpered at the forcefulness. Her delicate panting showed Kate she was ready for her. Consumed by passion, she pushed Jordan against the wall, and they stared at each other, Jordan's eyelids heavy as she submitted to Kate's control. Slowly Kate kissed her, flicking her tongue around her lips, teasing her almost vindictively. When Jordan's hands began roaming up her back, Kate restrained them.

"I want you so bad," Jordan whispered.

Holding Jordan's hands behind her back and her body against the wall, Kate devoured her neck and earlobe, prompting a loud moan of pleasure.

What was happening to her? She was going all *Fifty Shades of Grey* on Jordan, tossing her around like a blow-up doll. But the power and eroticism in the control she had over this sultry, beautiful young woman was an aphrodisiac right out of an Aphrodite myth.

As Kate continued to taunt her, Jordan started to wriggle her arms free. She slowly backed Kate toward the bed as her mouth and hands explored with hungry determination. With every stroke of Jordan's fingers, every part of her body came alive. They stopped at the edge of the bed long enough for Jordan to unbutton Kate's silky shirt.

"Kate…" Jordan whispered again.

"What?" Kate whispered impatiently.

"I know it's been a while since—"

"Don't worry. This is definitely like riding a bicycle."

"But if you're not ready, I don't mind wai—"

Kate clutched a fistful of Jordan's belt buckle and jerked her down on top of her, caressing the taut muscles in Jordan's upper back.

She shivered as Jordan kissed her chin and descended slowly down her neck, across her collarbone, any part of exposed skin her lips could access. The longing was almost too much to bear, especially when Jordan's tongue discovered that magic spot behind her ear. She glided her hands around Jordan's hips and pushed their bodies together into a grinding motion. Where had this passion come from? If she had experienced it to those heights before, memories of it were nowhere to be found. Only Jordan. That wild hair tickling her skin and luscious lips she'd daydreamed about biting. It was more than just the release after years of deprivation. With Jordan, her spirit felt as satisfied as her body was about to.

Kate gasped when Jordan grabbed her wrists and pinned them down above her head.

"Everything okay?" Jordan asked.

"Yes, fine," Kate said, writhing beneath her.

"I mean if we're moving too fast—"

"Jordan, another minute of you kissing me like that, and I won't be responsible for my actions." She freed herself from Jordan's control and rolled on top of her.

Jordan moaned softly as she wrapped her long legs around Kate. "Make love to me, Kate. I can't take it anymore." She ripped Kate's shirt out of her pants and dug her fingers into her back.

Kate pulled a fistful of her hair. "You're gonna have to be more patient," she whispered as her tongue glided up her neck.

"Don't stop," Jordan breathed in her ear. She fumbled with the zipper on Kate's pants as Kate pulled Jordan's tank top off over head.

"Turn off the light. Please," Kate said.

After she sent Kate's shirt sailing across the room, she reached over to the chain hanging off the lamp on the nightstand. With one yank, the room went dark, save the shimmer of a voyeuristic moon peering in through the window.

"By the way," Kate whispered. "I like your rendition of dinner with a friend."

As the sun imposed its way in and across Kate's eyelids, she awoke with a start. Jordan's arm extended across her stomach, and her head was nestled firmly into her neck. How was she supposed to extricate herself and slip out of bed without waking her, according to the plan she'd devised before falling asleep sometime after one a.m.? She was sure her left arm was somewhere in the vicinity, but it was numb from the shoulder down, sleeping more soundly than Jordan. What a night. A slide show of passion and pleasure flashed through her brain as she delicately lifted Jordan's arm off her. Now to somehow dislodge Jordan's face from the crook of her neck and shoulder while simultaneously sliding out from under her.

Last night had been incredible, sensual and cathartic in more ways than Kate could attempt to delineate at that moment. This morning, life pulsated through her, all her senses reawakened. Only one thought existed in the entire universe that could send her rocketing toward earth, crashing and burning on impact. What had she done? Yep, there it was, that old familiar cocktail of worry and dread laced with uncertainty, the one that stole the joy out of any guilty pleasure in which a morally principled woman might dare indulge. She'd been determined to keep it simple, but now that they'd done the deed, she'd unequivocally involved herself with Jordan. Maybe sneaking out and calling her later would clearly convey that while last night was special, it didn't signal a plunge into something more intense than either was prepared for.

Tiptoeing down the hall, shoes in hand, Kate was confident she was in the clear; not even a creak of the hallway floor could deter her from reaching the refuge of the apartment door. *There you are, you beautiful creature.* The metal, dead-bolted gateway to her salvation was only a few tips of her toes away.

"Good morning." A perky male voice sang out from the dining-room table, a bowl of cold cereal and the latest issue of *Backstage* arranged in front of him.

Her shoes clunked to the floor.

"Good morning," she whispered as she stooped to pick them up. "I'm sorry. Have we met?"

"No, but I'm William, Jordan's bestie from New York. And if you're not Kate, I'll be awfully chagrined."

"I am," she again whispered, hoping he'd take her cue and tone it down.

"Care to join me in a bowl of Cocoa Puffs?"

"No, thanks. I'm watching my carbs." Her wired eyes darted down the hall.

"But you have to try Jordan's cinnamon-raisin French toast. It's U.F.B."

"What's U.F.B.?"

"Un-Fricking-Believable. Say, you're a lawyer, right?"

"Uh-huh."

"Do you do entertainment law? Once my career picks up, I'm going to need competent legal representation to handle all that unpleasant contractual stuff."

"Actually, my area of expertise is family law, human rights, that sort of thing. But I'd be happy to recommend someone. Listen, I have to get—"

"That would be terrific. Jordan's still asleep?" The tenor of his inquiry seemed to accuse her of something.

"Uh-huh." *Think fast, Kate.* She was about to fold like paper in an origami class. "Well, I have an appointment this morning, and since she was sleeping so soundly, I decided to leave her a note."

"A note?" His voice dropped several octaves as he narrowed his eyes.

"Yes. A note."

He shrugged. "Usually you'd never catch me up at this ghastly hour, but I came in from the City early for an audition this morning." He held up two sets of crossed fingers.

"I won't keep you then."

"It's a speaking part in a union production at the Long Wharf Theater."

"Fantastic. Good luck. I mean, break a leg. I, uh, good-bye."

She stretched her hand for the doorknob; freedom was only inches away...

"You're leaving," Jordan asked sleepily from the hall.

Kate rolled her eyes before turning around. That friggin' kid and his Cocoa Puffs.

"Good morning, Jordan. Yes, I have to get to the office early, and I didn't want to wake you," she explained with a pleasant smile.

"She left a note," William offered from the table.

"I wouldn't have minded," Jordan said softly. Her bare feet padded toward Kate. "I had a wonderful time last night," she whispered in her ear.

"So did I." Kate smiled self-consciously in William's direction after Jordan gave her a peck on the lips. "I'll call you."

"I hope so." Jordan kissed her again.

Once Kate closed the door behind her, she collapsed against it for a moment and sighed. Crisis narrowly averted. Next item on the agenda: getting home, showered, and back to the office in ninety minutes for her ten o'clock appointment. And she thought sneaking out on Jordan after a night of mind-scrambling ecstasy would be the day's greatest challenge.

❖

Kate rapidly flicked a ballpoint pen as she walked out of her office with the ten o'clock appointment she'd kept waiting, a lesbian couple and their five-year-old son. Donna and Willa Ulman-Gravino were in the process of finalizing Willa's adoption of their son born to Donna.

"Everything will be ready for your signatures on Friday." Kate rubbed Willa's back as they stopped at the door.

"Thank you, Attorney Randall," Willa said. She shook Kate's hand profusely. "I feel so much better now that I'm legally able to look out for Ethan's welfare."

"I'm thrilled to help. Nothing brings me greater pleasure than validating a non-biological parent's right to Cub Scouts, car pools, and brawls with Little League umpires."

"Maybe he'll play violin instead," Willa said.

"With all that energy?" Donna said with a grin.

"I'm betting on baseball," Kate said. "Good luck, ladies, and good-bye, Ethan." She patted the little boy's head.

"Thank you again." Donna smiled as she led her family out of the office.

Kate closed the door after seeing them off and turned to Didi who was printing documents at her desk and cooed. "Isn't he cute? With that towhead, he looks just like a mini Anderson Cooper."

"Where were you this morning?" Didi was all manner of business, entirely unmoved by the little tike. "You never stroll in late."

"I don't want to talk about it." Kate poured a cup of coffee from the coffeemaker on the credenza next to Didi's desk and gulped it black.

"You slept over at Jordan's." Didi leapt to her feet with the accusation.

"I said I don't want to talk about it now."

"You slept with her. Yes," she exclaimed with a fist pump. "Next happy hour's on you, moneybags."

"I really screwed up."

"How? Did you forget how to do it?"

"Don't be an idiot. I slept with her on the second date," she said. "Technically, the first, since lunch wasn't really a *date* date. It was just like a preliminary 'getting to know you' thing, a 'you're not a psycho so we can have dinner' thing." With a sudden attack of nerves, she paced the reception area like a nervous shelter dog.

"Ooh, you dirty little whore," she teased with a fake Brooklyn accent. "You ah two steps away from the gutta, missy."

Kate ignored the vignette, lost in contemplation. "I can't believe I did that. Where was my sense of decorum? I must've been temporarily out of my mind."

Didi laughed as she sat on the arm of the sofa. "Kate, if you were able to resist her, then I'd question your sanity. You're such a prude."

"It's so easy for you to be blasé about this, isn't it? You didn't sleep with a girl that's seventeen years younger than you."

"You bitch. Nobody likes a bragger."

Kate rolled her eyes. "Once again you fail to grasp the gravity of the situation."

"Kate, I'm trying to be a friend here," she said sincerely. "For the past week and a half, I've tried to be sympathetic to your dilemma, but frankly, I'm having trouble figuring out the dilemma."

"You're not sympathizing. You're mocking me." Kate stopped pacing long enough to knock back another swig of coffee.

"Kate, I swear I'm not," Didi said, raising her hand to God. "You're looking for things to stress about. So what if she's younger? You're not shopping for someone to marry and have kids with."

"I'm not shopping for anything," Kate shouted. "Dammit, I was so adamant about taking this slow, and in one moment of weakness, I kicked the whole thing into warp speed."

"It wouldn't have happened if you didn't want it to."

"But I didn't want it to." She paused for a moment to see if Didi was going to buy that. No dice. "All right. I did want it to. I just shouldn't have let it."

Didi sighed. "There's no reasoning with you when you're like this. But try to look at it this way: maybe you weren't any good, and she won't ever want to have sex with you again."

"You're a regular Sister of Mercy," Kate said. She retreated to the other arm of the sofa. "I suppose I'm being presumptuous about all this, aren't I? It's quite possible that's all she was out for, and now that she got it, she won't want to see me again."

"Kate, I was kidding. I'm sure you two had outrageously hot sex, but that doesn't mean she's going to expect something serious. Maybe this could be a wild and wonderful summer fling that'll make you the target of every single lesbian's unadulterated scorn."

Kate grimaced at the suggestion. "I don't do flings. You know that."

"How do you ever enjoy yourself being so absolute about everything? A steamy summer love affair could be the most therapeutic thing you've ever done for yourself."

"Or the biggest disaster."

"I could just bask in the warmth of your optimism all day long."

"Come on. You can't possibly believe there's even a remote chance this could work."

"I'm not saying this *will* work. All I'm saying is if I had an afterglow like you have right now, you bet your ass I'd give it a try."

Kate loosened her shoulders and let out a sigh that blew up her wispy bangs into the air. "I do tend to get a little ramped up over things sometimes, don't I?"

"Maybe just a smidge."

"Which is a funny thing because I'm usually so rational."

Didi made no attempt to hide her eye roll.

"I had a glorious evening with Jordan," Kate said. "No need to read anything else into it."

"Now you're finally starting to make sense." Didi slid down on the sofa and patted the cushion for Kate to join her. "Now you just sit right down here and tell Auntie Didi every filthy detail of your naughty night of lust."

Kate smacked her on the back of the head and went into her office.

"All right. Have it your way. Let's talk about me then." She jumped up and stalked Kate into the office.

"Now there's a subject that never comes up."

"Don't you want to know why I can't go with you to the AIDS benefit Friday night?"

"I don't know. Do I?"

"Rhea Marquez asked me to go with her to this jazz bar in Harlem. How awesome is that?"

"Very. I guess sometimes they do buy the cow after getting the milk for free."

"That's unnecessarily cruel. I told you I'm planning on joining CrossFit."

"I didn't mean you're a cow. It's a…never mind."

"Funny how your sense of humor always returns once you're no longer the topic of discussion. Joke if you must, but you were all wrong about online dating. She's fantastic."

"Unlike someone I know, I can admit when I'm wrong. When do I get to meet this dreamboat?"

"Next Saturday night. We're going to Sheila and Amy's for margaritas, the six of us."

"What six of us?"

"You're bringing Jordan."

"The hell I am."

"The hell you're not." Didi's face lit up. "Oh, we're going to have such fun, Kate. This is the first time in the whole three long years we've known Sheila and Amy that we're all going to be paired off. Finally, you won't have to sit there like a pathetic third wheel while they finish each other's sentences. It's annoying after a while, isn't it?"

The more Kate considered the idea, the sweatier her palms became. "I'll have to see if Jordan's free that night. She's very busy on the weekends. I'll bet she has a show."

"Kate, this is the litmus test, the night when our friends meet the significant others. It's judgment day, a make-or-break proposition. It lays the foundation for the future of our relationships."

"I don't have a significant other, nor do I have a relationship. I'm not certain what I have, but I can tell you it's neither of those. Does Viv want to come with us?"

"She's meeting with potential sperm donors."

"She's really going through with this?"

"It seems that way. She's been hanging around outside the Ford modeling agency for a week."

"I'll think about asking Jordan, but I'm not making any promises. This is already moving faster than I'm comfortable with."

"Whatever, Kate." Didi got up and strutted to the door. "Live in your vacuum of loneliness forever if you want, but if you blow this opportunity with Jordan, I refuse to listen to you complain about being single anymore."

"When have I complained about that, to you or anyone else?"

"I'm just making a point."

Kate lowered her reading glasses and studied Didi for a moment. "You know, normal people use facts when making a point."

Didi gave her the talk-to-the-hand gesture. "I'll be trying to get some work done if you need me."

Kate smiled and slid her reading glasses up the bridge of her nose. She loved Didi to death, but she definitely lacked foresight when it came to relationships. If she was comfortable diving headfirst into something with a cyberdate, well enough, but Kate preferred to use reason when making decisions of the heart. Well, not counting last night.

After a deep breath, she attempted to refocus her attention on work—although it wasn't easy with visions of Jordan and their night of passion igniting in her mind like a fireworks display.

CHAPTER EIGHT

Reality Check

Kate checked her appearance in the rearview mirror as she waited at a traffic light down the street from the posh St. Regis Hotel. Although her eyes twinkled like a girl's in the streetlights, her lids looked heavy, and the closeness of her reflection made her feel her age. If she had taken Didi's advice and invited Jordan, she wouldn't be alone in the car contemplating the rings in her trunk like an ancient redwood or how much her life had changed in the month since Didi had dragged to her Moxy's. But inviting Jordan would've meant a move to the next level. An introduction to professional associates Kate had known for years would mean she and Jordan were actual girlfriends, significant others, or, more frightening, in a full-on, legit relationship.

She thought about Jordan again and felt a twinge in her stomach. Lately, every time she thought of her she'd experienced a twinge somewhere. Jordan was amazing in so many ways, namely in her power to keep Kate grounded in the moment. When they were together, the simple pleasure and richness of the present prevailed. Jordan's eyes, brimming with candor and possibility, chased away any temptation to agonize over the past or an uncertain future. Life was what it should be, and when Jordan left, something in Kate left with her.

Suddenly, Jordan's cell number popped up on her car's navigation screen. She touched the Bluetooth icon to answer.

"Hey." Jordan's sultry voice thundered throughout the car.

"Hey, yourself. What's going on?"

"Working at home, but I'll be done in a couple of hours. Can I see you tonight?"

The question jarred her as though she'd nailed a raised manhole cover in the road. Now she was going to have to explain. "I'm heading over to the St. Regis for the evening."

"Oh."

"It's the Bar Association AIDS fund-raiser. Didn't I mention that yesterday?" Kate asked casually, knowing she hadn't.

"No. I don't think so." Disappointment hung in the air like drugstore cologne.

"Well, these things are terrible yawners. Be grateful I forgot." Kate faked a laugh, then cringed at her lameness.

"That's fine. No big deal."

Apparently, it was a big deal. Hurt resonated in Jordan's voice.

"Actually, I bought the ticket back in April, and I don't think I could've..." The lie was starting to lump in her throat.

"Kate, it's okay, really. You had these plans before we even met."

"You're a sport."

"Do you think it will run late?"

"I usually sneak out by eleven, if not sooner."

"Okay. Whatever I do tonight, I won't be home late. Call me if you want," Jordan said, pausing. "I kind of miss you."

"Aww, that's nice," Kate said. "I kind of miss you, too. And wherever you go tonight, beware of middle-aged women playing wingman for their single friends."

Jordan giggled. "It didn't turn out too badly the first time it happened."

"No, it didn't," Kate said warmly. "We're still on for tomorrow night?"

"Absolutely."

"Okay. I'll swing by to get you around seven. You'll want something in your stomach for an evening like that."

"I'm ready for anything." Jordan paused. "I'm looking forward to seeing you."

Kate's tangled-up feelings dissolved into sweet repose. "Me, too." No shade required this time.

As she pulled into the hotel parking lot, she kicked herself for not inviting Jordan. For the last four years, she'd moped around the ballroom of the St. Regis, a sideline spectator as others cocktailed and dined with carefree ebullience, dancing until midnight with all kinds of partners. And this year she'd do it again, hopefully without patronizing smiles from a catty duo of personal-injury lawyers who knew Lydia from her days as the head of claims adjustment for Connecticut's largest auto-insurance company.

❖

The ballroom of the St. Regis sparkled in silver and white winter majesty, as this year's annual AIDS fund-raiser was themed *A Winter Wonderland.* Kate stood alone by an hors d'oeuvres table and ran a finger across a blanket of puffy white felt as she nibbled a scallop wrapped in bacon. The line between tacky and festive was blurred as someone had clearly spent way too much time adorning the room with paper snowflakes and strings of white lights. Feeling chic in her Halston beige pantsuit over a silky black camisole, Kate opted for festive.

She glanced around the room full of revelers drinking, dancing, and laughing and concluded she'd committed a faux pas by not inviting Jordan. What had she been so concerned about? Her beauty and grace notwithstanding, she could've protected Kate from the creepy life-size robotic Santa Claus staring at her from the side of the table.

"Hey, you," said a skinny young woman with short, wiry hair as she approached. She offered Kate a glass of champagne just grabbed off a passing waiter's tray.

"Sandra, how are you?" Kate beamed. She kissed the young court clerk she'd befriended last summer at a Lambda Legal cookout in the Hamptons.

"I'm great. Rumor has it you're off the market."

"You've obviously run into Didi recently."

"Is she here?"

"Didi?"

"No. Your new paramour."

"Oh. Uh, no. It's a casual thing. We're just dating."

"Didi said she's a musician. That's awesome. Would I have heard of her?"

"Maybe. Jordan Squire. She's performing at the Charlesworth winery next week."

"That's right. I saw that event listed. If I can check it out, I'm sure I'll see you there."

"Uh, maybe," Kate said, padding her response with indifference. "You know, if I'm free."

"I don't think I've ever seen you looking so radiant. She obviously agrees with you."

Kate smiled. "Thanks."

"Speaking of paramours, I'd better go find mine. Great seeing you again."

Sandra dashed off into the crowd, leaving Kate vulnerable to the women she'd made a point of avoiding since arriving. The predatory pair picked up her scent and meandered over to her at the bruschetta platter.

"Kate," Mitzi Fitzgerald trilled as she and Liz Greenwald flanked her.

"Hello, girls." She greeted them with a cautious smile and requisite air kisses.

"You're missing all the dish," Liz said, as if part of a conspiracy.

"Am I?"

"Did you see Judge Clark's new rug?" Liz asked. "It looks like a squirrel had an abortion." She giggled at the older man with the noticeable toupee resting above his shiny forehead.

"I guess I missed that one."

"So how are you, Kate," Mitzi asked. "Do you ever see Lydia anymore?"

Kate glanced at her quizzically. "Mitz, you ask me that every year. No. I don't."

Mitzi regarded her as though Kate was the grieving widow at a wake. "I'm sorry, Kate. I know it's hard. Someday soon you'll be over her and ready to get out there and meet someone else again."

Kate opened her mouth to rebut Mitzi's claim but considered the source and saved her energy.

"Did he really think no one would notice?" Mitzi said. "It's not even a good one, like William Shatner's."

"Perhaps he mistook his colleagues for adults," Kate mumbled, but they were already too far gone.

This was what an attorney had to look forward to after reaching the pinnacle of her career? Whatever happened to stimulating discussions in which great legal minds compared ideas about how they could use their powers for good instead of evil? Liz and Mitzi were fun gals, if you were at a sorority party, but together they worked like repellent against a reasonably intelligent conversation.

She checked her phone, only to receive the dismal news that it was barely eight o'clock. For fun, she texted Jordan.

Being held hostage by obnoxious women. Send help. Lol. ;-)

A few moments later, Jordan responded.

Lol!!! I'll send a carriage, Cinderella! Hang in there. <3

Kate smiled despite her limited options. She could ask one of the gals to hold her glass and run like the wind, or she could keep swiping champagne off the trays of passing wait staff. Maybe she should just tell Mitzi and Liz exactly what she thought of them.

"Oh, waiter," Kate called out, then snatched another glass from a passing tray.

"Look over there," Mitzi said. "It's Fred Hillcrest flaunting his pseudo-super-model wife."

Fred Hillcrest's distinguished silver hair stood out across the room as he socialized with his young, amply endowed spouse.

"I'll be surprised if she's the legal drinking age," Liz said in disgust.

The champagne pushed a burp up from Kate's diaphragm. Slamming down that second glass probably wasn't the brightest idea she'd ever had. "They look happy, though, don't they?"

"*He* looks happy. Look what he's getting."

"Yeah. She's gorgeous, thin, and sexy," Liz said. "What does she get out of the deal?"

"You mean besides his money?" Mitzi laughed.

"Maybe she just likes older men," Kate said, hoping they wouldn't smell her desperation.

"Come on, Kate," Liz replied.

"I swear something happens to a man's vision when he snags a younger woman. If he could only see how ridiculous he looks with her."

Liz and Mitzi broke into sinister laughter.

"Excuse me, ladies." Concluding that the mad dash was the best option, Kate thrust her empty glass at Mitzi and jetted off.

"Kate?" Liz called after her, but she'd already reached the cover of the ladies' room.

Thank heavens for soft lighting. Kate examined herself in the full-length mirror of the ruby velour lounge. Damn that Mitzi and Liz. She was allowing their mean-spiritedness to settle in her chest. The math on Kate's birth certificate might have equaled forty-seven, but her appearance hadn't yet caught up with her age. Thanks to regular elliptical workouts, a low-carb diet, and generous heredity, she still won glances from strangers. She was several years younger than Fred Hillcrest, but at that moment she couldn't seem to distinguish herself from him.

She tugged at her suit jacket and tried to reassure herself that she didn't look ridiculous with Jordan on her arm, in spite of the double take their pairing had registered from the waiter at the sushi restaurant. She studied the fine lines around her eyes and tapped the skin under her chin as she envisioned Jordan's taut olive complexion, the radiance in her youthful eyes, the fullness of her lips.

Her reflection taunted her. Sure, she finds you appealing now, but wait till you're sporting your first set of crow's feet. She sucked in her cheeks and exhaled, disappointed with the direction in which her thoughts had wandered. Superficial insecurity? Wasn't it a little late in the game for that?

She sniffed the flowery bowl of potpourri on the granite counter and forged onward to dinner.

By ten fifteen, Kate's restlessness got the best of her, and after making a quick round of good-byes, she left. As the elevator door opened to the lobby, she yawned, relishing the thought of a little late-night texting with Jordan from the comfort of her cozy bed. When the yawn cleared from her eyes, a mirage in the lobby came into view—Jordan glancing down at the phone in her lap. She moved closer to scrutinize the vision.

"Hi," Jordan said brightly. She jumped up from the sofa and engulfed Kate in a passionate hug.

"I should've known something was up when you asked what time I was leaving." She inhaled the tangy citrus body lotion on Jordan's skin, suddenly grateful for Mitzi's and Liz's harassment.

"You sounded like you could use some assistance, and the whole damsel-in-distress thing is a real turn-on."

"Really? Were you hoping to find me tied to the railroad tracks?"

"Maybe," Jordan said with a flirty smile. "I just knew I'd never fall asleep tonight if I didn't get to say good night to you."

"You could've called me."

"Is that what you'd rather I'd done?" Jordan gazed at her out of the corners of her big eyes.

Kate grinned. "No." After all, what was more appealing: texting Jordan from separate beds or sharing one with her?

Fifteen minutes later, Kate swiped the keycard through the door of room 814, lips firmly locked on Jordan's, hands fumbling with buttons and zippers. She flipped on a light switch so they could maneuver toward the bed without stumbling over the luggage rack.

Jordan stripped off Kate's silky beige blazer and threw it in the air where it floated to the carpet. "You're so sexy in this," she said, caressing the satiny material. "And you smell so good."

"It's balsamic dressing, walnut-crusted salmon, and cauliflower florets," Kate said as she pulled Jordan's shirt over her head.

"So the food was tasty?" Jordan said as Kate tore at the belt buckle on her jeans.

"It was almost worth dodging gossipy shrews all night," Kate replied while kissing Jordan's neck.

"No dessert?" Jordan asked. "Never mind," she said with a moan of pleasure.

Still entwined and devouring each other's lips, they shuffled over to the king-size bed. Kate tore down the sheets, and Jordan freed her from the last of her conservative ensemble. Clad in a peach lace bra and underwear, Jordan pushed her down on the bed, her body slowly creeping up Kate's until they faced each other, green and blue eyes blended in an ocean of desire. In a luxurious bed, skin on skin, bodies in one fluid motion, Kate shut out the complicated world of age difference and relationships and commitment.

Two hours later, they'd passed out in each other's arms. As Kate slept the sleep of the gratified, she dreamed of the ecstasy Jordan brought her, the softness of her fingertips tracing her face, the heat of their bodies together. Little by little, Jordan was quietly wearing down her defenses, working away her rigid reserve, and maybe, just maybe, that was okay.

CHAPTER NINE

The Margarita Test

In the calm before the party's official start with the pouring of the first pitcher, Kate watched Jordan gaze at the night sky, admiring the shine from the moon on her supple lips.

Right up till the afternoon of the meet-the-friends margarita summit at the downtown apartment of Amy and Sheila, Kate was still voicing her objections to Didi about introducing Jordan to their friends so soon. They'd only been seeing each other for about a month, even though it felt much longer on a spiritual level. Although Kate forgot about the minefield of potential problems before them when they were alone together, she still actively scouted for any red flags Jordan might have been waving.

Cynicism aside, she was happy Jordan had come along willingly.

"Look at that moon," Jordan whispered. "It's a big, ripe tangerine. A perfect accent for cocktails on the rooftop."

"It is," Kate said, smiling at Jordan's enthusiasm. "Except that it sometimes appears that color when the atmosphere is full of pollution."

"How festive."

"Amy and Sheila better stick with strings of Chinese lanterns," Kate mumbled, and they shared a clandestine giggle.

Gathered around the patio table draped in a tablecloth dotted with tiny sombreros and cacti, the ladies grazed on an enticing spread of chips, pita bread, two kinds of salsa, homemade guacamole, and a tray of Sheila's famous five-alarm jalapeño nachos. Three citronella candles placed around the perimeter warded off any bloodsuckers arriving to feast on a banquet of salty arms and legs.

"Your attention, please," Amy said with mock formality. "The 900 Chapel Rooftop Cocktail Club is now in session. Who's ready for some jailbait?"

Kate and Didi exchanged glances.

"What?" Amy said. "That's my name for my signature margarita." She brandished two pitchers as five hands thrust glasses at her.

"We're so pleased to welcome two more to our little klatch," Sheila exclaimed. "As you can see, tonight's theme is Tijuana 'til Dawn, and we'd like to thank Didi for her ever-popular black bean and corn salsa and Kate for making her customary raid on the liquor store on her way over."

The table broke into applause.

"You seem a little tense," Jordan whispered. "Everything okay?" She stole Kate's hand from her lap and held on to it.

Kate nodded and smiled, rendered speechless by Jordan's adoring eyes. But at the moment, everything wasn't okay. A tremor of anxiety was growing in her as she wondered what her friends were thinking about Jordan. She could've sworn Amy and Sheila were communicating telepathically, and it could only be about their age difference. Didi's date, Rhea, seemed particularly curious about her as well.

When Kate's mind returned to the conversation, Didi was delivering the punch line to a dirty joke.

"Ay, easy. There's a child in the room," Rhea teased, winking at Jordan.

The free-spirited flow of the evening ground to a halt as Jordan's and Kate's embarrassment reflected on everyone else's faces.

"I'm just kidding," Rhea said. "She knows she's not a kid. You're what, thirty-four, thirty-five?"

Didi winced, apparently feeling Kate's pain.

"Thirty," Jordan mumbled, then shoved a guacamole-heaped pita triangle into her mouth.

"Thirty?" Sheila said. "You were born the year we were all still drooling over Cagney from *Cagney and Lacey*."

"Um, speak for yourself," Didi said. "I was drooling over Rob Lowe in *St. Elmo's Fire*."

"That's right, the late bloomer," Amy said. "Who wasn't drooling over him? He was so pretty."

"Still is," Rhea added.

Everyone laughed, including Kate, who cringed from the lost look on Jordan's face regarding their pop-culture references.

"So Jordan's a singer," Kate said.

"Yes," Didi said, "a fantastic singer and guitarist. She's performing at Charlesworth Winery next weekend. We should all go."

"That sounds like fun," Amy said.

"What kind of music do you play?" Sheila said.

"Are they covers or originals," Amy asked.

"My sets have a mix of both. I call my originals lez-rock. I think I have a unique sound, but I include some notes of Brandi Carlile meets Melissa Etheridge seasoned with a little Janis Joplin."

"That sounds hot," Rhea said, directing her comment solely at Jordan.

"Yes, that's it." Didi slapped her thigh. "I've been trying to figure out how to describe you in meaningful phrases, not just 'fantastic' and 'awesome.'"

"I'll take fantastic and awesome," Jordan said with a humble grin.

"It certainly wouldn't be a lie," Rhea said.

Amy glanced over at Kate with a hint of confusion in her eyes. Kate grinned, relieved someone else noticed Rhea flirting with her date. So why hadn't Didi?

"Okay, Miss Fantastic and Awesome," Didi said. "Looks like you'll have yourself a special contingent in your winery audience."

Jordan smiled at Didi and threw her arm around Kate.

"Yeah, the cougar contingent," Rhea said, and everyone laughed. Everyone except Kate.

"I hate that term," she said, stern-faced. "Isn't it just another word for 'old whore'?"

"If the stiletto fits…" Didi said.

The group laughed again as Kate shifted in her chair.

"It's just a joke, honey," Jordan said. "You're not a cougar. You're much too elegant for that."

"Yeah, lighten up, will you?" Didi said out of the corner of her mouth.

Feeling like the butt of the joke, Kate drained her margarita and shoved the empty glass toward Sheila, who was seated by the pitcher.

"Let's have a toast," Amy said, raising her glass. "To a gorgeous summer night with refreshing margaritas and fine friends, old and new."

"Is that another age joke?" Didi said to Amy with mock seriousness.

"I'm looking around, and I don't see any old broads here," Rhea said.

"Especially Didi, who's living out her second adolescence," Kate said.

Didi mugged at the attention. "They weren't kidding when they said life begins at forty. Talk about a renaissance. I'm like a whole new person."

"A complete sexual reawakening will do that for you," Kate said. "Some of us experience rebirths of another, less auspicious kind."

"For some, it's divorce," Rhea said, turning pensive. "The inevitable implosion of the happily-ever-after myth."

Amy pulled a face. "Speaking as the senior member of the longest surviving couple out here, happily-ever-after isn't a myth. Twenty-four years and still going strong," she said, waving her thumb between herself and Sheila.

"Can you corroborate that?" Kate teased them.

"Don't look at me," Sheila said. "I just do what she tells me."

Amy swatted Sheila's arm. "We used Didi's renewed vigor for life as a paradigm for revitalizing our marriage. Thanks to her, Sheila and I have an appreciation for the value of each new day. Age doesn't define us, and it doesn't decide who gets to stay or fall in love."

Didi buffed her fingernails on her chest, delighting in Amy's acclaim.

Kate grinned. "What's this new life philosophy all about, Didi?"

"We've talked about this, Kate. It's about being," Didi said. "Seizing the present, reaching that higher tier of consciousness about life and identity. It's elusive to most people, but true fulfillment can only be found there." She stood up and drew everyone in with her enthusiasm. "Life is like a carousel, ladies. Ride it as many times as you want. As Viv would say if she were here, 'we up in dis bitch.'"

Kate stood, too, as though Didi's partner in the presentation. "A healthful alternative to the midlife crisis," she said.

"It's what comes after the crisis," Didi said, "in that moment of clarity achieved after you've gone through your Wellbutrin prescription and every flavor of Ben and Jerry's. It's the phoenix rising from the ashes of the former you."

"I feel something rising," Kate muttered as she sat, and everyone broke into laughter.

"True love and happiness exist, Kate," Didi said, "whether you want to believe it or not."

"I believe in true love," Jordan said.

"You're a kid. You haven't been down in the trenches long enough." Kate laughed, believing she'd made a sardonic observation, but Jordan looked like a mortally wounded deer and Kate, the hunter.

"Jordan, see what you have to look forward to many years down the road?" Rhea said.

"I have to use the bathroom." Jordan got up and walked into the apartment.

Suddenly, everyone was looking at Kate like she was the hunter, too.

"You're such an idiot," Didi muttered.

"What?" Kate asked innocently.

"You called her a kid," Amy said. "Kids find that very insulting."

"You better go after her," Didi said.

Kate continued professing her innocence with her eyes. "She's using the bathroom."

"Go in there and wait for her to come out." Didi shoved her in the direction of the door.

"I think we're ready for the lemon-lime ones now," Amy announced.

Didi said loud enough for Kate to hear, "If you don't have a name for those, how about 'foot in mouth'?"

Kate stood like the Queen's Guard outside the bathroom waiting for Jordan to come out. What was wrong with her? She made a living out of carefully organizing her thoughts and selecting her words before speaking only to say something totally inane and insensitive like that to Jordan.

"Jordan." Kate tapped lightly on the door. "Are you in there?"

"Where else would I go to the bathroom?"

"I mean is everything okay?" Kate asked.

A toilet flush seemed to answer the question. Jordan opened the bathroom door after a few minutes, drying her hands on the hand towel. "Are you sorry you brought me here?"

"What? No. Why?"

"You don't seem yourself tonight. You seem uncomfortable, especially when they were joking about age and stuff."

"If you ask Didi and Viv, they'll tell you 'uncomfortable' best describes me in most situations." Kate forced a laugh to lighten the mood.

"You don't seem that way when we're alone," Jordan said, looking deliciously vulnerable. "Maybe I should go. My apartment's only a few blocks from here."

Kate grabbed her hand. "No. Don't be silly. I don't want you to go. Look, I'm sorry for that dumb joke. It's not you. You're just the first person I've brought around to the girls so, you know, I'm a little out of my element."

"Are you sure?" Jordan's field-green eyes pleaded with Kate's.

"Yes," Kate said with a reassuring kiss on her lips.

"Hey, lovebirds, can I get some help in here?" Rhea called out from the kitchen. "Kate, can you take these outside?" She handed Kate a tray of quesadillas. "Jordan, you can help me finish the drinks."

After dropping off the tray at the table, Kate strolled over to the stone safety wall overlooking the green. The moon had drifted westward, perhaps to illuminate some other party under way on a different rooftop that balmy night. Didi joined her, cupping a handful of tortilla chips.

"What do you think of Rhea?"

"She's a no-nonsense kind of gal, strong personality. She's perfect for you."

"You think so?"

"Sure." Kate followed a faint trail of exhaust from a jet sailing across the sky, wondering if she should bother asking if Didi had noticed that Rhea was a horrendous flirt.

"I like her a lot," Didi said. "I admit I went into this with really low expectations, but she's an exceptional woman, driven, fun, straightforward. And the sex...sweet Jesus."

"I heard that," Kate said with a sober smile. "I'd almost forgotten what it felt like to be desired, to make love out of raw passion and not obligation."

"Do you think that's the fate of all long-term relationships?" Didi said. "Obligation?"

Kate pondered the idea. Even though that had been the case with Lydia and her, she wanted to believe it wasn't the rule. "I think it's different when you're with the right person. It has to be."

"I know I haven't known her long, but Rhea's everything I've always wanted in a person but never thought I'd find."

Kate was about to broach the subject of Rhea's flirting, but after observing the huge, mannequin-like grin plastered on Didi's face, she decided to shelf it for a future discussion.

Didi inhaled the night air as though it were recharging her soul. "Life is good, my friend."

"It has its moments." Kate turned away from the city and faced her. "Didi, I need you to tell me the truth about something. When I'm with Jordan, do I reek of midlife crisis? Do I scream it like the ubiquitous bald guy driving out to the Hamptons in a Corvette convertible?"

"What? No way. Listen, you are a living illustration of my philosophy. You're finally allowing yourself to live by your own definition—or no definition at all. I can't remember the last time I saw you this happy."

"Really?" Kate said, skeptical. "I feel more anxious and uncertain than anything else. I mean it looks so weird when an older person dates a much younger one. You have to admit they catch your attention."

"Yes. I've seen a few couples who take ludicrous to a whole new altitude, but that's not you and Jordan. If someone stares at you, it's only because you're stunning."

"Overanalyzing again?"

"Definitely."

"Thought so."

"You're just lucky I have Rhea," Didi said. "I'd be so jealous of you if I didn't."

Kate smiled, mildly appeased.

"Now if you're finding this dalliance with Jordan too much of a burden, I'll be glad to take her off your hands. I can handle both of them."

Kate chuckled. "I have no doubt you could."

The covert giggling at the wall drew Sheila and Amy over like the mosquitoes held at bay by wafting citronella.

"Well, kids, the jury's in," Amy announced as she and Sheila approached on either side of Kate and Didi. "We think you both have fabulous new girlfriends."

"It's so wonderful to see you both with someone," Sheila said. "How did you manage to find them at the same time?"

Kate raised her hands, denying all responsibility. "This one has Didi's stink all over it."

"Would you listen to her," Didi said, planting a hand on her hip. "Did I force you two to meet? Did I force you to invite her to lunch and then accept her dinner invitation for you?"

"Yes, yes, and yes."

Didi nudged Sheila's shoulder and grinned. "Kate's right. I should stop being so modest. I'm the one who orchestrated this fairy-tale romance."

"Does this mean all the cradle-robbing jokes have to stop?" a tipsy Amy asked.

"Amy." Sheila admonished her.

"That would be nice," Kate said.

"We should probably get back to the table so your girlfriends don't come back and think we're conspiring," Sheila said.

"Okay, but one last issue to settle," Didi said as they headed back to the table. "Whose girl is cuter, mine or hers?"

"Hmm," Sheila said. "Rhea's definitely the sexy sophisticate, but Jordan's got the market cornered on exotic. Is she Latina?"

"Half Greek on her mother's side," Kate said. "She definitely has a bit of the Greek goddess thing going."

"Kate, are you in love with her already?" Amy asked.

"We just met. Nobody's in love. This is just a casual thing."

"Maybe you're not, but Jordan is," Didi said. "I'm assuming." She amended her statement after Kate shot her daggers.

Amy and Sheila nodded in unison.

"You guys are all nuts," Kate said. "She knows we don't have a future. I'm old enough to be her mother."

"Kate, change the song," Didi said.

"Look, we're just dating." Kate's tone grew defensive. "And who even knows for how much longer. That's all this is."

Didi and Amy exchanged looks of shame, but the tension lifted as Rhea and Jordan returned with the trays of margaritas.

❖

As it neared one a.m., calmness floated in on a breeze. The ladies were still entertaining varying degrees of buzzes, but the conversation was waning, the lulls replaced by yawns.

"We should hit the bricks now," Kate said, peeling her legs off the chair.

"Time to call it a night," Sheila said, tapping Amy, who'd nodded off.

Amy shook herself awake. "We lifer couples need to go to sleep early, unlike you passionate lovebirds who can stay up all night."

"There's something to be said for longevity," Rhea said.

"You can keep your passionate, lovebird stuff," Amy said. "I wouldn't trade my cozy old pair of slippers here for anything in the world." She crushed Sheila's face in a robust hug around the neck.

Kate's evening glow faded, clouded over by the innocent flaunting of the partnership Amy and Sheila still cherished. It was tricky enough navigating the choppy waters of dating as a young woman, but starting over in her forties was a drag, especially when witnessing those playful moments between two people who knew every sunspot on each other's skin and every dream in their hearts.

"Anywho," she said brightly. "I better get out of here before someone refers to me as an old slipper."

"Timeless, maybe, but old? Never." Jordan caressed Kate's back.

Jordan's remark elicited a round of woos and cheers that reverberated between neighboring buildings.

"Come on, you," Kate said, tugging Jordan by the arm toward the table.

"This was a great time." Rhea's eyes fluttered toward Jordan.

"We'll have to do this again soon," Didi said. She joined the group gathering glasses, serving trays, candles, and other leftover miscellany.

Feeling the weight of Jordan's stare, Kate looked up and realized from the way Jordan was looking at her that Didi's assessment may have been spot-on.

❖

Kate and Jordan walked the few blocks back to Jordan's apartment off lower Chapel Street in unusual silence. Kate finally broke it with an affectionate punch to Jordan's shoulder.

"Why so quiet?"

Jordan sighed. "I'm contemplating whether I should open my mouth about something."

"If it's making you quiet, you probably should."

Jordan grabbed Kate's arm and swung it as they walked. "I think Rhea might have come on to me when we were making the drinks."

Kate considered the statement for a moment. "Is this based in fact or supposition?"

Jordan eyed her curiously. "Attorney Randall, are you trying to discredit the witness?"

"No. Protect her. There's a big difference between thinking and knowing. Opposing counsel would tear you apart if you said you 'think' on the stand."

"Okay," Jordan said. "I suppose the comment about my thong when I bent over can be considered hearsay, but I'm going to have to argue that her attempt to help me get more chips down from the cabinet was a come-on beyond a reasonable doubt."

Kate giggled at her quick mastery of the courtroom lingo as she resumed the cross-examination. "What's wrong with helping you get chips?"

"She's four inches shorter than I am. If I could barely reach the top shelf, how useful was she going to be?"

Kate went silent.

"Maybe I misinterpreted it," Jordan said softly. "I knew I should've kept my mouth shut."

"No, no, I believe you. I'm just deciding if it would do any good to share this information with Didi."

"Let's forget about it," Jordan said. "If you tell Didi, and she doesn't believe me, it will make things really uncomfortable, especially when we all get together again."

"If we *don't* tell her, things could get really uncomfortable for you. Do you want to keep being leered at and who knows what else against kitchen counters?"

"That depends on who's doing the leering." Jordan kissed Kate's neck.

"Then again, I'd hate to burst Didi's bubble," Kate said. "She's so psyched about Rhea."

"In that case, maybe you should tell her. What if she catches major feelings for her?"

"Didi's been around the block enough to know a player when she sees one, if Rhea really is one. She could've just been feeling the margaritas. Some people are awkward when they meet new people. We shouldn't judge her too harshly."

"I guess you're right. I could've misread the situation."

"It doesn't seem like it. You poor thing. You spent half the night getting insulted by Rhea and the other half getting harassed by her. I really threw you to the wolves, didn't I?"

"Yes, you did." Jordan pouted. "Next time I'm not leaving your side."

They shared a laugh, and Jordan draped Kate's arm around her shoulder as they strolled.

"She actually mentioned your thong?" Kate said after a moment. "I didn't even know you wore one."

Jordan giggled. "It was supposed to be a surprise for later."

"I see. Does that mean your friend, William, is gone?"

"Yes. He crashes now and then when he pops in from the city."

"Then what are we waiting for?"

Kate grabbed Jordan's hand and started jogging down the street, Jordan shrieking with delight.

The next morning Kate awoke to the smell of coffee wafting into Jordan's sunny bedroom. She'd been sleeping so well lately. Was it from the emotional exhaustion of fretting about a relationship with Jordan or from the sheer bliss of it? Whatever it was, leaving her bed seemed harder, and the days and hours between their dates, longer.

Jordan poked her face into the room. "Good morning, sleepy."

"Good morning," Kate said, rubbing her eye as she stretched.

Jordan jumped onto the bed and started kissing Kate's face all over. "Breakfast in bed or on the balcony?"

"You made me breakfast?"

"Spinach and asiago egg-white omelet and whole-grain toast with local honey. I figured it would keep you from running out on me so soon."

"It's Sunday," Kate said, brushing Jordan's curls out of her eyes. "I'm not running anywhere."

"Good." Jordan got back into bed and coiled her arms and legs around Kate as though she was guaranteeing Kate kept her promise. "Does that mean I have you for the day?"

"If you want me for the day." Kate squeezed her tight and kissed her head, feeling right at home.

"I do," Jordan said, and pecked at her lips. "I don't care if we stay in bed all day. I just want to spend it with you."

Kate sighed as Jordan nestled even closer, sliding her toes across Kate's legs. She closed her eyes, as serene and steady as the flow of a stream in springtime. How thoughtful of Jordan to cook for her. Everything Jordan had done over the past month seemed to leave Kate feeling special, wanted, and appreciated. She was becoming accustomed to it. Too accustomed to it. What if she was slipping back into her old ways? Becoming emotionally dependent on Jordan—codependent. No, that couldn't happen again. She wouldn't let it. In fact, now might be a good time to check herself—to slow the velocity of their relationship down to something more manageable.

Suddenly, Jordan's head popped up, and she gazed at Kate as though she were about to make an announcement of national importance. As her lips parted, panic swept through Kate. Oh, please don't say it, she thought. Please, not yet.

Jordan smiled and kissed her instead.

"Let's have breakfast out on your balcony." Kate scrambled out of bed and reached for her shirt from the night before. "It looks like a gorgeous day. Maybe we can take a ride and find a nice seafood restaurant later."

"Sure," Jordan said, seeming confused by Kate's abrupt shift in demeanor. "How about a hike or something after we eat?"

"Sounds great." She hauled up her pants and hustled out of the room like a busted poker player after a losing hand.

Chapter Ten

Overanalyze This

I was surprised I could snag you on a Sunday afternoon." Kate twirled her linguini and clams around her fork at their outdoor table on Wooster Street, New Haven's Little Italy.

"Rhea had a few showings today," Didi replied casually as she split a meatball in half.

"Got another workaholic in your life, huh? You'll see it's the price we female entrepreneurs must pay for our success. Are you seeing her tonight?"

"I'm supposed to. She said she'd call my cell when she's free." Didi then beamed at Kate. "Look at you. You're positively radiant."

Precisely timed with the compliment, Kate shoved a forkful of rolled linguini into her mouth. "Why do people keep telling me that? Am I radioactive or something?"

"You've got this whole aura about you. It's kind of endearing and nauseating all at the same time."

"This is turning out to be some summer," Kate said. "It's almost surreal."

"What is—being in a normal, healthy relationship?"

"I don't know how to explain it. Sometimes, I'm not sure what to think or feel." She brushed her napkin across her mouth and took a break from her mammoth plate of pasta. "I've been caught up in this whirlwind for the last month and a half, like I'm watching myself with Jordan from the outside, and I can't quite believe it's me."

"That's not a bad thing. Once in a while, a little unexplained phenomenon can be a beautiful thing."

Kate glanced out at the boiling air undulating on the pavement. "I suppose."

"But?" Didi said.

"You'd think, considering how I feel when I'm with her, that everything's perfect, but I don't know. I can't shake this unsettled feeling."

"Kate, you just met her in June. You have to give it some time."

"How much time? Long enough for us to get so emotionally invested that someone's devastated when it ends?"

"It seems like you're both already there, emotionally attached I mean."

"Maybe." Kate glanced at pedestrian traffic in and out of the Italian ice shop as she deliberated Didi's suggestion. "It's funny how in those moments when it's just Jordan and me, I'm a different person. Since she's come along the emptiness that resided in my chest for so long is just gone. It's a lovely distraction. I'd become so accustomed to it that I forgot it was possible to feel anything else.

"Her heart is so open, and she gives all of herself so freely. I envy that about her, that courage or naïveté—whatever it is." She squinted upward as a batch of cumulous clouds settled in front of the sun. "This is so confusing. She's so young, and we're so different. Am I ever going to get over that?"

Before Didi could answer, an elderly couple holding hands shuffled past their table. "See? Look at that," Kate said. "That's what I'm talking about."

"What about them?"

"When I'm their age, Jordan will only be our age now. Can you imagine what we'll look like together in twenty years? People will think she's my home-health aide, for Christ's sake."

Didi stared at her like she was ridiculous until she finished chewing. "Why are you stressing out about twenty years from now? It makes no sense. The government's gonna bring about the apocalypse long before then anyway."

Kate sighed in frustration. "Because this is what I do."

"You're wasting a lot of mental energy searching for reasons why this won't work. Can't you focus on the many positives you have going for you?"

Kate smiled as she sipped her prosecco. "We have plenty of those."

"Now you're talking," Didi said.

"You wouldn't believe what this girl has me doing," Kate said through a chuckle. "She got me onto a paddleboard. Not a kayak, mind you, where you sit snug and safe beneath the skirt, but actually standing and paddling down Branford River. Oh, and I dragged her to the Met last Saturday for the opening of the new Dali exhibit. It was a pleasure watching someone else be the fish out of water for a change. She was so thrilled to be there, studying every form and brushstroke of every painting in the exhibit. She wore this gorgeous, curve-hugging black dress—man, she was a vision—until you saw her wobble around in a pair of heels. It was just precious. Of course, when she stumbled into me and her liver pâté on milk toast slid down the front of my new Versace couture pantsuit, that wasn't so precious."

She sat back and laughed as she recalled the evening.

Didi smiled. "That's more like it."

Kate grinned, embarrassed by her enthusiasm.

"Look, I'm done lecturing you about having a meltdown over everything. My sincere wish is that you'll see in yourself what I've seen these last several weeks. It's all her."

"I'm happy to take this slowly. The last thing I need to do is go leaping before I look, especially into that fountain of youth."

"I couldn't care less whether you're in love or not, which by the way, I'm convinced you are. I'm just pointing out the glorious change in you."

"Thank you for that," Kate said. "And for the complimentary psychoanalysis you provide during nearly every meal we share. It never gets old," she said, rolling her eyes.

"You're an amusing topic of conversation. You get so tense and uncomfortable whenever anyone mentions feelings. So how about some details about Jordan in the sack?"

"And there it is." Kate tossed her balled-up napkin onto the table.

"Give me a break. It's not like I'll ever get a woman that young or that hot."

"Now what kind of attitude is that, Ms. Positivity Ray-of-Sunshine pain in the ass?"

"I came off the bench late in the game. I'll never make up for all that lost time."

"I think you'll make it all up with Rhea and then some, don't you?"

"You think? What do you mean?"

"Nothing," Kate said. "Well, I mean, she's a little friendly, maybe bordering ever so slightly on flirtatious."

"She's a realtor," Didi said. "She has to be friendly. Pop your head out of your cocoon once in a while, and you'll see how regular people interact with each other."

"Okay," Kate said, holding up her hands in surrender. For the sake of preventing her head from being entirely bitten off, she decided to drop that topic. "So how are things with her?"

"Fine," Didi said, almost too quickly. She hesitated for a moment, and then said, "You independent businesswomen have a personality type all your own. She doesn't see the fun in wearing her heart on her sleeve or blindly leaping into a love affair either."

"Imagine that," Kate muttered into her wineglass.

"But we're having a great time hanging out. And the sex is spectacular. I just can't say that enough—spectacular sex, spectacular sex. It has such a delightful alliterative ring to it, doesn't it?"

"I'm painfully aware of that part. It's all you ever talk about."

"Let me ask you this." Didi hunched forward and whispered, "Do you think I'm too needy?"

Kate contemplated the question while the busboy cleared their dishes. "I don't know you in a romantic sense, but I would hazard a guess that you might be a little high maintenance. Why do you ask?"

"Then it must be me."

"What must be you?"

"I was kind of hoping she'd become more affectionate and attentive. You know, cuddling in bed, late-night phone calls when we're not together, all that Hallmark propaganda that sucks you in during this stage of the relationship. She's sort of aloof, a touch ambivalent. She hasn't even invited me to her house yet."

"Maybe she's afraid you're one of those lesbians who'll show up with a toiletry case and ask for a drawer in her dresser."

"Please, girl. I may be a sucker for the happily-ever-after fantasy, but I've been around enough to know that's only guaranteed for pretty blond girls named Tiffany and their college sweethearts named Brad. I'm fine with pacing myself."

"Maybe she's like the '71 Torino I used to drive in high school.

Remember that car?" Kate suddenly drifted off in nostalgia. "That baby took a long time to warm up, but once all her pistons were firing, she was hell on wheels."

"You just compared my woman to an old Ford."

"Huh. Yes, I did. Look, lousy simile aside, maybe you should casually mention your concern to her—if you don't think it's too soon to have the conversation."

"I don't have much experience in relationships like this, you know, ones that I actually care about. What do you think?"

"I don't think it would hurt," Kate said. "My problem is prying Jordan off me." The thought amused her. "Whenever we spend the night together I feel like I have a Siamese twin."

Didi's face scrunched up. "I hate you."

"Sorry," she promptly offered. "It's only been a month, so I say give her the benefit of the doubt."

"Actually, six weeks, and thirteen days texting before we met, but who's counting? She's a remarkable woman, Kate, and I can see this going somewhere. For the first time in my life, I feel whole, like the mixed-up bunch of pegs that used to be me finally fit in the right holes."

Kate reached across the table and clasped Didi's hand for a moment. "I'm so happy you're finally experiencing this. You've waited so long."

They regarded each other with kindred smiles.

"You said 'holes,'" Kate said.

She and Didi shattered the tender moment with hearty laughs. Then Kate wondered whether Rhea was worthy of the credit Didi was giving her. The not-so-distant memory of her accosting Jordan at the margarita party resurfaced in her mind. If she was ever going to enlighten Didi, this would be the time. But how could she? If anyone was radiant lately, it was her. What would be the point of crushing her spirit now?

Didi checked her vibrating phone as a maniacal gleam tripped in her eyes. "Hey, you. What's going on? Oh, you can't? All right. How about tomorrow night? Okay. Thursday works. I can't wait to see you." She paused to glance at Kate before ending the call with, "I love you."

"I love you, already," Kate remarked casually, not to arouse alarm. "Does she say it back?"

"Does 'you too' count?"

Kate tried to mask her reaction. "Not sure. I suppose?"

"I said it first last night, and that was her reply. She's a Torino, remember?"

Kate nodded and mustered her most convincing smile. "If you're not seeing her tonight, come over for a glass of wine or something. Jordan's doing some rehearsing for her upcoming show, so Ruby and I will be relaxing on the couch watching *Sixty Minutes*."

"I can't tell you how appealing that sounds," Didi said with a giggle. "But no, thanks. I've got big plans of my own—binge-watching season two of *I Dream of Jeannie* on Netflix."

Didi's nonchalance couldn't hide the demons of doubt pitching about in her eyes. If somebody had the power to cast such a dark shadow over her glowing disposition, then it had to be love. Kate resisted the temptation to swing into overprotective big-sister mode; she didn't do meddling very well. And if a sexy genie didn't have the power to make Didi smile, nothing did.

Kate and Didi arrived at Charlesworth Winery early to claim a table facing the softly lit corner where a microphone stand and acoustic guitar awaited their mistress. The tasting area was packed with wine-tasters, mainly throngs of lesbians who'd gathered to catch one of Jordan Squire's notable standing-room-only performances. After watching the early evening sun sneak behind trees surrounding acres of grapevines, Kate made note of the varied ages of the women in attendance. Some were her age, but lots more were younger, and many of them appeared to be single. With Jordan's popularity growing to seemingly unknowable heights, how long before someone her own age swooped in and connected with Jordan on her level?

"Ay," Didi said, smacking the table. "You want a nipple for that?"

Kate snapped out of brooding over audience demographics and compared her nearly full glass with Didi's nearly empty one. "No. Just a little distracted."

"Aww, don't worry. Your little lady'll be out any minute."

Kate grinned into her wineglass, preferring to stow away her latest round of insecurity rather than unpack it with Didi right there.

"I thought Viv was coming up for the weekend," Didi said as she poured another glass of chardonnay.

"I thought so, too," Kate said. "She's been MIA a lot lately. I hope she's not up to something shady."

"Other than having fertility doctors mine her aged ovaries for the last vestiges of viable eggs?"

Kate laughed behind her hand to avoid spraying Didi with moist cracker crumbs. "I don't know why she's going through all this now. It's over with Maia. If she'd just behaved like an adult instead of a spoiled heiress while they were together, it never would've taken such a nasty turn."

"I felt so bad for Maia," Didi said. "She loved Viv so much, but in the immortal words of Patty Smyth and Don Henley, 'sometimes love just ain't enough.'"

Kate regarded her curiously. "I guess it's still too soon for you to quote Jewelle Gomez or Adrienne Rich."

"Huh?"

Kate smirked at Didi, then did a double take when Jordan entered the room. She licked her lips as Jordan sauntered toward their table, her black tank revealing the Wonder Woman symbol tattooed on her beautifully sculpted shoulder.

"I don't know how this is possible," Didi said, "but Jordan looks sexier every time I see her."

Kate nodded. "I can't figure out if all these recent hot flashes are from her or I'm starting menopause."

"Hey, baby," Jordan said as she wrapped her arms around Kate and gave her a big smooch. "Thanks for coming, you guys."

"It's our pleasure," Didi said. As Jordan hugged her, Didi made a lusty face at Kate over her shoulder.

"Have a great set, honey." Kate kissed her on the cheek and sent her off with a pat on the rear end.

As Jordan made her way to the microphone, numerous women stopped her to chat her up, delaying the start of the set.

"Do you see that?" Kate asked. "Should I be worried?"

Picking an olive off their charcuterie plate, Didi shook her head. "If my girlfriend had groupies, I'd be sitting here with the biggest goofy-ass grin you could ever imagine. And those skinny jeans…" She fanned herself with a napkin.

"Keep your eyes to yourself." Kate playfully swatted the napkin out of Didi's hand. "Where's your girlfriend, anyway?"

"Supposedly on her way. She had to work late again."

Kate ignored her suspicion about Rhea's latest absence as she swooned from the tingles Jordan's sultry voice fired through her. As she crooned Carly Simon's "Nobody Does It Better" and smiled at her, Kate momentarily forgot anyone else was in the crowded room. Sometimes the way Jordan looked at her left her breathless, like Kate was the sweetest note she'd ever sung.

Later, when Jordan announced she was taking a short break, Kate stood up and stretched in anticipation, but various women offering compliments and flirtatious smiles delayed Jordan's arrival.

"I'll be right back," Didi said. "I'm going outside to give Rhea a call. She's not answering my text."

Kate nodded, preoccupied with everyone swarming Jordan, particularly the two women acting rather familiar with her. Why was she feeling so possessive? It was not a good color on her and hauntingly reminiscent of another relationship she'd thought she'd learned from. Obviously, they were Jordan's friends. Against her better judgment, she meandered over to make her presence known.

"Hey," Jordan said, finally noticing her.

"Hi." Kate eyed Jordan's friends.

"This is Kate," Jordan said, sweeping her hand across Kate's back. "And this is Taylor and Andie, friends from Boston."

As the women exchanged greetings and handshakes, Kate didn't like the way Andie was looking at Jordan. Her lawyer instincts were picking up a strong whiff of collusion. Or was it just a case of good old-fashion jealousy?

"I'll let you ladies catch up," Kate said. "I'm gonna get in line for the ladies' room."

"You don't have to…" Jordan said, but Kate was already on the move.

As she waited in line, she tried to stop stewing about the pretty young women who'd grabbed Jordan's attention. The last thing she wanted was to turn into *that* woman, the insecure, smothering, control-freak girlfriend. No way could she allow that to happen—again. After Lydia, she'd worked too hard with her therapist to purge those old habits and beliefs to fall back into them so easily now with someone she was just getting to know.

Meanwhile, as she was admonishing herself, disembodied voices proclaiming how hot Jordan was floated past her ears. Where were her two best friends when she needed them?

As if on cue, Didi approached her in line as she waited for the next available stall. "Can I borrow your car?"

"My car? For what?"

"Rhea's not answering my texts or my calls. I need to go check on her. What if she fell at her office and is lying in a pool of blood dying from a clot or something? Or even worse, what if she's with someone else?"

"Didi, you haven't been dating long enough to stalk her," Kate said.

"So it's okay for Viv to stalk Maia but not for me to look in on Rhea? You always take her side."

"No. It's not appropriate for anyone to stalk for any reason. Now please, Didi, I don't want to have to defend another friend in court on such an embarrassing charge. My schedule's busy enough."

Didi leaned against the wall and pouted as Kate entered the stall.

"I'm sure she's fine," Kate said, before closing the door. "If she's working, she'll get back to you as soon as she's free. It's only eight fifteen."

By nine thirty, Jordan had finished her set, and Kate had sufficiently talked Didi down from her ledge. As Jordan packed up her equipment, the two friends from Boston hovered by her. Kate tried to ignore the pangs caused by wondering why Jordan hadn't introduced her as her girlfriend.

"Have you heard from Rhea?" she asked.

"No," Didi said, "but I'm following your advice and giving her the benefit of the doubt. See how evolved I am?"

"Why are you listening to me? I don't know everything."

Didi glared at her and thrust out her palm, into which Kate dropped her car keys.

"Be careful," Kate warned her. "I just had it detailed."

"Gotcha." And Didi was out of there.

Kate strolled outside to Jordan, who was loading the car. "Do you think you could give me a ride home? Didi needed my car."

"Sure. Is everything okay?" Jordan said, appearing distracted by Taylor and Andie.

"Fine. Do you have plans with them? I don't mean to interfere."

"Uh, no. They asked if I wanted to join them somewhere else for a drink, but this gives me the perfect reason to say no."

"Your friends drove two hours to see you. Shouldn't you go have a drink with them?"

Jordan sighed and stared at Kate for a moment. "I don't really know Taylor that well, and Andie is, uh, she's my ex."

"Your ex," Kate repeated dumbly. She stood like a boxer straining to recover from a left hook. "Don't let me stand in the way of your reunion."

Jordan pulled her aside. "I don't want a reunion with her. I was trying to think of a way to ditch them."

"She apparently wants a reunion with you. Why didn't you introduce me as your girlfriend?"

"I don't want any drama at places where I perform. I'm not saying she'd start anything, but she's got a sharp tongue, and I just want to avoid any possibility of an exchange."

Kate's dander was rising. "I'm not worried about an exchange," she said coolly. "Just say you can't join them because you have to take your girlfriend home—unless you really want to go, and I'm the one you want to avoid drama with."

"Kate, no, I don't want that at all. Andie just wants to be friends, but I don't."

Kate wasn't about to buy that with someone else's money.

"C'mon. Let's go over there." Jordan pulled Kate by the hand and led her to Taylor and Andie. "Thanks for the invite, ladies, but I can't make it for that drink. My girlfriend and I have special plans tonight."

Kate shot her a smile dripping with satisfaction as Andie's eyes sized her up.

"No problem," Andie said. "Maybe some other time." She glazed her comment with a smug glance at Kate, as though suggesting the battle wasn't over.

As Kate helped Jordan carry the rest of her equipment cases to her car, she realized what had just transpired, and her short-lived feeling of victory turned to shame.

"Were you going to tell me that was your ex?" she asked as they loaded the last guitar case into Jordan's trunk.

"Yeah, but it was so chaotic in there, I planned to tell you on our way home."

"When did you break up?"

"About ten months ago."

"That's the four-year one?" Kate shouted and then reined herself in. "She's definitely here to get you back, and not just as a friend."

"Honestly, I'm surprised she's here. We hardly ever talk, and if we do it's just a quick happy birthday or holiday text. I thought Taylor was part of the reason we broke up. But whatever her deal is, I don't want anything to do with it."

"Are you sure? I mean I know it hasn't been that long with us, but I'd still like to know where I stand." Kate wanted to kick herself at the desperation in her voice.

Jordan crunched across the gravel, slipped her arms around Kate's waist, and looked deep into her eyes. "All right. You want to know where you stand? Right here with me, a woman who's crazy in love with you."

Kate swallowed hard, neither expecting nor ready to hear that. She thought about poor Didi, who'd said it to Rhea recently and was left flapping in the wind like granny panties in a tropical storm. She didn't want Jordan to feel like that.

"I love you, too," she whispered.

While Jordan beamed, Kate's stomach knotted up again, this time from feeling backed into a corner. Was she really in love with Jordan or just infatuated with Jordan's attraction to her?

She began resenting being pushed into saying it as Jordan kissed her passionately in the parking lot.

"You don't mind sleeping over another night, do you? I have an early meeting tomorrow morning," Kate lied.

"On a Saturday?"

After a beat, "The client works long hours all week. I said I'd meet her at eight."

Jordan kissed her softly on the lips. "You're so compassionate. That's one of the top fifty things I love about you."

What was that? Was Jordan going to start frosting every sentence with that word now that it was out?

"I'm just doing my job," Kate replied, suddenly claustrophobic. "Shall we go now?"

"And so humble." Jordan smiled as she opened her car door. "You're the whole package, Kate Randall."

Kate forced a smile, but at that moment she felt the contents of that package ready to explode.

CHAPTER ELEVEN

The Ex Factor

The next morning, Kate dragged Didi to a gym several towns away, a precautionary or paranoid measure after telling Jordan the night before she was meeting with a client that didn't exist. As they pedaled their stationary cycles, Kate attempted to sort out the business of Jordan's ex appearing out of the past like a bunch of unpaid parking tickets.

"I don't know what you're worried about," Didi said after a squirt of bottled water. "They broke up a long time ago, and you're clearly an upgrade."

"It wasn't that long, and Jordan had this weird look on her face."

"Most people have weird looks on their faces when their ex- and current girlfriends are in the same room." Didi shuddered in repulsion.

"It was more than that. It was stolen glances laced with longing and regret. I was wondering if I should let her go, so she can figure out this thing with Andie. She can't process her feelings for her with me around."

"Aww, aren't you selfless," Didi said, wiping her forehead with a paper towel. "Give me a break."

"What? I'm serious. What if seeing her again has left her second-guessing her decision? Maybe she needs some space to sort things out with her."

"Did she tell you that? Or give you any indication whatsoever that she's still hung up on the ex?"

"Nothing other than what I saw."

"Given your general state of mind lately, I wouldn't completely rely on your eyes if I were you. If Jordan was giving off sketchy vibes with this chick, I would've picked up on it."

"You weren't even there," Kate said. "You were out plotting to run Rhea over with my car." She jacked up the resistance on her machine and pedaled harder. The push-pull of conflicting emotions was one thing she hadn't missed in her single years—that raw, aching vulnerability, like using Purell on a fresh paper cut.

"Kate, you're not threatened by this girl," Didi said. "I mean, would you ever consider taking Lydia back if she came around?"

"Definitely not."

"Then why assume Jordan wants that?"

"Because I was with Lydia a lot longer. You know my relationship with her had more than enough time to run its course. She hasn't even been an adult long enough to have had a relationship that long."

"Kate, you're phishing for rationalizations, and I'm not biting. I refuse to be your enabler. If you want to ruin this with Jordan, do it on your own."

"Is that what I'm doing?" Kate said as they got off their machines. "It's called self-preservation, Didi. You've never gone through a painful breakup and, therefore, haven't had the need to develop the instincts to protect yourself emotionally. You even said when your marriage ended you were relieved."

"I was relieved," Didi said as they headed toward the treadmills. "Mike and I were married fifteen years, but I knew I wasn't happy with him after the first five."

"That's my point. What did you have to fear?"

"One of the biggest ones of all: the fear of change. Besides, I was with Georgie for almost a year when I first came out, and I was devastated when she broke up with me."

"Devastated or kind of sad? There's a big difference."

"Sometimes you're so condescending. What do *you* have to be afraid of? A beautiful young woman who's totally into you? This may come as a surprise to you, Kate, but nobody wants their heart broken. Nobody wants to be deceived or lied to or dumped."

"I realize that, but we can all reduce our risk of heartbreak by paying attention to the warning signs and learning from our past mistakes. Our instincts are rarely wrong."

"Unless there's something you're not telling me about Jordan, I haven't noticed any signs other than her having a major crush on you.

Your chemistry is palpable."

"Yeah." Kate broke into a full sprint at the thought of nights with Jordan.

"And second of all," Didi said, "who ever learns from their mistakes the first time around?"

"I was trying to be the first," Kate said dryly, slowing to catch her breath.

"Good luck with that," Didi said. "What are you guys doing this weekend?"

"Jordan has another show at a restaurant on the water in Clinton."

"She's been busy with gigs lately."

Kate nodded. "Lucky for me, she plays great places. So how did you leave it with Rhea?"

"After she apologized profusely for falling asleep on me last night, we had a rather lovely time in the car."

"Whose car?" Kate bleated in horror.

"Hers. We met at the commuter lot."

Kate stared at her for a moment in revulsion. "How I envy your man-like ability to have sex in any circumstance. I would've been grilling her all night about how and why she'd fallen asleep when she knew we had plans."

"That's because you suffer the cynicism and complete lack of trust from being a lawyer your entire adult life. You should've had your shrink fix that, too, while she had you in for an overhaul."

Kate laughed. "We're two very different people, Didi. That's what makes us such great friends. We complement each other so well."

"I just thought it was because we met when we were too young to know any better."

"That too," Kate said.

"What does Sylvia think about your relationship?"

"I haven't discussed it in detail with her yet."

"It's been almost two months, and your mother doesn't know?"

"She knows I'm seeing someone, but I'm saving the surprise of the age difference for when she meets her next weekend. Jordan's irresistible charm will soften the blow."

"You're taking Jordan to meet Sylvia?" Didi gave a whistle of surprise.

"She won't stop hounding me about it. Anyway, I'm not viewing it as a formal introduction or anything. I'm simply having lunch at my mom's and taking along the woman I happen to be dating."

Didi regarded her with skepticism.

"And you always say I'm afraid to live on the edge," Kate said.

"That ought to be a gas. Can I come and watch from the hedges?"

"No," Kate said. "You'll be busy trying to keep your girlfriend awake on date nights." She giggled at herself as she stepped off the treadmill.

"I think that last night I more than proved the worth of her staying awake for me from now on."

They walked over to the locker room to gather their things and wash their hands. Kate checked her phone and then went into her work email.

"What the fuck?" she shouted over the piped-in workout music.

"What's the matter?" Didi said, sounding alarmed.

"I think I know why our dear Vivienne has been MIA lately," she said. "I just got an email from Maia's lawyer saying she's filing a motion on Monday to drop the restraining order against Viv."

"Are you serious?"

"No. I thought this would be a hilarious joke," Kate said with an eye roll. "I cannot believe her."

Didi grinned. "Theirs is a love affair for the ages."

"It's a love affair for the DSM, and I'm the one who's going to get the text the next time they implode."

"Stop being so cynical," Didi said. "Maybe this time they're ready to work it out for real. Viv really seems committed to settling down with her."

"Right. What can possibly go wrong with going back to the ex who had a restraining order against you?"

❖

After spending the afternoon on the phone with Viv reviewing the pitfalls of trying it again with Maia, Kate was ready for a relaxing evening, first having dinner and cocktails with Jordan, then being transported by one of her magnetic acoustic performances.

Jordan picked on a small seafood salad as Kate explained the backstory of Viv and Maia, anticipating her full support that Viv was clearly deluded and vigorously avoiding the big picture.

"Aww, that's so romantic," Jordan said.

"Romantic? Several adjectives come to mind—unhealthy, dysfunctional, doomed—but not romantic."

"Kate, that's a little judgy, don't you think? Who's to say what makes people fall in love. I think it's wonderful when couples try with all their heart and soul to make it work."

She softened into a smile. "I love your optimism. It's so refreshing. I, on the other hand, am of the firm belief that you can't make chicken salad out of chicken shit."

Jordan giggled. "I've never heard that one before, but its relevance isn't lost on me. I do deal with the public in my day job."

"You deal with them at night, too, but they're of a decidedly different persuasion."

"Oh? And what's that?"

"Fans. They fawn all over you. You realize you can have any woman you want?"

Jordan's curls flopped in her face as she bowed in a blush. "There must be some truth to that, because I'm sitting right across from her. And hopefully going home with her tonight."

Kate privately reveled as she studied the flawless physical specimen before her, still amazed that she was the woman who had captured Jordan's affection. Those earthy green eyes and that delectable chin dimple were enough to lure anyone in, but what she had on the inside was a pearl hidden in an elegantly sculpted shell.

"You better finish your salad, or you'll be late starting your show."

Jordan rested her chin in her palm. "I wish I could sit here and stare at you all night."

"I wish you wouldn't." Kate crossed her arms in front of her chest, self-conscious of Jordan's probing eyes.

"But I love to," she replied in a seductive tone. "Sometimes I feel like I can't get enough of you. If I were a museum curator, you'd be my prized work of art."

"Yeah. *Whistler's Mother.*"

"Kate, I'm serious." Jordan sat back in her chair, obviously deflated. "I'm trying to show you how you make me feel, and you're cracking jokes about it."

She reached across the table for Jordan's hand. "I'm sorry. It's been a while since I've experienced compliments, never mind ones as beautiful as yours."

"That's a real shame," Jordan said.

Kate looked away, puckering her lips to fend off a smile.

Jordan shrugged as she rose from the table. "I don't mean to make you feel uncomfortable. Something comes over me when I'm with you, and it just spills out."

Kate rose, too, and faced her. "You can win a girl's heart with talk like that."

Jordan stroked the back of Kate's arms. "Good to know. Would it make you feel uncomfortable if I kissed you right here, in the middle of the restaurant?"

Kate offered a sultry smile. "It will make me feel many things, but uncomfortable isn't one of them."

Jordan clasped Kate's hands as they hung at her side and gave her a long, sensual kiss. "I'll miss you when I'm gone."

Kate chuckled. "I'm going to be sitting right here."

"It's still too far away," Jordan said as she pecked at Kate's lips.

"You better get up there before I steal you out of here," Kate said, studying her sparkling eyes.

"Do it," Jordan whispered.

"Get up there." Kate gently, reluctantly pushed her away.

Jordan hopped up on the small platform, slung her guitar over her shoulder, and strummed the strings as she greeted her intimate audience. When she stood behind the microphone undulating in rhythm with her guitar, she delivered Kate to a place of multisensory abandon. What it did to her libido was a given, but Jordan's velvety voice and suggestive glances on the sensual lyrics launched Kate into an unexplored galaxy of emotion.

After the performance, they snuck away from the venue and back to Kate's house. They lay in bed under silky sheets as a sea breeze whistled them a love song through the open doors.

Nestled into the crook of Kate's arm, Jordan nearly crushed the air out of Kate's torso. "This is the best feeling in the world," she purred.

Kate moaned her agreement and gripped Jordan's shoulders tighter against her. Jordan's devotion and passion filled her with contentment she'd never experienced with a lover. How could she have spent so many years with Lydia and not have felt that? What did Jordan have that she'd never found in anyone else?

"You're so quiet," Jordan said.

"I was just thinking about that time you sang that Carly Simon song and were smiling at me through most of it. It was so romantic. I fairly swooned."

Jordan giggled and kissed Kate's neck. "Song lyrics never had as much meaning to me as they do now."

"I can't believe you've even heard of her, never mind play her music."

"My taste in music is wide-ranging, to say the least. I also like old movies, in case you're wondering. *Mildred Pierce* and *Calamity Jane* are two of my absolute faves."

"I guess it proves the classics never go out of style," Kate said.

"It also proves that age isn't always a factor in what we connect with." Jordan ran her nails over Kate's arm. "Or who."

Kate giggled. "I'm glad I don't have to go up against you in court."

"Why? Because I make such good arguments?"

"No, because you're so sexy. I could never keep a jury's attention with you in the room."

As Kate jabbed her sides, Jordan yelped and writhed to get free. She continued searching for more ticklish spots until, after a long, torturous span, Jordan finally arrested her hands.

"I loved singing that song to you," Jordan said as the moon peered into the window and illuminated her sleepy face. "The lyrics are perfect, especially the part about feeling sad for the rest—the women who lost you and the ones who can't have you now that you're mine."

Mine? Kate choked up on the sweetness of her sentiment and the fear it conjured. She wasn't aware they'd reached the possessive-pronoun stage already. Jordan probably hadn't meant it that way. It was just a lovely, romantic thing to say.

"You have quite a way with words, too," Kate said.

"They come from the heart. You can't be a songwriter without it."

"It's a wonderful talent."

Jordan propped herself up and stared into Kate's eyes. "I mean every word. You inspire me to express everything you make me feel. That's how I know you're the one."

Kate swallowed hard. "The one?"

"Uh-huh," Jordan uttered softly then cuddled her tighter.

"Oh, come on." Kate laughed it off. "It's a little soon to know that for sure. I mean, look at me—I'm full of faults."

Jordan giggled. "Relax, baby. I'm not about to get down on one knee or anything. Especially since I'm stark naked at the moment."

Kate laughed in relief. "I knew that."

"Did you?"

"Pffft, yeah," Kate said.

"Okay, good." Jordan began kissing her neck. "So, listen, as long as we're naked…"

Chapter Twelve

Mother Knows Best?

The backyard Kate grew up in always seemed so small whenever she gazed out from the deck during visits with her mom. Still surrounded by a perimeter of forsythia bushes on each side and a robust wall of shrubbery edging out from the woods in back, it always offered Kate a respite when the real world felt like it was bearing down on her.

At that moment, it wasn't the world bearing down on her, but her mother's occasional but obvious inquisitive glances at Jordan. The idea seemed harmless enough—a lazy afternoon and a lunch of steak and veggies on the old three-legged charcoal grill on which the late Mr. Randall had worked his outdoor culinary magic. But the late-August humidity wasn't the only form of oppression dogging Kate.

Jordan sat beside her at the umbrella table oblivious to Kate's discomfort as Mrs. Randall regaled her with quaint Randall-family anecdotes.

"Mr. Randall told me he'd never rest in peace if I didn't learn to use this grill before he died," Sylvia said. She imitated her husband, shaking a bony finger at Jordan. "'And don't you dare sell out for one of those gas jobs either,' he said."

Kate smiled. "Barbecuing was a competitive sport for Dad."

"I get that impression," Jordan said. "Thank you for lunch, Mrs. Randall. It was delicious."

Buddy, the chubby, aging yellow Lab sitting patiently by Jordan's chair, barked in agreement.

"You're welcome, Jordan. Thank you for bringing the trifle. I can't wait to try it. I hope you have room for dessert."

"I think I can force it down."

"Let me get the coffee started."

"I'll help you." Kate gathered the plates and silverware.

"I'll help, too," Jordan said.

"Both of you stay out here and relax," Mrs. Randall insisted. "Besides, Jordan, I don't think Buddy will like it very much if you leave him."

"Is that right, Buddy-boy?" Jordan asked the dog as she scratched his ears. He dropped to the patio so she could rub his belly.

Kate grinned at the charming scene. "If you keep pampering him like that, he'll never leave you alone."

"I'm not worried," Jordan said. "I've got plenty of affection to give you Randalls, especially the furry ones."

"Should I stop shaving my legs?"

"Ha-ha. Uh, no." Jordan smiled as she patted Buddy's chest. "It was a really nice surprise when you invited me here to meet your mom. That's kind of big."

Kate shrugged. "It's just a little lunch."

"But it's lunch with your mom. Unless you have a girl-of-the-month club I'm not aware of. When was the last time you brought someone to meet her?"

"Hmm." Kate pressed her finger against her lips as she calculated the answer. "Twenty-three years ago."

"Two decades? Yeah. No big deal." Jordan shot her the cutest smirk.

"She's seventy-five. Tomorrow she probably won't even remember meeting you," she said with a wink.

"I doubt that. She's wicked sharp."

Kate enjoyed their teasing banter, but it really was a big deal. Bigger than she'd wanted to make of it only two months in.

"Does this mean you'll meet my parents now?" Jordan asked.

Suddenly, Kate's self-assurance plunged like the cabin pressure in a nose-diving airplane. Meet *her* parents? Who said that was part of the bargain? "Uh…"

"I don't mean like tomorrow. You know, I mean when we're all free to arrange something. Whenever that might be."

"Sure, yeah, definitely," she sputtered when she'd recovered her ability to process language. "Let me see if my mother needs any help in there. Be right back."

Kate peeled out into the kitchen through the sliders.

"I think you might have to give Buddy up to Jordan," she said to her mother after a deep breath.

"Ah, he's always been a pushover for pretty girls," Sylvia said, heading for the coffeemaker. "Like everyone else in this family—except me."

"It's never too late to break into something new, you know," Kate said. "And it's more fun than learning conversational Spanish."

Sylvia smirked. "I'll give it some thought."

Kate tossed out the lunch scraps and arranged the dishes in the dishwasher, tracking her mother's every move with anticipation. Finally, with contrived nonchalance, "So, how are things?"

"What do you mean, 'how are things?' You know how they are. We talk three times a week."

Kate rolled her eyes. "It's rhetorical. I'm trying to start a conversation with you, about something serious."

"You haven't been this clumsy with words since you came out to me in college. What are you, going back in?"

"No," Kate said with a laugh.

Sylvia stopped and whirled around with the coffee scoop still in hand. "Kathryn, please tell me she's just a friend," she said, as if she already knew the answer but was hoping she was mistaken.

Kate frowned. "Why are you saying it like that?"

"Does her mother know where she is?" Sylvia was apparently teasing, but the look on her face was of genuine concern.

"That was tacky, Mom, even for you."

"I'm sorry. I'm old. My mind isn't it what it used to be," she said after noticing Kate's expression.

"Who are you kidding? You're more on the ball than all of us."

"I love these cheeks." She pinched Kate's face before heading to the faucet to fill the coffeepot.

"You have a problem with the age difference?"

Kate joined her mother in gazing out the window over the sink. Jordan was rolling around in the grass loving up Buddy, who wriggled on his back.

"You're a big girl, Kate. You don't need my opinion."

"I know I don't, but I always talk to you about what's going on in my life. Is this really a problem? We're just dating."

"That's it? Just dating?" Sylvia gave her that *I'm gonna keep letting you lie till it blows up in your face* look she recognized too well from her adolescence.

"That's all." Kate let her eyes lock on her mother's in defiance. "Who knows if we'll even be together in six months, or next month?"

Sylva's stare felt like a Taser.

"Listen, kid," she said. "I know you're an ace in the courtroom, but your trial expertise is no match for a mother's instincts. You're crazy if you think I can't read in your face, in both your faces, that this is more than just casual dating."

"Whatever, Sylvia," Kate said. "I'm living in the moment, and I'm happy. That's all that matters."

"Good. I'm glad you're happy."

Kate stared at her mother's back for a moment and then said seriously, "Would you just say what you want to say?"

Sylvia turned around again and leaned against the counter, arms folded. "Okay, so you're having the time of your life right now, but what about in three years when you turn fifty and she's only in her early thirties? Where's this coming from anyway? Is this a delayed Lydia rebound?"

"What are you talking about?" Kate said dismissively. She sat in the chair where she'd spent numerous summer evenings of her youth forcing down creamed spinach at dinner as part of the bargain to go back into the swimming pool.

"Kathryn, ever since you were a little girl, you wanted everything just right. No one could touch your international doll collection because you had it arranged by continent and then by country. All your albums were alphabetized, and that time your brother spilled soda on your favorite paper-doll set, I didn't think I'd ever get you to stop hollering. You do things a certain way because it suits your personality. That girl out there is marvelous but, honey, she's a stack of albums entirely out of order."

"Yes, Mom," Kate said with an exaggerated nod. "No one is going to dispute my propensity toward anal-retentiveness, but Jordan is a person, not a thing. I love spending time with her. I think it shows tremendous personal growth that I haven't dumped her because she doesn't fit into a specific mold."

"Obviously, your mind is made up."

"Look, you have a point, to a certain extent. But I'm surprised at how narrow-minded you're being. That's so not you."

"Oh, Kate, these May-December things never work out." She ambled to the table and sat down with her.

"How can you say that? Bogey and Bacall were your favorite Hollywood couple."

"You can't count them. He died before anything had a chance to go wrong."

Kate scoffed in exasperation.

"What kind of future do you think you can have with someone that young? What happens if she meets someone her own age?"

"If you'll recall, I planned a future with Lydia, who was my age, and we all know how well that turned out. As for her meeting a younger woman, well, now you're asking me to answer questions no one can."

"You're both in such different places in your lives. You must see that. Think about how much you've changed since you were her age. Isn't that why you and Lydia broke up? You hit your forties and grew apart."

"That's a gross minimization of my situation with Lydia, but yeah, that was part of it."

Sylvia looped her fingers around Kate's. "Honey, you think I'm being narrow, but you don't have children. You don't know what it was like for me to look at you and watch you suffer the pain of a broken heart and know I couldn't do a thing for you. I never felt so helpless in my life. With this girl, you could be setting yourself up for more of the same."

The weight of her mother's words crushed her confidence like glass.

"Kate, the deeper you let yourself fall..." She got up and resumed busying herself with the dessert preparations. "I don't know. I just don't want to see you to go through that again."

Kate's head throbbed. She could've easily flustered herself at home with these unpleasant musings without braving miles of summer highway traffic so her mother could reinforce them.

"Look, there's no reason to worry. This isn't serious." She pushed away from the table and padded to the counter.

Sylvia eyed her.

"We better hurry up and eat the trifle," Kate said. "Things seem to turn sour awfully fast around here."

Sylvia feigned her classic maternal frustration. "Fine. I'm just your mother. What do I know about anything? I've only survived on this planet for seventy…"

Kate took the large trifle bowl from her as she ranted and breezed out the sliders.

Jordan jogged over to her. "Is everything all right? You look a little flushed."

Kate soothed herself with the aroma of freshly mowed grass. "I'm fine. It's just a little hot out for coffee and an inquisition."

"Your mom still gets on your case," Jordan said through a chuckle.

Kate narrowed her eyes. "Was that a crack about my age?"

Jordan clapped her hand over her mouth. "No, no. That's not what I meant. I mean, mine does, too."

"Forget it." She hooked her hand under Jordan's arm and led her to the table. "Let's swelter in the heat now with dessert and my mom's hot coffee."

"Sounds like heaven," Jordan said.

The ride home did little to restore the normal color to Kate's face, despite the continuous blast of air-conditioning. Sylvia knew exactly where to dig to strike a nerve by reminding Kate what was and wasn't suited to her infamously uptight personality. So, she was serious. Big deal. Where would the world be without a few conscientious, even-keeled people like her to balance a universe filled with impetuous fools?

But what if by some strange cosmic shift her mother was right? As horrible as it was to comprehend, Sylvia had presented an airtight case. Before Jordan burst onto the scene, life might have been occasionally dull and lonely, but at least it was ordered, and Kate had full sovereignty over her emotions. Before Jordan, the international dolls and albums were precisely where they belonged.

"She hated me, didn't she?" Jordan said, staring out the window.

"Huh?" The question jolted Kate out of her rumination.

"Your mother. She hated me."

"She did not hate you. She said you're a doll, and that's a direct quote."

"She liked the trifle anyway."

"She loved it. And you tripled your market value when you said your grandmother taught you how to bake."

Jordan smiled. "She did. We always made desserts together—cookies, pies. She always let me get my hands right in it."

"And playing with Buddy all afternoon? Forget it. You're golden."

"It just seemed like there was some tension in the air, especially during dessert."

"You were probably just a little anxious about making an impression."

Jordan nodded, seeming satisfied with her answer. But as the sun slipped into the smoky orange horizon, Kate's little exchange with her mother still had her on high alert. As she and Jordan strained for conversation on the ride home, she struggled to convince herself that the disquiet inside was the handiwork of an overactive imagination.

"If I'm the anxious one, how come you haven't reached for my hand once since we got in the car?" Jordan set her hand on Kate's thigh.

All along, Kate had measured her safety in this by guesstimating how she'd feel if Jordan decided to stop seeing her. No big deal, she'd told herself. She'd reclaim her independence after a brief interlude of melancholy—nothing she couldn't manage. But the truth was finally confronting her. She'd miss her. A lot. And what if her mother's projection came true? How would she feel if Jordan had a midlife crisis at forty and wanted to move on with someone her own age, more in tune with her life goals? It might not even take that long. If the way women flocked to Jordan at her shows was any indication of things to come, a better match for her was only a performance away.

❖

All had returned to normal with Kate and Jordan in the couple of weeks since visiting Kate's mother. She'd managed to compartmentalize her mother's doomsday predictions far enough from her consciousness that they'd eventually lost their bite. Jordan had even offered to turn down a gig invitation so they could spend an entire weekend together, but Kate had insisted that she take the Sunday-afternoon lesbian social event at a local brewery. The selfless deed had made her feel magnanimous and emotionally secure. Of course, she'd gone along with Jordan to the gathering, but that was a minor detail, not to detract from her good-girlfriend magnanimity.

Now as they drove to the restaurant for Sunday dinner with Jordan's parents, Kate contemplated the feasibility of bolting from the passenger seat at the next stoplight. She wished she'd thought it through more before she'd invited Jordan to meet her mother. It left the door wide open for something like this.

Jordan clutched Kate's thigh from the driver's seat. "Stop shaking your leg like that. You're making me nervous."

"Okay, sorry." She replaced the leg-shaking with drumming her fingertips on the passenger-side door panel. Dinner with Jordan's parents. Why had she agreed to this? Certain implications were made when one meets the parents, heavy implications—unspoken, binding promises. The roller-coaster speed at which things were progressing made her feel like she was a passenger who realized right before the first drop that her seat belt was undone.

"Kate," Jordan snapped. "Come on, babe. You don't have to be so nervous."

"I don't? You've essentially described your parents as judgmental elitists."

"They're judgmental with me. You're an attorney. They'll love that I'm dating you. They'll probably say something like they hope your professional status will influence me to go back to school for a more prestigious career—such as greedy, soulless CEO or corporate yes-woman like my sister."

"I'm sure it was awful growing up feeling like you had to fill the shoes of a sibling, but you're an adult now, with a mind and dreams and goals of your own. Hopefully, they'll learn to respect that fact sooner than later."

Jordan glanced over at her from the driver's seat.

"Come on," Kate said. "They can't be that unreasonable."

"They sent me to a therapist when I came out to them at fifteen."

"I'm sure they just wanted to make sure you were okay with your preference emotionally. It's gotta be a hard thing for a parent to hear—

at least it was back in the nineties." Suddenly, panic rifled through her. "This may be a bad time to ask, but are they okay with it now?"

Jordan nodded. "The bigger disappointment to them is having a child in such a low tax bracket."

Kate sank back into the passenger seat. "I don't dare suppose they know my age and love the idea of their underachieving daughter dating a woman so much older than her."

"I haven't mentioned how old you are."

"Jordan," Kate wailed. "You're just going to spring it on them by walking in with me?"

Jordan shrugged. "It's not a big deal, Kate. Look, if you're worried about winning them over, tell them you're trying to talk me out of a music career." She laughed, but Kate sensed Jordan hadn't found the suggestion amusing in the least.

When they walked into the restaurant, Kate was already ordering a drink in her mind. One glass of wine or a flavored seltzer was the proper first beverage during dinner with the girlfriend's parents, but in light of recent disclosures, a martini or three would be necessary to avoid another concert of drumming and bobbing at the table. Although Kate had become an expert at masking her nerves in court, Jordan's captain-of-finance father would undoubtedly smell the fear.

"There they are," Jordan said, waving into the dining room.

Kate searched the couples seated in the general direction Jordan indicated, but all she noticed was an attractive, middle-aged couple. Who waved back. And smiled. At them.

"No," Kate whispered as Jordan pulled her by the arm to their table. "It can't be," she whispered again. Where was the stuffy, gray-haired old couple? Where was the big pocketbook her mother was supposed to be stuffing dinner rolls into? This couldn't be. They weren't supposed to look like that…like her!

After the exchange of cordial introductions and Kate's first dirty martini, she'd settled into her seat and relaxed enough so that she was in command of all her extremities in front of Mr. and Mrs. Squire.

Jordan gave her thigh a squeeze of reassurance under the table, but Kate couldn't stop her eyes from darting between Jordan's parents, both so refined and attractive. Her second dirty martini helped wash down the disturbing observation that if Jordan's mother was a lesbian, they'd probably hit it off quite famously and lunch in trendy bistros after spa days in the same salon as Kathy Lee Gifford.

"Jordan tells me you love the water," Mr. Squire said. "We'll have to get you out on our boat before the summer's over. We dock in Stamford."

"We like to do our Sunday brunches out on the Sound," Mrs. Squire said. "Lox, bagels, and mimosas."

"That sounds fantastic," Kate said, starting to feel a little buzzed. She stared into Mrs. Squire's face, dying to know how old they were. They had to at least be fifty. *If there's a god or goddess in heaven, they'll at least be fifty.*

Mrs. Squire appeared to be puzzled at Kate's prolonged glance. "Do I know you from somewhere? What year did you graduate?"

"No, I don't think so," Kate said casually. Way to go with the staring, genius, she secretly scolded herself. "Uh, ninety-one," was her answer to the second part. Hey, she didn't specify high school or college. "So how long have you folks been married?"

"Thirty-three years in October," Mrs. Squire said, smiling at her husband.

"We hadn't planned to get married that soon," he said, "but when Jordan's sister decided to show up, we managed to make it in right under the wire." His chuckle softened the scandal.

"He always blames my sister," Jordan said. "It's not like she was the one who was supposed to stop at the drugstore."

Kate was impressed by her quick-witted, feminist defense of womankind.

Her father smirked. "I think Mrs. Squire just wanted to get her hooks in an up-and-coming future business mogul."

"I already had them in you, darling," Mrs. Squire said, dragging manicured fingers across his hairy forearm.

"Wow," Kate said as she sipped her third martini. "You guys don't look old enough to be married that long."

"I'm fifty-three," Mrs. Squire said, and made a face, which hadn't really translated into *a face*, thanks to Botox. "Sounds so old, doesn't it?"

"Yup, especially when I'm only a few years away from fifty myself."

"Really?" said Mrs. Squire. "I thought you were only around forty. You look fabulous. Who does your skin? I only allow Yvette at Salon de Paris in Westport to touch me."

"Mom, nobody wants to talk about facials," Jordan said.

"Sure we do," Kate said with a slight slur. "In about ten years you'll have to start worrying about fine lines, too. Would you excuse me for a sec?"

Kate rose and swayed a little as she headed to the ladies' room. Running her hands under cold water, she shuddered as she imagined Jordan's parents imagining her in bed with their daughter. Could anyone's parents actually be progressive enough not to get queasy? Her own normally open-minded mother threw a fit over their age difference. What would the final analysis be after Jordan's parents had time to review their daughter's latest liaison?

Jordan came in and rushed over to her. "Are you all right?"

Kate nodded and forced a smile.

"You don't seem it. You're getting a little bombed." She brushed Kate's hair away from her face.

"Why wouldn't I be all right? I've only just discovered that my girlfriend's parents are only six years older than me. We could've been in the same grammar school together."

Jordan lit up. "No way. What school did you go to?"

"Jordan, focus. I can't even think about what they're saying about me right now, this old woman dating their thirty-year-old daughter. How gross."

"Kate, they think you're great. I can tell." She tugged at Kate's hand. "Come back to the table and finish your dinner. You need to eat something."

"What I need is to be ten years younger if I want to date someone your age. And even then I'd still be older than you."

Jordan's eyes grew dark and sad. "Why are you making this an issue again? I thought we'd settled it weeks ago. I love you and want to be with you. Neither one of us can change our birthday, so why waste energy obsessing about it?"

She sighed and leaned against the counter. "I don't know."

"Kate, are you having second thoughts about us?" Jordan's brow wrinkled with worry.

"No." Kate pulled Jordan closer to her. "I feel like I've been zooming through the sky on a flight I didn't know I bought a ticket for. I'd just like to know the ground is still beneath me. Do you know what I mean?"

"I suppose," Jordan said. "A situation made worse by your fear of flying."

Kate was suddenly annoyed with herself. Even if this was an issue that needed further exploration, now was neither the time nor place.

"Okay, enough of this." She lifted Jordan's chin and kissed her with slow sensuality, propelling them both beyond the clouds. "Let me present the facts: your parents are great. And two, the night was going along without a hitch until I got all phobic and whatnot." She smiled to reassure Jordan. "You want to go finish dinner?"

Jordan nodded, threw her arms around Kate's neck, and squeezed her. She rejected Kate's gentle attempt to pry her off until she was good and ready.

"By the way," Jordan said. "After a kiss like that, it's going to be quite a challenge to make it all the way through dessert."

Kate agreed to stay over at Jordan's that night as a conciliatory effort since she'd nearly ruined the meal with her parents that Jordan had been so enthusiastic about. Letting her know that she'd been feeling a little overwhelmed about the pace of their relationship seemed to release some of the built-up pressure. So had their tryst that had begun against Jordan's kitchen counter when they first got home and wended its way over to the couch.

As she lay in bed reading and responding to some work emails on her phone, Jordan was in the bathroom brushing her teeth. When she came in and landed on the bed wearing a sexy camisole and lace bikini underwear, Kate hadn't looked up until the scent of her body lotion flipped her switch from business to pleasure.

"Busy?" Jordan purred.

Kate's mouth hung open as she surveyed Jordan over the rim of her reading glasses. "Well, hello."

"Hello," Jordan said. She grabbed Kate's phone and straddled her to toss it onto the nightstand. She remained in Kate's lap and started to kiss her sensually. Moments later, Kate reached for the side lamp and tugged the small chain.

After their second vigorous romantic interlude of the day cleansed away the remainder of memories still brewing from dinner, she lay with Jordan in her arms listening to her breathe. Her eyes grew heavy in the serenity of darkness and warmth of Jordan's body against hers. Just as she was about to drift off to sleep, Jordan's chest rose and then stopped.

"You know how earlier you said that you wouldn't mind feeling your feet on the ground again?" she asked softly.

"Yeah, listen, I hope that didn't upset you—"

"No, it's okay," Jordan said. "I understand what you mean."

"You do?" Kate turned on the light.

"You make me feel like I've been zooming through the atmosphere, too," Jordan said. "The only difference is I've been enjoying the ride."

Kate touched her hand, her heart deflated by Jordan's sullen tone. "Jordan…"

"Kate, I'm fine. I'm grateful for your honesty. But I think I have a solution to your problem. I have to go to LA for ten days."

"Oh? What for? Website business?"

"No, music business. A rep from a small company out there, Swag Music, wants me to cut a demo."

"That's so great," Kate said. "How did this come about?"

"I got the call a couple days ago. I didn't say anything because at first I thought it was a joke. But apparently, some muckety-muck who was at my Moxy's show in June contacted the rep and said she should check out my YouTube video. I Googled her and the record company, and they're legit."

Her? "I'm so happy for you," she said flatly, deafened by the alarm bells ringing in her head. If this rep wasn't plotting something of her own for Jordan, surely the lure of LA's music scene would keep her out there. What's more, her graphic-design business was the kind that traveled.

"I was going to ask if you wanted to take a little vacation and come with me for part of it, but I guess it's a good opportunity for you to have some space."

"Me?" She wasn't about to let Jordan stick her on the hook for a break, if that was, in fact, what she was about to suggest.

"Yes, you. I don't need space," Jordan said, her eyes steeling over. "The shorter the distance I am from you, the better."

"From a business point of view, wouldn't it be better if we're apart? You'll need to focus on what you're doing."

"I'm a musician, not a neurosurgeon. Besides, it's a proven fact that musicians are much more creative when they're around their muse." Jordan crawled up and rubbed her nose against Kate's.

"I'm your muse?" Kate grinned at the suggestion.

"You are. Matter of fact, I've been working on a new tune for a couple of weeks now."

"About what?"

"You."

"Get out of here," Kate said. "No, it isn't."

Jordan tantalized her with a cocky look. "Fine. Don't believe me. You'll know it when you hear it. It's one of the songs I'm recording for the demo."

"It better be a flattering portrayal, or you're gonna have a libel lawsuit on your hands."

Jordan screeched with laughter as Kate nibbled at her collarbone to drive home the threat. When they finally settled down, Jordan snuggled up to Kate and slipped her arm around her torso.

"Think about taking a long a weekend or something, if you can sneak away," she said. "Ten days is a long time not to see you. I don't know if I'll make it."

"I'm certain you'll have plenty of activities there to keep you busy. You probably won't even remember my name."

"I will if you come with me. I'm leaving Tuesday."

"This Tuesday?"

"It's sudden, I know, but everything's happened suddenly."

"I'll have to check my calendar tomorrow and see what's up. A long weekend away in sunny California might be nice, if I can swing it with my caseload."

"I hope you can," Jordan said and closed her eyes.

Kate switched off the light but lay wider awake than before. Jordan's solution to Kate's problem hadn't felt like it solved anything. But the time apart would give her a chance for some much-needed reflection. She was in love with Jordan, and while it felt utterly fantastic, this fact also resurrected aspects of herself she'd thought were dead and gone. Jealousy. Insecurity. Anxiety. Viv and Didi acted like they'd unearthed their own private diamond mines when they were in love. Why had she felt the specter of doom and gloom floating overhead?

Maybe because the very young, very beautiful singer she'd fallen for was now on the verge of becoming a rock star. And the only place for a middle-aged lawyer in the life of a young, beautiful rock star is behind a desk reviewing her contracts.

She lightly removed Jordan's arm from around her and rolled over, hoping to muffle the sound of her mother's words about fifty-five-and-over communities blaring in her brain.

CHAPTER THIRTEEN

Unhappy Hour

As Kate sipped her cosmo at their favorite alfresco table facing the bustling street, she stared at Didi and Viv, her mouth curled in a downward horseshoe and feeling about as heavy. Didi and Viv practically convulsed with giddiness as they texted and FaceTimed their girlfriends, mugging with goofy smiles and kissy lips. How embarrassing.

She shook her head at the young, downtown happy-hour crowd, as if commiserating with their imagined disgust. She tapped her butter knife on the table to signal the breach of social etiquette and force their mental presence on her more pressing dilemma, but apparently it would be a frosty day in August before they'd realize that on their own.

"The next person who picks up her phone is paying the check," Kate finally barked.

"Gotta go, smoochie-pants," Viv said to Maia through FaceTime.

Didi locked her phone and tossed it into her giant purse resting open beside her on the patio.

"I see someone's still trying to recoup her losses from our bet," Viv said as she carefully raised her martini glass to her lips.

"I don't care about the money, Viv," Kate said. "I'd like to have a conversation with slightly more depth to it than a few wows and oh yeahs? while you two grin like idiots at your phones."

"Sorry, Kate," Didi said. "I just thought you'd be on yours, too, since your mamacita's all the way across the country."

"She's busy singing and recording and whatever they do out there."

"Selecting the groupies that get to get on the tour bus for a night with the…" Viv said.

Didi skewered her with a look.

"Even if Jordan ever did become famous, she'd never cheat on you," Didi said.

"You don't have to do that," Kate said.

"Do what?" Didi said.

"Act like her PR woman. I know she wouldn't. I trust her. She has a strong character."

"Then why are you so miserable?" Viv asked.

"'Cause she misses her little snuggle bug," Didi said. "I love this tender side of you, Kate. It reminds me that you are human after all."

"I'm starting to think I like robot Kate better," Kate said. She swiped her fork through the brussels-sprouts-and-bacon app they were sharing and stuffed a large gob of it in her mouth.

"She'll be back in a week, won't she?" Didi asked.

Kate kept them in suspense as she deliberately chewed longer than necessary. "Yes, she will," she finally said, "but that's not what's bothering me."

"She's not gonna cheat on you," Viv said. "I was just busting 'em on you." One side of her mouth drooped. "Unless she already has—"

"Viv, what's the matter with you?" Didi snapped. "Not everyone cheats."

"Girls, this isn't even about her cheating," Kate said. "I'm thinking about extending the break even after she gets back."

"No," Didi said. "You can't do that."

"Yeah. What's the point?" Viv asked.

"This," Kate said, her hand drawing circles between them. "I'm sitting here with you guys while she's off recording a song demo for a real record company, not some CD she could sell locally at her shows. This is just the beginning for her."

"I know, and it's so exciting for you," Didi said.

"It's exciting for her, and she shouldn't have to worry about keeping the home fires burning while she's embarking on this incredible journey. It would be selfish of me to expect that of her."

"Lots of celebrities have relationships with people who aren't in the business," Viv said. "This isn't something you break up over."

"It's not like we were planning a wedding," Kate said. "We've only been together a couple of months. We'll just back-burner it for a while so she can focus on her music." She sat back in her chair, pleased with her rationale.

Didi and Viv exchanged puzzled looks.

"You guys know I'm right."

"I don't think you're right at all," Viv said.

Kate whipped her head toward her. "You're on relationship-advice probation until I see how this reconciliation with Maia turns out."

"Is this what Jordan wants?" Didi said.

"I haven't talked to her about it yet, but by the time she gets back, I guarantee you she'll see things my way."

Didi glowered as she picked at her salad. "I think you're just missing her, and it's making you loopy. Wait till she gets home before you make any life-altering decisions."

"Jordan's probably missing you even more," Viv said. "I'm gonna text Daddy and see if we can borrow the company jet to pay your girl a visit—well, you can. Didi and I can go shopping at the Grove."

Didi's face lit up. "That's the most romantic idea I've ever heard."

"She's there on business," Kate said. "I can't just swoop in on her."

"I was talking about shopping at the Grove," Didi said.

"Look, nobody said nothing about swoopin' in on nobody while they're working," Viv said. "The three of us can wing it out to the left coast for a long weekend without anybody's permission, can't we? You can meet up with Jordan when she's free."

"Come on, Kate," Didi said, her eyes demonic. "When was the last time we cashed in on the obscene wealth of our friend's parents? We can hit every A-list restaurant and club in LA and act like entitled douchebags throwing Viv's money around. It'll be a blast."

Kate glared at her. "Yes. That's exactly how I'd like to spend the weekend."

"Viv is right in that we haven't had a weekend away together in ages."

Viv checked her phone. "Daddy says the jet is free this weekend. What do you say?"

"You're going to leave Maia for three whole days?" Kate said.

Viv swallowed hard and flipped her hair over her shoulder. "Sure. If Didi can leave Rhea for the weekend, I can do it, too. Remember, I'm a new Vivienne."

"Rhea won't mind at all," Didi said with a frown. "Last night she said I'm smothering her."

"She was speaking figuratively, right?" Kate asked.

"For now," Didi said with a mischievous wink at Viv.

"Look, I'm warning you both—I'm through representing anyone on domestic charges. Pull yourselves together, and stop acting like emotionally stunted adolescents."

Didi and Viv exchanged glances as they tried not to smile.

"If this one wants to sit home and brood all weekend," Didi said, pointing at Kate, "let her. I'll be happy to join you on a left-coast jaunt. I have vacation days." She glared at Kate for effect.

Viv pouted and bit into the orange slice at the bottom of her glass. "It won't be the same if it isn't the three of us."

"Nice going," Didi spat. "You just screwed me out of a free summer vacation."

"All right, fine," Kate said. "I'll go, but I have to be home by Sunday night. I'm on the docket Monday morning."

"We'll leave Thursday and be home by Sunday," Viv said. "Here's to a girls' weekend."

As Didi and Viv raised their glasses and made a small, rowdy scene, Kate shielded her face from the patio patrons with her menu.

❖

They arrived in Los Angeles Thursday night and were checked into the Beverly Hilton by eight p.m., West Coast time. As soon as they entered the suite, Kate plopped onto the sofa and began taking off her watch and jewelry.

"What are you doing?" Didi asked as Kate turned on the TV.

"What does it look like I'm doing? I'm settling in for the night. I want to return Jordan's text."

"You bitches ready?" Viv emerged from the bedroom glammed up for a night on the town. "What is this?" She pointed to Kate stretched out on the sofa like she was a piece of installation art.

"It's eleven o'clock in Connecticut," Didi explained.

Viv rolled her eyes as she threw lip gloss into a bedazzled Coach clutch. "'Bye, Felicia." She grabbed Didi's hand and headed toward the door. "Order room service if you get hungry."

"Stay out of trouble, girls," Kate called out from the sofa. "Remember, Viv, you're not single anymore."

"Neither are you," Didi said. "Instead of texting, why don't you call her and see if she's free tonight?"

"Didi, you're keeping your sugar mama waiting." Kate blew her a kiss and then gave a dismissive wiggle of her fingers.

When the door shut, Kate picked up her phone and texted Jordan, contemplating if she should tell her she was in town or go for the romantic-surprise glimpse across a crowded room tomorrow night.

Hey sexy songstress, how's it going?

I miss u!! <3 Rehearsing now for my acoustic set tomorrow nite.

Miss you, too. I'll let you get back to it.

Noooooo! Talk to me ☹

Lol. Ok but I don't want to disturb your rehearsal.

You're not. Alexandra's keeping me on a tight schedule, but I can take a well-deserved break.

I'll bet she is, Kate thought. Her throat tightened as she wondered about what other plans Alexandra had for Jordan.

You're gonna be a star by the time she's done with you.

Not likely. She already explained it's a one in a mil chance but def. thinks I have a sound that could catch on.

You definitely have something, alright. ☺ Is there still such a thing as a recording couch??

Kate was grateful their conversation was taking place through text as her rising jealousy would've been impossible to mask in a phone call.

A what?

Never mind. Still coming home Sunday?

Yes. Can't wait to see u!!!! <3

You too!! <3. Break a leg tomorrow night!!

After they said good night, Kate felt slightly better about the situation. Jordan seemed herself, but she'd only been out here for seven days. Once her song and video reached a mass audience, that would signal the end of Jordan Squire, website designer, and the emergence of

Jordan Squire, the music industry's next It Girl. Then how long before Jordan outgrew Connecticut and Kate? It wasn't a question of if but when.

Kate couldn't even fault her. She knew what was in her heart, but as Jordan's star rose, she wouldn't be able to keep her feet on the ground. Kate loved her enough and cared enough about her dreams not to stand in her way. No matter how much it hurt.

❖

Kate kept the secret of her presence in LA for the twenty-four hours until she'd found out the name of the club in West Hollywood where Jordan was playing her acoustic set. Disguised in a fedora and sunglasses, she slipped into Harlot's Web on glimmering Santa Monica Boulevard, trailing behind Viv and Didi, who sauntered in with all the subtlety of a Lady Gaga music video. Peering around them, she ripped off her sunglasses as she inventoried the array of gorgeous young women in the packed nightclub. It was like Connecticut's entire lesbian population had assembled in one space.

She put her sunglasses back on to sulk incognito.

"Will you take that shit off, Kate," Viv said. "You're not Bette Davis walking into the Brown Derby."

"I don't want Jordan to know I'm here till after the show. I might distract her."

"Yeah," Didi said, "because you don't look like a distraction now wearing sunglasses inside a dimly lit club."

"You said you wanted to make believe we're entitled douchebags, didn't you?"

"Uh, I was kidding," Didi said.

"Make up your mind," Kate said. As they settled at their reserved table off to the side of the stage, she took off her hat and pushed her sunglasses up into her hair. "I don't know what made me think I could be low-key with you guys around anyway."

A waitress brought over a bottle of Cristal, and Kate relaxed into the environment after several large, consecutive sips that tickled her nose.

"Hey, is that Jordan over there?" Viv asked.

Kate glanced over and caught the unmistakable sight of her

girlfriend huddled with trendy-looking people who had an air of style, sophistication, and power. An older woman, older than Kate, had her arm around Jordan's lower back and appeared to be lightly rubbing her as they engaged in lively conversation and laughter with two young men with hipster pompadours and tight suits. Alexandra, Kate thought. Her lips puckered at the taste of her name. And she was worried about all the young, beautiful women in the club? That tall, dark, and sexy *Vogue* cover cutout was all over her like a knock-off Versace pantsuit.

"Aren't you going to go over there and say hi?" Didi asked.

"Can't you see she's busy? They're probably offering her a contract as we speak."

"All the more reason she should have her girlfriend slash lawyer by her side," Didi said. "Go surprise the leather pants off her."

"That tall bitch look like she making her an offer, all right," Viv said. "But it don't look like recording got anything to do with it. If that was Maia with a woman hanging on her like that, I'd be over there toot sweet, puttin' a bitch in her place."

"Well, it was nice knowing you, 'new Vivienne,'" Kate said. "I'll talk to her after the show. Besides, how will I see what might happen between her and Alexandra if she knows I'm here?"

Didi glared at her in disappointment. "Et tu, Kate?"

"It's possible, Didi. You seem to have placed her on this pedestal of perfection, but how well do we really know her? It's only been a few months."

"Mm-hmm," Viv uttered. "And if she like older women, she struck gold with that old, mummified hack."

Didi's jaw hung open for a moment. "Kate, you were just defending her honor the other day."

"That was before I saw her out in this element. She looks so natural out here, like this is exactly where a woman like her belongs." Kate sighed, forgetting her surroundings. "She probably won't ever come back."

"Kate," Viv said, pressing her hand.

When she snapped out of her unpleasant musings, Viv and Didi looked genuinely concerned.

"Don't project too far ahead here," Viv said. "They haven't offered her a contract yet. They're just demoing her, seeing how she does in a live performance."

"Look at her," Didi gushed, gazing off at Jordan in the distance. "How could they not?"

"Didi," Viv said. "You're not helping." She turned to Kate and caressed her shoulder. "Look, sista, we joke with you. We like to see you get all worked up, but all teasing aside, we love Jordan, and we love you in this relationship with her. Don't write it off yet."

"Thanks," Kate said. "But ironically, your jokes have injected some much-needed reality into this situation. I don't know why I let you two talk me into coming here."

"We're in LA for the weekend," Didi said. "We're supposed to be having fun, and we were until your doom and gloom showed up and pissed out our bonfire."

"We thought spending a little time with Jordan would make you feel better," Viv said, "not question things even more."

"I can't help it," Kate said. "I've been trying to live in the moment with her, but every time I think I can do this, something else reminds me how ridiculous it is to try. When you strip away the layers of romantic fantasy, the unvarnished reality is that Jordan and I just don't make sense."

"You're not really going to break up with her," Viv asked.

Kate shrugged. "I'm afraid that's the direction it's headed whether I'm the catalyst or not. She won't have time to devote to a relationship, and I certainly don't want one with a touring musician."

"No, no, no," Didi said, her eyes glued to Jordan, who was making her way over to them. "Please don't do it now."

"Kate!" Jordan charged at her through the crowd. She flung her arms around Kate's neck and nearly choked the air out of her.

"Surprise," Kate mumbled, lost in Jordan's effervescent smile.

"I'll say. I can't believe this. It's so awesome to see all of you," she said, passing hugs around to Viv and Didi. "I'm not so nervous about performing now that I know I'll see your faces in the audience."

"You're going to be great," Didi said, eyeing her like a groupie. "Nice pants," she muttered. "Turn around."

Kate whacked her arm.

In her zeal, Jordan grabbed Kate again and hugged her with all of her body. Kate inhaled her hypnotic scent as the tingling from Jordan's touch radiated through her. In that moment of sensory overload, breaking up with her was the furthest thing on her mind.

"Thank you for coming, baby," Jordan whispered. "I've missed you so much."

"Me, too," Kate said softly. And it was the truest thing she'd said all night. She'd missed Jordan to the point of distraction all week, finally realizing she was in much deeper than she'd admitted to anyone, least of all herself.

"Jordan," the husky voice called out. "We have to get you backstage now, honey." Alexandra stood smiling at Kate and her friends, her hand extended for Jordan to take it.

"Alexandra, this is my girlfriend, Kate, and her friends, Didi and Viv."

"Hey, how's it going?" she said and hadn't waited for their response. "We have to get your hair and makeup touched up now. Your stylist's waiting."

Kate stood steaming as elegantly as possible watching Alexandra drag her girlfriend away like she was hers and Kate was some fawning sycophant.

"Stylist?" Didi muttered.

Kate and Viv smirked.

"She's got handlers already. Impressive," Viv said.

"If I know Jordan, the novelty of having her ass kissed will be short-lived."

Didi glared at her. "Who gets tired of being treated like a queen?"

Kate's and Didi's eyes fell on Viv for the answer.

"So, who's ready for another round?" Viv asked, displaying a wall of gleaming white teeth.

When Jordan finished her near flawless five-song set, she had the audience cheering long after the reverb faded. Kate clapped her hands raw, but inside she was wound up tighter than the strings on Jordan's Ibanez Talman, a condition three cosmos should've easily remedied. As Alexandra, her PR minions, and various newly won fans descended on Jordan, Kate began to feel the way Alexandra had looked at her, like just another fan clamoring for her attention.

Jordan approached and took Kate's hand. "We're going to my producer's house for a party. She's up on Sunset." She said it like she'd been living in Los Angeles forever. "I'll ride with you guys, and we can follow them."

Will Alexandra allow that, Kate wanted to say but took the safe, passive-aggressive route instead. "Uh, we sort of have plans for tonight," she lied. "Viv's cousin over on Roxbury is having a party, too."

"Oh."

Kate savored the disappointment in Jordan's eyes. It was a shameful victory, but it was all she had to cling to as her grip on her emotions steadily slipped away.

"Where are you staying? Can I come by tonight and stay with you?" Jordan asked.

"We're at the Beverly Hilton, but don't alter your plans because I showed up. Do your thing, and we'll catch up when you get home."

"When I get home?" Jordan's tenuous smile faded to black. "Let's have dinner tomorrow night. Come with me to the dinner party."

"What dinner party?" Kate asked, unable to conceal her growing frustration.

"Swag Music's VP is having us over for dinner. Please come with me."

"Are they offering you a deal?"

"I don't know. It's up in the air right now. They have a couple of acts they're considering, so Alexandra says that while they like my sound, it's not guaranteed they'll sign me."

"What's going to happen if they do? Will you have to move out here?"

"Alexandra says I'll have to come out to cut the album, but no. I wouldn't have to move here."

By this point, Kate felt the vein in her temple pulse. "When you get a chance tonight, ask Alexandra what she thinks about you keeping your lawyer girlfriend back in Connecticut. My guess is that it won't fit into her agenda for you."

"What do you mean?" Jordan glanced over Kate's shoulder as

something seemed to summon her attention. She looked back at Kate. "What's the matter, Kate?"

"Nothing. Just kidding," Kate said and forced a smile.

"You don't sound like you're kidding. Or seem like it."

"Okay, so I was a little serious, but there's no point in getting into it here."

"Then why did you bring it up?"

"Jordan, don't act like I'm being unreasonable. Look where we are right now. Look where you're headed. Things are going to change. I can't move to accommodate your new career. I'm only licensed to practice law in Connecticut and New York."

"Whoa. What new career?" Jordan's eyes darkened with apprehension. "I'm a graphic design artist from Connecticut."

Kate softened her demeanor. "For now, baby. These people seem serious about what they do, and I doubt they would've invested the time and money in getting you out here if they didn't see real potential." She turned to see what was vying for Jordan's attention. Alexandra was motioning Jordan over. When she turned back, Jordan's eyes floated in pools of tears. "Go to your party," she said, cupping her face in her hands. "We'll get together for breakfast tomorrow if you want."

"What about dinner?"

"We'll talk about it over breakfast," Kate said as she thumbed away the tears under Jordan's eyes. "Now go have fun, and spray some hag repellent on yourself to keep Alexandra off you."

"Promise we'll be together tomorrow?"

"Promise." Kate kissed her forehead and then her lips.

Jordan smiled and headed back into the evil clutches of Alexandra the Mediocre and her flying monkeys, glancing over her shoulder at Kate. Didi and Viv ambled over once Kate was alone.

"What's going on?" Didi said.

"Nothing much," Kate said, still staring as her view of Jordan became obscured. "Jordan's only about to become a rock star."

Viv grabbed Didi's shoulders. "Oooh, girl, we gonna hang with Beyoncé."

"Kate, that's so exciting," Didi said and then paused. "Isn't it?"

Kate nodded, straining to seem unfazed as a vortex of record-company bodies swallowed Jordan up in their mass. The fog of uncertainty began lifting, allowing Kate a sharper view of where the road was leading.

"So," Viv chirped, cutting through the tension. "Looks like the party's over in this joint. Wanna hit the road?"

"Back to the hotel?' Kate asked hopefully.

Didi and Viv exchanged guffaws at the absurdity of her suggestion.

CHAPTER FOURTEEN

The Hangover

Absorbed in the hot, sweaty air of their next nightclub of the evening, Kate squinted against flickering strobe lights as her ears throbbed from the assault of house music. She and Didi waited behind Viv, who was procuring the first round of drinks.

"We're leaving after this one round, right?" Kate asked. "None of us are single so let's observe proper dating etiquette and get back to the hotel at a decent hour."

"Uh, speak for yourself," Didi said. "Do you know what Rhea said when I told her I was jetting off to LA for the weekend?"

Kate shook her head.

"Have fun. Can you believe it? She told me to have fun."

"How dare she?" Kate said, not sure what tone was appropriate.

"Kate, she just let me go. Didn't say, 'Oh, honey, don't leave me for a whole weekend' or anything that at all indicated she gave a crap where I went or for how long."

Viv turned around. "Maia and I needed an extra therapy session after I told her."

Didi extended her hand as though thanking Viv for the support. "You see?"

"I owe Viv an apology," Kate said. "I've waited every day for your powder keg of a relationship to blow sky-high, but it's not happening. The two of you are actually making it work."

"You mean the three of them," Didi mumbled when Viv turned back to the bar to grab their cocktails. Kate snorted, trying to hold in her laughter.

"I heard that, bitch." Viv glared at Didi as she handed the martini glasses around. "I'd rather have the third party in my relationship be a therapist than some other woman like Rhea's probably with now that you gone for the weekend. Or some ghost from my past," she said, nodding to Kate.

"Rhea's not with another woman," Didi said.

"She ain't with you either," Viv drawled. "And that's most of the time."

"Jeez, Viv, we were just kidding," Kate said. "You didn't have to come out swinging."

"You always messing with me about Maia. Maybe I'm getting sick of it. Yes, we had our problems in the past, but don't anybody deserve a chance at redemption in your eyes?"

Kate slumped, feeling like every bit of the schmuck Viv had intended her to feel. "Yes. Of course you do. I'm sorry, Viv." She patted Viv's back, glancing at Didi, who looked as punched with remorse as she felt.

"I guess we didn't think how it would make you feel," Didi said. She led them to a tall table that had just been vacated.

"To be fair," Kate said, "none of us ever really bother to do that, so…"

"Yeah," Didi said. "Do we really want to start something new now?"

"Aww, hell no," Viv said, and lifted her glass. "Let's get all banged up on these and then strut out to the dance floor."

"I can't get banged up. I have to meet Jordan for breakfast at nine tomorrow."

Viv sucked in her cheeks. "That's if she hasn't met someone already at all these soirees that malnourished old white woman is dragging her to."

Kate joined them in their laughter, mostly to hide the pain of Viv's innocent crack that irritated the wound of worry she'd been nursing all night. Instead of venting to them and bringing down the mood, she signaled a passing waitress to bring them another round.

By the fourth round of cocktails, they were tangled together on the dance floor, arms flailing like they were stuck in the agitation cycle of a demon-possessed washing machine. During a house version of Alicia Keys's "This Girl Is on Fire," a woman had slowly maneuvered near Kate and was undulating provocatively close to her. Even in her bleary state, Kate knew the woman was up to more than just dancing. When they made eye contact, Kate noticed the woman was around her age—tall, slender, self-assured, wearing a striking slicked-back hairdo and figure-hugging black dress. Probably does something in show business, she thought. Former model or game-show prize girl. Or fashion designer. Whatever it was, she had an undeniable appeal and a self-confidence that defied anyone to take their chances with her.

The woman wedged herself into their clique and undulated in front of Kate, never missing a beat of the throbbing music. Kate made eye contact with Viv and Didi over the woman's shoulder as she moved in rhythm with her. They seemed confused, surprised at her behavior. Didi tried to signal her off the floor, but she stayed, closing her eyes and swaying with the woman, who was close enough now to exchange a breast brush with Kate. She slipped her arm around Kate's waist and grinded into her pelvis. Kate thought of Jordan, wishing she was there, wishing they could go back to a hotel room overlooking the Hollywood sign and make love until they fell asleep in each other's arms.

The wet softness pressing on her lips jolted her back to the mass of sweaty bodies and blinding strobe lights.

"I'm Yvonne," the woman said. Her hot breath was damp against Kate's ear.

"Thanks," Kate said as she stepped rather ungracefully toward their table. Something in her wanted to stay, to continue the kiss, to forget that the woman she was in love with was somewhere in that strange city among beautiful, powerful people with the ability to make her dreams come true.

"Why did you let that happen?" she said to Didi, eager to appoint a scapegoat.

"Yeah, like I could've stopped it," Didi said.

Viv circled a finger around Kate's face. "Woman, now you are officially off the relationship-advice roster, too."

"What were you doing out there?" Didi asked. "What if Jordan ended up here and saw you?"

"She's got other things vying for her attention right now," Kate said bitterly as she checked her dead cell phone. "That chick out there, now that's someone I should be with. She's our age, sophisticated—"

"That barracuda would eat you alive," Viv said with an arched eyebrow.

"You're such an ass." Didi scoffed. "You already have the greatest girl in the world who's attentive and devoted. You want to switch with me so you can see just how good you have it with Jordan?"

"Girl, you wasting too much life trying to figure this Rhea woman out," Viv said to Didi. "Respect yourself enough to move on."

"Gee. That advice sounds familiar," Didi said. She pinched her chin, pretending to recall. "Oh, yes, now I remember. We've only said that to you about a thousand times apiece over the last twenty-five years."

"Then practice what you preach," Viv said.

Didi glared at her. "You're like the convict that finds Jesus and then suddenly wants to convert everyone."

Viv shifted her weight to lean toward Didi's face. "That's no worse than a bigmouth always giving advice but never following it in her own mess of a life."

"Whoa, whoa. Easy, girls." Kate struggled to slide off the stool and land on her feet between them. "We have to leave now."

"Yes, we do," Viv said, giving Didi a parting glare. She then indicated a waitress coming toward their table. "Right after this round of lemon-drop shots."

"I really shouldn't," Kate said, lifting the shot to her lips.

"Wait, wait, wait." Didi raised her shot and stumbled into Kate. "What do we drink to?"

"Our three beautiful ladies," Viv said, "wherever they may be."

They knocked back the shots and then slammed the glasses on the table like cowboys in an old Western.

Yvonne then appeared and drew Kate aside. "If you'd like to grab some lunch sometime, give me a call." She pressed a business card into Kate's hand.

"Uh…" Kate stammered as she attempted to gather her wits. "I'm just here for the weekend. I live in Connecticut."

"Then come back to my house tonight. I'm not too far from here."

"I, um, don't think that…"

"Don't worry. I'm not a serial killer," Yvonne said, but her inviting smile was about to slay Kate right there on the spot.

"I'm sure you're not, but I'm here…"

"If you came with your friends, I'll make sure you get back to your hotel safely."

"It's not that," Kate said. "I have a girlfriend. She's at a party."

Yvonne regarded her like she was awaiting the rest of the reason.
"We can have a little bash of our own."

"I can't," Kate said. "As attractive as you are, I just can't."

She leaned in and kissed Kate on the cheek. "As attractive as you are, I'd never choose a party over you."

Buzzed and confused, she stared into Yvonne's penetrating eyes that locked onto hers. She might not have been a serial killer, but with the fixation in those black, gleaming stones, Kate wouldn't have ruled out vampire.

"Are you sure I can't convince you?" Yvonne said.

Before Kate could answer, Didi and Viv had a hand under each of her armpits and hauled her out to the sidewalk to wait for their Uber car.

"Now I'm drunk," Viv said, "but this bitch gonna need her stomach pumped."

Kate closed her eyes and leaned face-first into a thick wall of shrubbery lining the sidewalk in an attempt to outsmart her spinning head.

"Kate." Didi spun her around and slapped her face lightly. "You're not gonna pass out on us, are you?"

"Nooo," Kate slurred. "Don't be *ridicalous*. I'm not gonna pass out on you. But I am gonna throw up on you."

Didi lurched back, and the dense crowd waiting for valets to bring their cars around parted before Kate as though she were Moses vomiting over the Red Sea.

❖

The muffled pounding on the hotel-suite door finally roused Kate from her slumber beneath a pillow. She pried open an eye. The digital clock read a blurry 10:34. Was that a.m. or p.m.? After she opened both eyes, the sun shining into the bedroom solved the mystery.

Another round of pounding. Was that in her head or on the door? She sat up slowly and pushed her forehead into her palms.

"Kate, I know you're in there. Open the door," Jordan called from the hallway.

"Oh, no," she said, fumbling to emerge from the cocoon of sheets and blankets. When she finally opened the door, Jordan's look of fury melted like a watch in a Dali painting into bewilderment.

"Good God," Jordan said.

"Hi?" Kate replied.

"I think it's safe to assume breakfast is off," Jordan said after a moment studying her.

"Jordan, I'm so sorry."

"Why didn't you answer any of my texts?"

"My phone died last night while we were still out, and I forgot to charge it before I went to sleep."

"I see you also forgot to set an alarm. Is there some reason why you're not inviting me in?"

"No, no, come in." Kate stepped aside and scratched at her bed head. "I'm so sorry about oversleeping."

"What happened last night? And don't say 'nothing' because you're a wreck this morning."

Kate rushed to a mirror to assess the damage. "Holy mother." Her hair looked like she'd been riding a motorcycle without a helmet all night and her face like a street with a hundred feet of skid marks. "We had a few cocktails."

"Where?"

"Some bar in West Hollywood. I was ready to go home after your show, but the girls wanted to go dancing."

"Did you?"

"Yes, we all did."

"With who?"

"Jordan, I feel like I'm being cross-examined. What's the matter?"

"You flew all the way out here, allegedly to see me, yet it seems like you're doing everything in your power to avoid it. You totally blew me off this morning."

"I didn't mean to, babe." Kate approached her and took her by the hands. "It was a strange night that began with the fatal error of allowing Didi and Viv to plan the itinerary. We can still grab something downstairs. It'll only take me a few minutes to shower."

Jordan sighed as she slipped her hands from Kate's grip. "I'm just gonna go. It'll be noon by the time you're ready." She crossed her arms over her chest, her face tight with disappointment.

"Please accept my apology, Jordan. I didn't give myself the mother of all hangovers on purpose."

"Are you mad at me for coming out here and doing this?"

"Mad? Are you kidding? This is so great. I'm so happy for you." Kate enveloped her in a hug and felt Jordan's tension release in her arms. As she kissed her, she sensed she'd be forgiven.

"I love you, Kate," Jordan whispered. "So much."

"I love you, too." She held her tight and allowed herself to relish the sensation, to feel comfortable saying it back knowing she'd meant it. Maybe she'd been too reactive last night when she contemplated breaking up. It seemed rather drastic in the morning light.

"I have an idea how I can make it up to you."

"This better be good," Jordan said with the cutest pout. "I'm still mad at you."

A trace of vitality returned to Kate's hangover-deadened limbs as she nodded toward the bedroom. "Why don't you order up some room service while I jump in the shower, and then we can eat in there?"

Jordan snaked her arms around Kate's neck and sucked at her lips. "I'm starting to forgive you already."

As the pilot leveled off the Gulfstream, Viv popped the cork on a bottle of pink champagne and topped off flute glasses half-filled with orange juice. Kate directed her attention out the window, as the mere sight of the bottle produced a nasty gurgle in her gut.

Didi offered up two glasses for Viv to fill. "Aren't you having any, Kate?"

Kate slowly pivoted her head around. "I drank about six months' worth of alcohol in the last two nights and somehow didn't wake up in the ER. I'm gonna take the win and sip water for the rest of the day."

"You wouldn't have been able to get hammered two nights in a row if you'd come with me to the dinner party last night," Jordan said.

"Babe, I already told you I didn't want to intrude," Kate said. "Besides, the girls would've been furious if I ditched them on the last night of our girls' weekend." She fired off a warning shot with her eyes to Viv, who looked as though she was about to make a smart remark.

Didi handed Jordan a mimosa. "I hope you've forgiven us for

luring Kate into an evening of debauchery Friday night and ruining your breakfast date."

Jordan smiled. "It's hard not to be forgiving when you're drinking mimosas on a private jet. It turned out better than expected anyway," she said, tapping Kate in the leg with her foot.

"So we heard," Viv said with a grin.

"I guess you'll be getting accustomed to traveling by private jet soon enough," Didi said.

"I don't know about that," Jordan said. "It's a nice idea though."

"When are they going to offer you the contract?" Viv asked.

"Do you have an agent yet?" Didi asked.

The sudden barrage of questions piqued Kate's curiosity. She remained facing the window but kept her ears aimed at the conversation.

"No. I don't have an agent yet. Alexandra suggested I hire one and a business manager, even if the company doesn't offer me a contract now."

"That sounds like good advice," Didi said. "Kate, as a lawyer, what would you advise?"

Kate looked over, feigning ambivalence. "I'm not an entertainment attorney, but I'm sure Alexandra has it all worked out for Jordan whenever you say the word."

"I still value your advice, Kate," Jordan said. "What do you think?" It sounded like a challenge.

Kate broke open a bottle of sparkling water. "It all depends on how actively you want to pursue this."

"The ball's rolling," Viv said. "Why would she stop now?"

"Only you can answer that, Jordan," Kate said. "You came out here to see where things would go. What if they don't offer you the contract? Will you continue pursuing performing at a professional level?"

"I honestly haven't thought that far ahead."

"Maybe they're going to offer her a contract," Didi said. "Then this conversation will be moot."

Kate shifted in her seat. "Either way, you'll have to think about it. You can't go back to the way things were before you left—unless you don't want to pursue stardom."

Didi gave Kate a look.

"Stardom?" Jordan said. "Look, all I want to do is write and play music. I used to daydream about being a rock star when I was a kid, but that was a long time ago. I have different priorities now."

Kate was about to ask where she fit into that scheme, but after noticing the uncomfortable looks on everyone's faces, she shelved it for a land conversation.

"I think whatever's meant to happen will," Didi said. "No sense stressing about all the 'what ifs.' Let's all just sit back and ride that rainbow wherever it takes us."

"Amen, sista," Viv said. "And when this one hits the big time, we'll all be flying high on her jet stream."

Kate raised her bottle of water. "Here's to Jordan. May all her dreams come true."

As she tapped her bottle against everyone's glass, she smiled over the unrest she was feeling. This time, Jordan's claim that she didn't care about fame or the big time lacked the same conviction she'd displayed before leaving for California. She'd better start relying more on her own intuition than Jordan's words.

The next morning Kate walked into the office cranky, her eyes slits from a nasty combination of jet lag and sleep deprivation. By the time she'd finally drifted off somewhere near the witching hour, the internal debate still hadn't resolved itself. Why was it all so complicated? Why had falling in love again with a kind, sensitive soul like Jordan seemed less like the proverbial stroll along a beach at sunset and more like a decathlon of neuroses presenting a new hurdle at every turn? It wasn't just a matter of the age difference anymore. Now there loomed the real possibility that Kate could end up becoming an obstacle to Jordan's success—or a liner note on her past.

"Morning," Didi said, way too perky for Kate's mood. "There's a fresh cinnamon-croissant doughnut on your desk."

"Thanks. That'll only cost me two extra hours at the gym this week." She marched past Didi into her office.

"You told me to get you one the next time I went to that bakery. The one time I actually do obey your wishes, and this is what I get."

Kate huffed when she consulted her calendar and realized she was behind in preparing for a family-leave case that was fast approaching.

Didi appeared in the doorway. "So when is Jordan going to know about her record deal?"

"Is that all we have to talk about anymore? I have no idea, and even if she's offered one, it's not going to mean a reality show for all of us to star in."

Didi cocked her head to the side. "Why are you so bitchy?"

"I'm tired," Kate said. She rubbed her face as if that would erase the angst cluttering her mind.

"We landed on the same plane, but you don't see me biting your head off." As Didi stormed back to her desk, she shouted, "And by the way, you still owe me for that dry-cleaning bill."

Kate slumped back in guilt. "I'm sorry I'm a bear today," she called out. "Just give me the receipt."

Didi reappeared at the door. "Fight with Jordan?"

"No, but this contract thing adds a new, unpleasant dimension to us. I was awake all night."

"Have you talked to her about it?"

Kate shook her head. "I don't want it to become an issue. What if her infatuation with me interferes with her decision-making process? I'd hate to know her fear of losing me caused her to sabotage her chances at a professional career."

"Kate, it's already an issue between you. You're obsessing about the 'what-ifs' instead of appreciating what's real and in front of you. How long can you keep that up?"

Kate reclined in her chair and exhaled. "I hate it so much when you're right."

"You know what might help?" Didi said. "If you stopped giving her reasons to fear losing you. You weren't very supportive on the plane yesterday. In fact, you were kind of douchey."

"Why? Because I didn't gush over her like a tweenie like you and Viv? To you it sounds sexy and exciting, but I'm realistic. I don't want to date a rock star. I'm forty-seven years old. I should be with someone on the same page as me, someone working toward a stable, permanent relationship. Not a kid who wants to chase a dream all over the globe."

"Kate, I've known you most of our lives, and if there's one thing you should try before you die, it's chasing a dream."

"It's her dream, not mine."

Didi rolled her eyes. "Honestly, I don't think I've ever known anyone who's worked as hard as you are at ruining a good thing. You're so engrossed in protecting yourself against all these perceived hazards that you're completely missing what you have with Jordan."

Kate swiveled in her chair as she contemplated. She smiled as thoughts of Jordan crept in—who she really was behind the scenes of circumstance, her open heart, her level head, her captivating talent. Yeah, she'd had it pretty good. "Maybe I'm just in desperate need of a good night's sleep."

"At the very least," Didi said and walked back to her desk.

After a moment, she called Kate into the reception area. A delivery man was standing in the office holding a lavish rose bouquet. After thanking and tipping the guy, Kate ripped the card out of Didi's hand and read it to herself.

"Aww, Jordan wants to know if I'm free in two weeks for a romantic weekend away." Kate fanned herself with the card like a coy Southern belle. "Maybe I do need to relax," she said, grinning in fond recollection. "Recent events aside, I have to say that in the last two months, she's acted as though my happiness is her main priority."

"Oh, bite me," Didi said and sat down at her desk.

Kate placed the flowers on a side table to lessen the blow. "So, how's Rhea?"

"So *not* Jordan. She's had an excuse ready the last couple of times I suggested getting together, and it's always the same: she has to show a house."

"In her defense, realtors have to keep weird hours sometimes. They have to meet clients when it's convenient for them. I can relate to that."

"I want to have a heart-to-heart with her to see where it's going, but I want to do it in person, not by text."

"It really could be nothing more than a busy buying season. On the other hand, she may be indirectly answering that question by being unavailable, not that I want to be a harbinger of negative vibes or anything."

"You, a harbinger of negativity?" Didi smirked. "Of course, I've thought of that possibility, but right now I'm still in the denial stage. Can you let me wallow here for a while?"

"This whole conversation reminds of something my therapist

once told me: you'll never have a healthy relationship if you try to fit someone into the mold you think they belong in."

Didi cupped her hands over her ears. "Lalalalalala. Not ready for logic. Lalalalala. Still in denial."

Kate laughed and grabbed her flower arrangement before heading to her office. "By the way, Viv is coming up Friday, so don't make any plans."

"Don't think that'll be a problem," Didi said with a frown.

They exchanged thumbs-ups, and Kate buried her nose in the fragrant roses all the way to her desk. Did Jordan have some sort of superhuman intuitive powers? Lately it seemed whenever Kate was shadowed by doubt, Jordan somehow found a way to lighten the darkness of worry.

"Hey, you," Jordan said when she answered her cell.

"Thank you for the roses. They're gorgeous."

"Not nearly as gorgeous as you. So, what do you say—can you run away with me for a weekend?"

"I'd love to," Kate purred. "Do we have to wait that long?"

Jordan sucked air through her teeth. "I have a gig this Saturday night, babe. It's a private party in Greenwich. Some New York finance exec is paying me eight hundred dollars to play at his daughter's coming-out party."

"Rich debutantes. How fun."

"No. He's literally throwing her a party to celebrate her coming out of the closet. I know it's last-minute, but I just couldn't turn down that kind of cash for an hour-and-a-half set."

"You're worth every penny of it," Kate said. "How about dinner at Chez Kate later?"

"I thought you'd never ask."

"I'll whip up an Asian stir-fry, and you can bring dessert."

"Okay. Any particular place you'd like to me stop for it?"

"Nope. What I want goes wherever you go."

"Ooh, on second thought, we might want to have it as an appetizer."

Kate ended the call with a smile, suddenly longing to hold Jordan in her arms.

CHAPTER FIFTEEN

Ms. Wilmington Goes to Bizarro World

When Friday arrived, Kate was more enthusiastic than usual for happy hour with the girls. Her wintry heart was finally beginning to thaw in the security of feeling like she and Jordan were at last in synch. As she recalled their romantic dinner earlier in the week and anticipated their upcoming getaway, she grew antsy for Jordan to arrive.

After grabbing the happy-hour menu from Didi, she eyed the bistro's entrance as they engaged in a tug-o'-war.

"Get your own menu," Didi said. "I was reading that."

Plucking it from Didi's grip, Kate passed it to Viv and Maia, huddled closely in their large round booth. "You guys pick the apps," she said. "Didi wants all the fattening ones."

"I need some comfort food," Didi said. "And their buffalo nachos and poutine go splendidly with tequila."

"Didi, why don't you just cut your losses with Rhea?" Kate asked. "No woman is worth carbing yourself to death."

"No, no. It's all good. We have a lunch date tomorrow."

"Then don't you think you ought to pass on all that cheese tonight?"

A bubbly, pierced, and tattooed waitress appeared at their table. "Evening, ladies. The usual?"

"Yes, but we'll also be ordering some food," Kate said.

"Oh?" the waitress said.

Didi leaned toward Kate. "Should we be worried that every waitress in New Haven knows we have a 'usual' drink order?"

"Just some sparkling water for me," Maia said, beaming.

"I'll have the same," Viv said.

Didi and Kate exchanged looks as they mentally grappled with their unprecedented alcohol-free drink order.

Viv gripped Maia's hand. "We're going for the sperm implantation on Tuesday. I'm just supporting my lady." She gave Maia a wrinkled-nose smile that Maia zealously returned.

Didi pantomimed a gag reflex.

"I'm sure it also cuts down on the risk of a domestic call to your apartment," Kate said.

"You're so fresh." Maia giggled as she brushed Kate's hand with a pretend slap.

"I, for one, am happier than a billionaire finding a new tax loophole that you kids got it together and are starting a family," Didi said. "I've said for a long time that's exactly what Viv needed. And I can't wait to babysit your little turkey-baster bundle of joy when the timer goes off."

"I can't wait to watch Miss Vivienne change her first dirty diaper," Kate said.

"Don't say that," Maia teased her. "You'll scare her off."

"No, baby," Viv said. "I'm in this for all the right reasons this time."

"Me, too, baby." Maia leaned over and they kissed.

"Boy, there really must be something to this therapy racket," Didi said. "Where the hell's my margarita?"

The waitress arrived with a tray of drinks as Jordan breezed into the restaurant. "Sorry I'm late, everyone." She bent to kiss Kate. "I got caught up in some last-minute work."

"Songwriting?" Kate asked with an ever-so-slight whiff of resentment.

"No, work-work. A local Mom and Pop wants to go viral." She turned to Maia and offered her hand. "Hi. I'm Jordan."

"The musician," Maia squealed. "I've heard so much about you."

"Yes, likewise." Jordan sent Kate a secret smile.

"It's so nice that we're all finally able to get together," Maia said as Viv played with the ends of her hair. "I was just telling Vivienne we should have everyone up to the penthouse for cocktails some Friday night."

"We will, baby girl," Viv said, "as soon as Mother Nature and Dr. Silberstein give us the good word. We'll throw the biggest, baddest baby shower the Upper West Side's ever experienced."

Jordan leaned toward Kate's ear. "These are the poster girls for lesbian drama you were telling me about?"

"You're gonna have to trust me on this one," Kate whispered back. "If I didn't know better, I'd think we're drinking at a cocktail lounge in Bizarro World."

"They're adorable, and they seem so excited about the baby."

"I'm happy for them," Kate said. "Lord knows I've seen stranger things happen lately."

"What are you two whispering about over there?" Viv asked.

"Jordan was just saying how adorable you guys are." Kate raised her glass with a smile at Maia. "It's wonderful to see you again, Maia, and I think I speak for the rest of us when I say we're all rooting for a successful fertilization on Tuesday."

The table erupted in cheers.

"Aww, you guys are the best," Viv said. "I can't tell you how much it means to share this with my girls."

"While you're waiting to hear from the doctor, we need to discuss your parental-rights options," Kate said.

"It's New York," Viv said. "My name automatically goes on the birth certificate."

"Only if you two are married."

An awkward silence descended as four sets of eyes zeroed in on Viv and Maia.

"We can always file adoption paperwork," Kate said to defuse the tension. "That's easy enough."

"Well," Viv said, looking at Maia. "I guess my woman and I will have to review our options and get back to you."

"Yes," Maia said with such exhilaration that Kate recoiled, fearing her head was about to explode.

Viv wrinkled her perfectly sculpted brows. "Yes, what?"

"Yes, I'll marry you," Maia said.

Viv smiled, kissed her passionately, and wrapped her in an embrace.

Didi and Jordan shouted and collapsed into each other.

"Okay, on the birth certificate you go," Kate said. Sipping her drink, she smiled at their jubilation.

❖

After the delirium of Vivienne's impromptu marriage proposal, Kate and Jordan reset their serenity buttons on Kate's veranda as the sun returned to earth over Long Island Sound. Kate reached for another handful of grapes as she watched Jordan sitting with her tanned knees up to her chin, slowly chewing, watching a seagull hop across a hunk of beached driftwood.

She could stare at her, posed sculpture-like, all night, long after the sun's light faded to moon glow. While her physical beauty was mesmerizing, the light of her genuine soul had slowly revealed itself over the last two and a half months and tightened its grip on Kate's heart.

Jordan did a double take when she noticed Kate's expression. "What are you staring at?"

"You," she answered with a loving smile.

"Why? Is something crawling on my face?" She swiped at her cheeks with a napkin, then dabbed strawberry juice off her fingers.

"No, you're clear," Kate said, still smiling.

Jordan stretched across the arm of the wicker patio chair and kissed her. "You make me feel so special," she said as a light breeze tousled her curls.

"You are special." Kate took her hand and stroked her palm with her free fingers. "If I had your creative way with words, I'd write you a song or poem or something that would show you how I feel about you."

Jordan's eyes twinkled in the moonlight as they brimmed with tears. She jumped into Kate's lap and hugged her until the wicker love seat creaked under their weight.

"I love when you say things like that," Jordan said, her lips against Kate's ear. "I love you, baby, so much."

"I love you, too." Kate kissed her tenderly, savoring the trace of fruit on her lips.

They rested their heads together and gazed out over the water. What a feeling, Kate thought. If only being in love felt that way all the time, like strawberry kisses and fiery sunsets.

"That was a unique experience earlier," Jordan mused as she shifted to the cushion beside Kate. "I've never witnessed a marriage proposal in real time before."

"Theirs is one of the most unique relationships I've had the pleasure to...well, let's just say it wasn't that surprising to me."

"I can't imagine what the wedding will be like."

"I'd venture to predict as outrageous as they are, especially since it's the first marriage for both of them."

Jordan tickled Kate's leg with her bare toes. "Well, if you need a date, I'm available."

Kate grabbed her foot and pulled her legs into her lap. "Are you sure? You may be off somewhere on your world tour by then."

"I doubt that. In fact, I'm so sure I won't be you can mark me down on the RSVP for the fish right now."

"Speaking of that, have you heard anything from Alexandra?"

"Actually, I did this morning. She said that Swag is going to pass on me right now, but I shouldn't give up hope, blah, blah, blah."

"She's right. You shouldn't." Kate smiled to conceal the guilt that sprang from feeling relieved. "I'm sorry, baby. Are you okay?"

"Oh yeah," Jordan said. "I knew it was a long shot anyway."

Kate pulled her close for a consoling cuddle. "Still, it had to hurt when she told you."

"Not as much as the thought of losing you."

Kate kissed her head. "What does that have to do with anything?"

Jordan shrugged. "Just sayin'."

"Did Alexandra have any advice as to where you could go from here?"

After a moment of what Kate interpreted as truth-appropriating hesitation, Jordan replied, "Uh…not really. Just to keep writing and booking shows as often as I can."

"Good advice." Ignoring the twinge of doubt, she laced her fingers through Jordan's. "The girls and I love your shows, even when one of your exes shows up trying to win you back."

"You don't have to worry about that, baby. My exes could never compete. You've set the bar way too high. I honestly don't know what Andie had in mind, but when I told her how crazy in love with you I am, she stopped texting me."

"Oh, she was texting you?"

"The day after she came to my show, and only until I started gushing about you." Jordan stretched to kiss Kate's lips.

"So you're crazy in love with me?" Kate said, kissing her back.

"Totally." She sucked at Kate's top lip.

"I'm pretty crazy about you, too, kid."

"Let me freshen up, and we can get crazy on each other under the moonlight."

"That sounds lovely," Kate said, stroking Jordan's forearm.

Jordan leapt up and bounded inside, leaving her phone face down on the table.

Kate stared at it, trying to dismiss the shameful compulsion that popped into her head. Don't do it, she admonished herself. Don't let yourself sink into the abyss.

On the other hand, Jordan was her girlfriend. Would it really be such a crime to take a quick peek at it? It wasn't that Kate distrusted her, but it seemed like Jordan hadn't wanted her to know she'd received texts from Alexandra and Andie. Why hadn't she mentioned either of them sooner? If Kate hadn't brought them up, would Jordan have ever told her? Maybe Jordan had a sketchy side. Musicians didn't usually have the most promising history with fidelity. If she was so inclined, she certainly wasn't going to reveal that to Kate. Wasn't that something she should find out sooner rather than later?

She lifted the phone without turning it over, then placed it down again. What was wrong with her? Jordan hadn't an ounce of deceitfulness in her; she knew that.

So if that was the case, there shouldn't be any moral dilemma in taking a little peek, just to alleviate her concerns. She picked up the phone again and swiped it. She opened the text from Alexandra and scanned up until she'd found the beginning.

> *Don't be discouraged, J. This happens all the time. I'm serious about you moving out here. A and R peeps are always around the clubs.*

J? She's got a nickname for her now?

> *Don't think I can just move across the country. I'm close to NYC. Isn't it kinda the same?*

> *No way. I'm out here ;-) lol. Seriously, think about it. U can stay w me until you get settled.*

Aww, wasn't that generous of Alexandra to offer free housing to Jordan while she waited to be discovered? That old hoe was itching to get her claws into Jordan and wasn't even trying to be sly about it.

"Aren't you coming in, baby?" Jordan called from the living room.

Kate closed the text and replaced the phone on the table as Jordan appeared at the French doors. "Uh, yes, just cleaning up." She collected their wineglasses and stacked the small plates and forks.

"I'll finish with that later," Jordan said as she nudged Kate toward the door. "Meet me under the sheets, and don't keep me waiting."

"Roger that." Kate smiled as she fought the distraction of Jordan summoning her in a peachy camisole and bikini underwear. She needed to know Jordan's reply to Alexandra's offer. Now. How was she supposed to concentrate on the worldly pleasures Jordan was about to lavish upon her if her mind raced with all kinds of dreadful, apocalyptic relationship scenarios?

As she trailed Jordan and her tight, incredibly appetizing rear end up the spiral staircase, she hadn't lost sight of the urgency in getting her hands on that phone. But a butt on the stairs is worth two in the bush.

After Jordan had fallen asleep in her arms, Kate lay watching the night breeze off the sound tango with the curtains through the open doors. Now would've been the perfect time to slip out of bed and finish reading Alexandra's text, but after such a steamy interlude, Kate wanted nothing more than to lie skin on skin, lulled by the rhythms of high tide and Jordan's breathing. Besides, like her Grandma Winnie used to say, "Don't go lookin' for nothin' you'd rather not find."

The night before they were to leave for a cozy, historic inn in Newport, Kate packed items into an overnight bag. As she rifled through drawers, she discovered a black lace bra with the tags on it, purchased as a symbol of hope not long after her breakup with Lydia. Twirling the bra on her finger, she smiled. She'd come full circle. She was finally over Lydia and the fear and self-doubt that had crippled her emotionally. And it was all thanks to Jordan, the woman who'd come along with her caring heart and fiery passion and blowtorched her way through the walls Kate had built to freeze out everyone.

This getaway was important, their first real chance to spend time alone connecting and getting fully reacquainted with all the aspects of each other that had attracted them in the first place. It pleased her to imagine the smile on Jordan's face when she told her she was ready to entertain whatever future possibilities Jordan had in mind. She smiled at the peace washing over her from the mere thought of the words *future* and *possibilities* in the same sentence.

As she cut the tags off her sexy brassiere, her phone chimed with a text. She grabbed it, thinking it was Jordan. But it was Didi.

What are u doing?

Packing. Leaving for Newport tomorrow.

Lucky. Have fun. ☺

You ok?

Yeah. Saw Rhea tonite. She came over.

Did you talk things out?

Not exactly. We were a little busy.

All night? You couldn't talk after?

She had to leave. Early staff meeting tomorrow.

Lol. I used that excuse when I panicked the first time I slept w Jordan.

It's not an excuse!!!!

Ok ok. But you really need to get to the bottom of this!!

You're right. I'll call her tomorrow!

Good girl. Now let me finish packing <3

She felt bad for Didi, but if she always insisted on fighting uphill battles, she'd have to fight some of them alone. After all, the sexy apparel she planned to wear to seduce Jordan wasn't going to pack itself.

Suddenly, her cell phone rang.

"Hey. I was just about to call you to say good night," Kate said.

Jordan hesitated.

"What's the matter, babe?" Kate asked.

"Kate, please don't be mad at me."

"For what?"

"I, uh, I have to postpone our weekend. I'm so sorry, honey."

"Why? What happened?"

"Well, um, there's this talent showcase in New York tomorrow night, and Alexandra called in some favors and got me a performance slot. All the big A and R people will be there, as well as talent agents."

Kate's disappointment overwhelmed her.

"Kate, are you furious?" Jordan asked. "Do you hate me?"

"No, no, of course not." More silence. It was the only way to handle the news with grace.

"Come with me," Jordan said. "We can stay overnight in the City and spend the day—"

"I don't think so. I'll just be in the way."

"No, you won't."

"Yes, Jordan. It'll be like it was when you were in LA. It'll be better if you just do what you need to do."

"But Kate, I want you to—"

"I said no, Jordan," she snapped. "I'm not gonna follow you all over like some groupie."

It was Jordan's turn to be silent. She was quiet for so long, Kate thought for a moment she'd hung up on her.

"I'll cancel it then," Jordan finally said. "I'll just wait for the next one to come around."

"When will that be?"

"I don't know," she said, her voice hollow with defeat.

Kate was about to hold her to the offer until her conscience rose up and slapped her ego down.

"You can't cancel this, Jordan. Just go."

"Are you sure?"

With life infused back into Jordan's voice, Kate couldn't stop the "yes, I'm sure" from spilling out even if she'd tried. The least Jordan could've done was resist a little more.

"Thank you, baby," Jordan gushed. "I promise I'll make it up to you."

As they ended the conversation, Kate wondered how many more times Jordan would have to make up for broken promises. And how many more times she'd be willing to wait.

After ending the call, she launched her phone, aiming for the bed, but sent it rocketing into the side of her dresser, cracking the screen. Before her eyes completely clouded with tears, she glanced at her open suitcase. The clothing and sexy lingerie folded neatly for a romantic getaway were now covered in the trail of exhaust left by Jordan's rising star.

CHAPTER SIXTEEN

The Good-bye Girl

After the defunct weekend getaway that was supposed to symbolize their move into semi-permanence, Kate still hadn't rebounded from the disillusionment. Fancy dinners for two, making love, and a night at the theater hadn't recalibrated the off-kilter feel between them like she'd hoped.

She felt Jordan's body heat radiate against her back as she trailed her into the darkness of her house. Like a scene in a slasher film right before someone gets a machete to the face, her heels slowly, eerily clicked on the hardwood floor on their way to the nearest light switch.

"I loved that play," Jordan said, as the lamp illuminated the room. "It was a Broadway-quality show."

"It was, and at an eighth of the ticket price." Kate jingled her house keys in her hand, her insides in knots. This had to be one of the worst feelings in the world. If only Jordan was even an iota of the vixen her onstage persona suggested.

"Are you all right? You've been quiet all evening." Jordan tossed her phone onto an end table and her light jacket on the sofa.

"Fine," Kate muttered as she crossed the room and switched on a reading lamp.

"Okay." Jordan flopped on the sofa, but her eyes seemed to be noting every movement, every gesture as Kate writhed with angst in the suffocating silence.

The air conditioner kicked on, startling Kate. "Actually, I want to talk to you about something, Jordan." Her mouth remained open, but the words seemed to crawl back down.

As the color drained from her face, Jordan sloped forward, resting her forearms on her thighs. Kate could only stare at her like a stage actress going blank in the middle of a monologue.

"I know what this is," Jordan finally said softly. "You're breaking up with me."

Was this chick clairvoyant or what?

Kate faltered. "Well, I, uh…"

"C'mon, Kate, say it."

"It's not necessarily a breakup per se." She wandered away from Jordan, fearing the jury was about to become hostile. "I think we need to slow it down, you know cool it off for a bit, just until—"

"What? What does that even mean?" Jordan said. "Normally, when things are hot, people don't just randomly decide they need to cool off. Unless what they really mean is break up but don't have the balls to come out and say it."

Kate's big rebuttal was a meek shrug from across the room. "I guess that's what I mean."

Jordan bit her lip and gazed around the room, seemingly dazed. "I know it's my turn to say something right now, but I don't know what."

"Look. This must feel like a surprise after—"

"After what? The way we make love? The connection we have that I've never felt with anyone else? It didn't feel like it was only me."

"It wasn't only you," Kate said as Jordan paced the room.

"Then why don't you explain what this is really about?"

Kate was more upset than she'd anticipated being. She retreated to the window and watched the surf crash under the full moon, hoping to stem her emotions from rising over her protective wall.

"You know what?" Jordan flung her hair back with attitude. "I shouldn't be surprised at all. I mean how stupid could I be not to see this coming. You've done such a shitty job hiding your neurotic obsession with our age difference. But I kept telling myself that if we loved each other…" Her voice began to crack. "That's the reason, isn't it?"

Kate couldn't bring herself to look directly at her. "No, actually—"

"We've been together barely three months. You haven't given us a chance."

Jordan's eyes flared with indignation, and Kate suddenly regretted invoking her fiery stage persona.

"Jordan, let's be realistic. I'm seventeen years older than you.

That's practically an entire generation. My life is established, and you're just coming into yours, especially with—"

"You said age didn't matter on our first date. Was that a lie to get into my pants?"

"What? No," Kate stammered. "I mean, honestly, I had no idea where this would go at the time. And as we grew closer, I didn't want it to matter, but it's something we can't keep ignoring. We're in two completely different places in our lives."

"Kate, I moved back to Connecticut to settle down and build my business. I wanted to be closer to my family again and hopefully meet someone I could have a life with here."

"Until Alexandra came calling. Jordan, how do you expect to settle down and build a life with someone if you're off chasing your dream of a professional music career?"

"I don't have dreams of pursuing a music career. I love writing songs and performing for small audiences here and there, but I haven't dreamed of being a rock star since I was a kid."

"Then why did you go to LA and that New York talent showcase?"

"They were amazing opportunities that fell in my lap, so I followed through for the fun of it. It was a wild experience, and I don't regret going."

"You canceled our romantic weekend together for something that doesn't mean anything to you?"

"Kate, I didn't cancel our weekend. I asked you to come with me. We could've stayed in the City. You're the one who flipped out on me and said forget it."

"Jordan, who are you kidding?" Kate said with understanding. "You want to cut a record. Who could blame you?"

"Of course I would if I got the chance, but either way, it's not gonna change who I am or what I want."

"You're thirty. How can you know what you want?"

Jordan raged at her. "Could you be any more condescending? This isn't about age at all, is it? Act like you're under oath, Attorney Randall, and admit that you're scared to commit to anyone. Been there, done that. No complicated emotional entanglements for you. You just want to party with your friends and throw Viv's money around on expensive cocktails and use her father's private jet."

"What?" Kate exclaimed.

"Or maybe it's just about you not wanting to commit to someone like me, an unsophisticated underachiever who'll never fit into your world of elitists. It's not about how old I am. It's about who I am, and who you are."

Taken aback, Kate stammered. "Jordan, I don't know what you're—"

"That's why you didn't take me to that charity event at the St. Regis in Greenwich, and that's why you're dumping me now. Our little affair has finally lost its savor."

Kate moved toward her. "Jordan, that has absolutely nothing to do with this."

"You're so full of it. I may not have the wealth of life experience you've had, but I'm not an idiot." She stomped toward the door.

"Jordan, wait. My decision has nothing to do with status or any of that crap you said. I think you're a remarkable young woman with so much going for you. I don't want to stand in your way. I'm doing this for you."

"For me?" Jordan laughed in disgust. "Wow, Kate. I never would've expected something so entirely unoriginal from you."

"Jordan, that's how I feel, like lately I've been an obstacle for you to go around whenever some new opportunity comes along. Look, let's just throw it on hold while you explore where this music stuff is going."

"And then what? When I fall on my face and come crawling back, you'll be gracious enough to take me back?"

"That's the thing, Jordan," Kate said through a sad smile. "You're not going to fall."

Jordan smirked. "So, did Columbia U give away a free crystal ball with every law degree? Save the 'It's not you, it's me' defense for your next negotiation, Counselor."

Kate grabbed her by the arm. "Jordan, please don't leave like this. Let's talk about this calmly like…"

"Like what, adults?" Jordan's voice was shaking. "Sorry, but according to some people, I'm not capable of doing anything like an adult."

"I never said you were incapable of—"

"I can't believe you're doing this, Kate." She turned away and rested her forehead against the door as she cried.

Kate gently touched her shoulder. "Jordan, listen to me. I'm upset, too. Believe me, I am, but it's better to end it now before anyone gets really hurt."

Jordan wheeled around to face her. "I got news for you, Kate. You're too late." She shook Kate's hand off, yanked open the door, and stormed down the steps.

Kate followed her across the driveway to her car.

"Leave me alone, Kate, or you'll be the next one in your group to need a defense lawyer." Jordan slammed the door, threw the gearshift in reverse, and gunned the gas. Kate flinched at the stones and dust kicked up from her spinning tires.

"Jordan," Kate shouted into the night, but when the dust cleared, her car was already gone. She sat on the front porch steps absorbed in a perversely liberating state of sadness and relief. Time seemed dead as she sat, numb and vacated, in the dark.

When she went inside, she poured a glass of white wine and drank it too fast, forcing down the image of Jordan's disheartened face. As the wine slowed the reeling in her mind, she relaxed in the notion that she was regaining control. Life would become manageable and orderly again with nothing to distract her from the thoughts she preferred to think. No more sweeping surges of passion carrying her beyond the safety of her comfort zone.

Although she'd never anticipated such a dramatic scene, she found solace in the fact that Jordan was young and beautiful and would get over her. Why should she feel guilty? Jordan should've known that Kate needed to ease her way back into romance after so many years spent languishing in dry dock. She should've been more understanding of her need for a break, too. That's all she wanted, some time to regroup from the whirlwind. She hadn't intended to end it completely, but with Jordan overreacting the way she did, an end was the inevitable outcome.

Besides, it wasn't like they'd ever talked about a future or anything. Perhaps in time they could even become friends.

❖

The feelings of relief and self-assuredness that had powered her through the breakup conversation with Jordan the night before were nowhere to be found the next day. Instead, an overwhelming sense of loss loomed as she'd struggled for the emotional energy needed to simply get through the day.

As it finally neared its twilight, she raked a fork through the plate of leftover ziti she'd tried to finish for half an hour. Her eyes puffy and irritated from a deluge of crying, she smirked bitterly at the state she was in. She'd never felt completely comfortable in the relationship, so after thoughtful deliberation, she'd done what she believed was in her best interest, both of their interests. And as far as breakups went, she'd done it in style, buffering the heinous act by treating Jordan to dinner at a classy steakhouse and orchestra seats to a stellar touring production of *Hamilton*. But that did little to lessen the ache of missing her.

After putting the plate of pasta that had bested her on the coffee table, she buried her head into a sofa cushion and flicked mindlessly through the channels, settling on a thirty-minute infomercial, the best non-chemical sleep aid she'd ever known.

Ten minutes into a demonstration of the many ways a countertop rotisserie oven would improve her life, she'd dozed off on the couch with Ruby balled up on her chest. Sleep seemed to be the only way to drive Jordan's tortured expression from her mind, and after the miserable bout of punch-drunk insomnia she'd suffered through last night, a nap was the rarest of treasures. But before the limited-time-only price slash on the rotisserie oven blinked across the screen, her vibrating cell startled both her and the cat awake.

"Hey, Katie, you guys want to come to the *Rocky Horror Picture Show* with us tonight?" Didi's perky voice sliced through her.

"What?" she croaked, still foggy with sleep.

"You and Jordan. Meet us at the Landmark for the seven o'clock show. I bought these crazy hats and glasses." She giggled, unaware of Kate's downslide.

"Didi, we broke up."

"You what?" Didi shouted into the phone. "Oh, Kate, you didn't, did you?"

"I did," Kate said quietly, holding the phone away from her ear.

"But Kate, we talked about this—you, me, and Viv."

Kate opened her mouth to reply, but Didi was off and running.

"You agreed you were overthinking everything," Didi said. "Things were going so great. You could've dropped me a hint."

"I needed your permission?"

"No, but we always share this kind of stuff. What made you change your mind? Did something happen on Jordan's end?"

"Dee, I'm not in the mood to get into this now. Let's talk about it tomorrow."

"No way. Your schedule is full tomorrow, and you know it. I'm coming over there right now. I'm calling Viv. They're in town this weekend."

"Didi, please." She blinked her dry eyes. "I can't deal with a three-pronged attack from you guys right now. I just want to be alone."

"Kate, you can't be alone at a time like this. You sound terrible. You need your best friend to comfort you."

"What I need is some space and a friend who can respect that."

"How am I supposed to enjoy my movie knowing you're suffering all by yourself?"

"I know it's a lot to ask, but please do this for me. I'll be fine."

Didi hung on in silence for a moment. "Are you sure?"

"That's the one thing I am sure of. Enjoy your movie."

Kate tossed the phone onto the coffee table and scooped the sleepy cat up in her arms. As Ruby purred faintly, Kate let go of the emotion that had snuck up on her like a mid-summer thunderstorm. Inconvenienced by the breakdown, Ruby shook the moisture off her ears, jumped out of her arms, and stretched before moving to the other end of the sofa. Kate chuckled at the cat's indifference at her falling to pieces.

She absently checked her phone again for a text from Jordan.

Maybe tomorrow would be a better day.

CHAPTER SEVENTEEN

It Ain't Just a River in Egypt

Ready to call it a day after spending the afternoon writing a brief, Kate wandered out of her office and collapsed on the sofa. She ran her fingers through her hair and kicked off her shoes, imagining the first sip of a chilled cosmo passing through her lips as she waited for Didi to acknowledge her. But Didi was otherwise engaged stacking file trays and placing her stapler and paperclip holder in a desk drawer. She remained oblivious, humming as she shut down her computer and straightened up a mound of file folders.

Kate resorted to a loud sigh for attention.

Didi finally glanced over at her, looking like she'd just watched that Sarah McLaughlin animal-neglect commercial. "Any plans this weekend?"

Kate sighed again. "No. Just taking Sylvia to bingo at the casino Sunday morning."

"Ugh. Really?" Didi recoiled with disdain.

"What else would you like me to do? Go catch a Jordan Squire show?"

"Does she have a gig this weekend?" Didi joined her on the sofa.

"It doesn't appear so, according to her FB page."

"Ohhhh," Didi sang. "Weeks later and you're still creeping on her Facebook page. If that's not true love, I don't know what is."

"I wasn't creeping. A client was running a few minutes late, so I was just passing the time."

"You're looking to see if that ex is lurking around again," Didi accused her. "What are you going to do if she gets back with her?"

"Nothing," Kate said with a shrug.

"Then stop torturing yourself by looking at her page. On certain occasions in life, ignorance really is bliss." Didi beamed. "Unless you're contemplating going back with her."

"No. I doubt Jordan would even want that. She hasn't made any attempts to contact me, so she must've realized she's better off without me."

"I could tell how that girl felt about you. It's going to take her a lot more than a couple of weeks to get over you."

Kate didn't dispute the claim as her mood plunged even lower. Surprisingly, it seemed like that might be the case with her, too.

"Listen," Didi said. "Tomorrow is the annual Ladies with an Attitude's Gertrude Stein Book Club and Sky Dive. Wanna come along for the ride?"

Kate grimaced, her heart feeling as heavy as granite. And then it registered. "Sky dive?"

Didi nodded as though it were no big deal. "Only a fool would pass up the chance to watch me plummet toward the earth strapped to the back of a butch instructor dressed like Alice B. Toklas."

"Is Rhea going?"

"What's wrong with you?" Didi sprang into an upright position. "I thought we agreed never to mention that name again."

"I'm sorry. I just assumed you'd called her and were back on again."

"Why would you assume that? Because I'm so emotionally frail that I'd rather let someone use me than be alone?"

Kate looked at her innocently. "No. Because you like sex a lot."

"That's a very good point, but I liked her a lot. I wanted more from her than just a casual dinner and lay twice a week. Once she cut out the dinner part, I knew we were in trouble. I said '*hasta luego*, doll.' I deserve better."

"And you're okay with it," Kate asked.

"No, not really. I miss her and want to call her so bad. But if I do, I'll be sending the message that I'm okay settling for what little she's willing to give."

Kate offered a listless smile and a whack on Didi's thigh. "There may be hope for you yet."

"C'mon, Kate," Didi said, shoving Kate in the leg. "I don't know what's worse, the *you* you were before you met Jordan or this one."

Kate groaned and sank into the sofa. "You promised me you wouldn't keep harping about the breakup."

"And I haven't. You have to admit, I've been a pillar of self-restraint. But I just have to make one comment."

"All right. Out with it."

"You're working my last nerve. For the past two weeks, you've been bitchy, mopey, and depressing to be around. I've had to up my Zoloft dosage just to come to work."

"You said 'one thing.' That was like five."

"Kate." She closed her eyes for a moment and pleaded softly from the arm of the sofa. "I've endured your glib attitude all week whenever I've tried to have a normal conversation with you. Would it kill you to express a genuine emotion? What's going on? What are you feeling?"

Kate rallied a calm smile. "If you insist on moonlighting as a shrink, you should go lease your own office space."

Didi scoffed and leapt up from the sofa. "I'm so done trying to help you."

"Didi, please bear with me. I'll be my old self again in no time."

"That's what worries me."

"Here's an idea. Why don't you go brew yourself a fresh pot of go-fuck-yourself?" Kate arched an eyebrow at her. "There. How's that for self-expression?"

"Impressive," Didi said. "Rage may not be the prettiest, but at least it's a genuine emotion."

Kate stretched out, exhausted by the conversation. "I don't know what you want from me."

"Call her, text her, something." She dropped back on the sofa and placed Kate's feet in her lap.

"Why, pray tell, would I want to do that?"

"You're miserable without her."

"I'm not miserable. I'm just…I'm not miserable."

"Are you getting some kind of perverse pleasure out of this twisted self-denial ritual? You're not a nun. You're not even Catholic."

Kate glared at her. "Oh, yeah, that's exactly it. You've discovered my secret fetish. What time are you jumping out of that airplane?"

"I don't know what I'm gonna do with you," Didi said as she shoved Kate's feet off her lap.

"You can stop worrying about me. I've got it under control."

"This is asinine." Didi began pacing. "I don't know why you're doing this to yourself."

"It's not just about me. Jordan was getting serious too fast the way young, idealistic women will do. If I'd kept stringing her along, I would've really hurt her, and I'd never want to do that."

"Kate, you did hurt her. You're making her pay for something she has no control over. If she was some immature player type, Viv and I would totally be on board with you. But you're running scared and using Jordan's age as the perfect cover."

"Is there not one practical bone in either of your bodies? She is thirty years old. I am forty-seven. She wants to be a famous singer. This would never work out in the long run. And frankly, I'm tired of pleading my case to you guys."

"You're right, you're right. I'm sorry I brought it up again," Didi said as she grabbed her purse from her desk. "She's too young and unspoiled to be with a cynical old crank like you. You actually did her a huge favor."

"I wouldn't phrase it like that. You're acting like I'm yelling at kids to get off my lawn."

Didi rolled her eyes as if that was next. "Oh, no, not you. Listen, it's Friday night, we're both single, and we'd be a disgrace to the Women's March if we didn't get out in the world and at least try to have a good time."

"What do you have in mind?"

Didi pondered the thought for a moment, and then a glint of mischief brightened her eyes. "A bite to eat, a couple of cocktails, and a side of reconnaissance."

"On who? Rhea?"

Didi nodded eagerly. "I got her address. I want to do a drive-by."

"I can't look at Jordan's Facebook page, but you can do a drive-by?"

Didi grinned. "People expect this kind of thing from me. I'm not as emotionally stable as you are."

Kate smiled in spite of herself. "I hope I'm not going to regret this."

Didi lightly clapped her fingertips together. "It's no big deal. I just want to see the major renovations she was supposedly making to her house that prevented her from inviting me over. Ever."

"Oh yeah. No big deal. Nothing could go wrong there."

❖

As the September sun lowered into the trees, Kate's BMW turned onto Rhea's street. She slowed so Didi could count off the house numbers as they drove down the winding, tree-lined road.

"She really lives in the sticks," Kate said. "What does she need such a giant house for?"

"Maybe the houses get smaller the farther down you go." Didi scanned the numbered mailboxes on the right side.

"I doubt that."

"She is a realtor. I wouldn't expect her to live in a cramped little cottage."

"It should be coming up," Kate said.

"Yeah, slow down. I think this is it, the one with the fence."

Kate rolled to a stop. "Wow. Does she run a bed-and-breakfast or something?"

"What the…? Go up a little. Is that a swing set in the yard?"

"And a kiddie pool?" Kate noted, stretching over the steering wheel for a better look. "Are you sure you have the right house?"

"Positive."

"So what is all that?" Kate scanned the windows in the front of the house.

"That's what I'm about to find out," Didi said as she raised her cell phone to her ear.

"What are you doing?" Kate was unnerved by the look on Didi's face.

"Why is your yard full of kids' toys?" Didi demanded after Rhea answered.

"Didi, calm down," Kate whispered, ready to step on the gas. "They probably have security cameras on us right now."

"Oh, they're for your grandkids," Didi said into the phone. "Would you mind explaining why you never told me you had kids, let alone grandkids?"

"Dee, I'm getting out of here," Kate said.

"Don't you move," Didi warned her, grabbing the steering wheel. "Who's that guy on the side of your house? Yes. I'm parked outside right now. How about you come out and explain to me who the fuck I was dating for a month and a half."

"Didi," Kate said, panicked. "Come on, let's get—"

But before she could take off, Didi pushed open the door and jumped out onto the sidewalk. "You better get out here now and start explaining, Rhea, or I'm coming in."

Kate threw the gearshift into Park and jumped out after her. "Didi, get a grip," she said, latching onto her arm. "If she calls the cops, we're gonna get hit with trespassing and disorderly conduct."

"Don't forget assault," Didi said.

Rhea trotted out the front door and down the stone sidewalk to the gate. She appeared far less composed than she had at Amy and Sheila's cocktail party when she strutted around like a peacock flirting with Jordan.

"What are you doing here, Didi?" Rhea said. "You said it was over."

"I want some answers, Rhea, like who is the woman I met and almost fell for this summer?"

Once she realized a brawl wasn't going to break out, Kate retreated to the driver's side of her car and pretended not to listen.

"Didi, I'm sorry," Rhea said. "I should've been honest with you."

"Oh, you think? Rhea, what is all this?"

"I'm bisexual. I've been married to my husband for almost thirty years, but when I came out to him as bi, he was understanding."

"So he knows what you're doing online. It's just all the unsuspecting women you meet who don't. You're a real piece of work, Rhea, for manipulating and deceiving people like this."

After a menacing glare from Rhea, Kate slipped into the driver's seat but rolled down the passenger window to continue eavesdropping.

"Didi, I handled this all wrong, and I'm sorry," Rhea said. "Can you give me a minute to explain?"

Didi hesitated, then gave her a reluctant nod.

"You're only the second woman I've met online. The first woman didn't seem to care about my home situation. We had a brief affair, and then she went on her way. I thought it would be the same with you, so I didn't bother investing."

"How could you have assumed I'd just be another casual lay? I was so into you, Rhea. I told you I loved you."

"I know, and it shocked the shit out of me when you did. I didn't know what to do, so I pulled back and hoped things would just fizzle out."

"And when they didn't, you ghosted me," Didi said, her anger fading to sadness.

"I'm sorry, Didi." She seemed truly contrite. "I don't know how else to apologize, but if you'd like, you can come in for coffee, and we can talk more. I'll tell you anything you want to know."

"How many kids do you have?"

"I have one daughter. She has two little ones."

Didi stared into the yard for a moment. "I have to go."

Rhea brushed her hand on Didi's arm. "Can I take a rain check on that coffee?"

"I'll call you." She left Rhea standing on the sidewalk. When she got into Kate's car, she looked down in silence.

Kate chewed her lip, digging deep for the right words. "Um," she finally said, placing a comforting hand on Didi's. "Did I hear you say you'll call her?"

Didi responded with a nod.

Kate gave her hand a light squeeze and in the gentlest of tones asked, "Have you lost your fucking mind?"

Still looking down, Didi mumbled, "I probably won't."

"Probably? How are you even considering it?"

"Can we please drive?"

Kate pulled away, intentionally driving into and knocking over Rhea's plastic garbage and recycling bins. "What was all that talk earlier about you deserving better? What can a married woman possibly give you besides an inferiority complex?"

"I loved being in her company. When we were alone, she made me feel like I was the most beautiful, significant person in the world."

"How did you feel the rest of time when she was avoiding you, which, by the way, was most of the time."

"Look. I'm not judging you about Jordan. I'd appreciate you showing me the same courtesy."

"But this is idiotic. You're being an idiot. You have feelings for this woman, and you think you're going to be okay sharing her with someone else? Give me a break. This is by far the dumbest idea you've ever had."

When Kate finished ranting, she glanced over at Didi, who was staring straight ahead as tears rolled down her cheeks.

"Oh, hey, I'm sorry." Kate grabbed her hand again as she negotiated the dark road. "C'mon. Don't cry."

The imperative seemed to trigger a full-on eruption as Didi buried her face in her hands and sobbed.

"Dee, honey, I'm sorry. I didn't mean what I said. You've had much dumber ideas than this one. Please stop crying."

Didi chuckled. "I don't know why I'm crying so hard. I really liked Rhea, more than anyone since Georgie, but she's obviously not the one."

"I'm relieved it's obvious to you. You're one step ahead of Vivienne."

"It doesn't feel that way at the moment. I feel like dying, and Viv is with the woman she wants. Everything's going great. They're planning their wedding."

"Good for her. Maybe one of these days I'll stop seizing with panic when her name comes up on my phone."

"Gee. I thought finding love would be easier once I jumped the fence," Didi said. "It's so much worse. I actually feel bad when things don't work out."

"That's how you know you're finally on the right side."

"Really?" Didi pulled a napkin from the glove compartment and blew her nose like a foghorn. "If that's the case, I think I'll finally make my ninety-six-year-old nonnie's dream come true and join the convent."

"Smart move. No lesbians there," Kate said, and they both laughed.

CHAPTER EIGHTEEN

And the Award Goes To...

By the start of autumn, Kate was still in a funk but managed to rouse her spirits enough to attend the last major outdoor event at the Oceanview. The True Colors benefit drew a crowd not only for its importance to the LGBTQ community, but also for its stellar lineup of local entertainment.

At the moment, drag star Shelley Summers, the rotund mistress of ceremonies adorned in a flowing chartreuse sequined gown, monster brunette wig, and enough chunky costume jewelry to summon the ghost of Liberace, was opening the show.

"Boy and girls, we can't thank you enough for turning out for the final True Colors benefit of the year. And now I'd like to introduce you all to the fierce song stylings of Miss Penny Pincher, making her drag debut with us tonight," Shelley said into the microphone nearly hidden in chubby, nail-polished sausage fingers. "C'mon, kiddies. She likes her applause like she likes her sex, loud and vigorous." She wagged her meaty arm in a flourish and glided off into the wings.

The crowd cheered as Jordan's friend, William, vamped across the stage adorned in a blond bouffant wig, peach dress, and white go-go boots, lip-synching Doris Day's "I'm a Big Girl Now."

"That's Jordan's friend," Kate said into Didi's ear. "She's gotta be somewhere in the audience."

"No doubt," Didi said, scanning the crowd in the dim light. "I'm surprised you're here, considering she's the headliner."

"The headliner is True Colors and all the good work they do for the community," Kate said. "Besides, I'm the chairperson of the event. It's not like I had a choice."

"Like you would've missed this chance to twat-block Jordan," Viv said from across the table as Maia played with a strand of Viv's hair. "Get ready, 'cause she's gonna be pickin' 'em out of her weave all night."

Kate glared at them. "Don't you two have a turkey baster that needs your attention?"

"I'm rooting for you, Kate," Maia said. "I don't believe this is the end of what seemed like such a promising love affair."

"Maybe I can sneak out early," Kate said as her leg bounced under the table.

"Don't you dare," Didi said. "We're all in this together tonight."

"I'm having a good time," Viv said. "But if one more person mistakes me for a drag queen, she gonna get her nuts kicked up in her vagina."

"Well, if you didn't do up your hair like Divine..." Didi said.

"The only time I can do it like this is when I get a Brazilian blowout," Viv said. "Look at these tits. No way a drag queen is gonna have a rack like this."

"And you wanted to carry a baby at your age?" Didi made a face and chewed her cocktail stirrer. "They'd be slapping against your knees after you delivered."

"That was before we got back together," Viv said.

"I'll be carrying," Maia said. "I'm only thirty-eight."

"You broads in your thirties just own the world, don't you?" Kate said in disgust. "I have to use the can."

"You really miss her, don't you?" Viv asked.

Kate pursed her lips to control her rising emotions. Her mood was sinking lower every minute closer to Jordan taking the stage. She was going to look and sound incredible, and some woman would no doubt seize the opportunity to approach her.

"I have to use it, too, Kate," Didi said. "Let's go." She looped her arm through Kate's as they searched for the restrooms. "Are you okay?"

"Yeah. Just a little anxious. I haven't seen her in weeks, and I don't know how it's going to feel seeing her onstage."

"Shitty," Didi said. "It's gonna feel shitty, and then it'll pass."

"You're right," Kate said. "This ain't my first rodeo. I'll be fine."

"Uh, let's go this way." Didi pulled Kate by the arm in the direction from which they came.

Kate stopped her. "What's the matter? What's over there?"

"Nothing." Her eyes darted wildly as she attempted to drag Kate forward with her. "The bathroom is this way."

"Didi, stop shoving me." Kate jerked her arm away and headed back in their intended direction.

"Kate," Didi shouted.

She ignored Didi's plea, and when she rounded the curve, she saw what Didi was trying to protect her from. At a cozy table in the corner, Jordan sat with her ex, Andie, having what appeared to be quite a friendly conversation. Andie stretched toward her over their drink glasses and said something that made Jordan whip her hair back in laughter.

Kate's neck flamed with prickly heat as she licked her dry lips, waiting to bear witness to some hideous display of affection she was certain would happen at any moment. Suddenly, she felt hot breath spreading over each of her bare shoulders. She wheeled around to face Didi and Viv, apparently on a rescue mission.

"Kate, step away from the ex," Didi said calmly.

Viv swung around in front of her, raising her hands as a barricade. "Just do as we say, and no one has to get hurt."

Kate rolled her eyes. "Could you two be any more obvious? Get out of here before you blow my cover."

"We're not going without you," Didi said. "We leave no woman behind."

"I'm just going to go say hi," Kate said calmly. "See how she's doing. Maybe if I see that she's fine without me, I'll stop marinating in self-pity."

"She looks fine to me," Viv mumbled. "A whole lot of it."

Didi glared at her in astonishment. "Why? Why?"

"No, wait a minute," Viv said. "This is good. She can come to terms with this once and for all."

Kate gritted her teeth when Andie grabbed Jordan's hand, and they exchanged what appeared to be longing glances. A fire of jealousy spread across Kate's face.

"Uh, let's just go back to our table," Didi said, motioning to Viv. "I do not like the juju going on over here." They each looped an arm under Kate's.

Kate pried herself free. "I'll be right back."

Wearing her best poker face, she approached Jordan's table. Jordan looked up as the shock of her presence wiped the smile from her face.

"Hello, Jordan. What a nice surprise seeing you here," Kate said, perky as a QVC pitchwoman.

"How is it a surprise? You asked me if I would play this event."

Kate shrugged, faking indifference. "It's a friendly expression."

Jordan glanced at Andie. "Okay. It's nice to see you, too." She sipped her beer, seeming quite done with the conversation.

Kate found herself loitering at the table.

"Is there something else?" Jordan said, avoiding direct eye contact.

"Could I talk to you for a minute? Privately?" Kate glanced at Andie. "Sorry for the interruption. I'll have her right back to you."

Kate led her to the corridor near the restrooms.

"So," Kate said with a sigh. "How are you?"

"I'm doing great." Jordan shoved her hands into her jeans pockets and looked down.

"Great," Kate said, staring at her.

After a moment of silence, Jordan looked up. "I have to get ready to go on in a few minutes."

"Oh, uh, right," Kate stammered. "I just wanted to know how you're doing."

"Isn't that thoughtful," Jordan said, her words oozing out slow and thick with resentment. "I've never been better. How's the single life working out for you?"

"Okay." Kate glanced at the flowery framed art on the wall. "I must say, I'm a little surprised to see you on a date so soon. And really surprised it's with Andie. Maybe I shouldn't be."

Jordan glared at her. "Who said I'm on a date?"

"You're not?"

"What business is it of yours?"

"None, I guess. But after all the carrying on you did a few weeks ago, I assumed what we had meant a little more to you than this."

"Why did you even come over here? Morbid curiosity? You wanna survey the wreckage you caused?"

Kate was momentarily stunned into silence as Jordan's formerly innocent eyes blazed with anger.

"You know," Jordan said, "if you'd approached me a couple of weeks ago, I would've begged you to take me back."

"All it took was a few weeks to get over me. Nice."

"Aww, am I disappointing you, Kate? Exactly how despondent would you like me to be after a summer fling?"

Kate sighed. "That's all I meant to you?"

Jordan scoffed. "Don't play the victim. Someone like you could never pull it off."

"What do you mean, 'someone like me'? Don't you think I had feelings for you?"

"I honestly don't know what I was to you, Kate. Maybe something to cross off your midlife-crisis bucket list. You're probably still high-fiving Didi and Viv over it."

Kate grabbed Jordan's arm as she started to walk away. "I hope you don't really believe that."

"It is what it is," Jordan said with an icy stare. "Now if you'll excuse me, my date is waiting."

As Jordan walked off, something in Kate broke free. "And I thought singing was your talent. You're quite the actress. You should be up on stage with the drag queens the way you can work a room."

Jordan stopped and spun out on her. "Is that right? Well, somebody got worked over in this relationship, that's for sure."

When Jordan darted off down the hall toward the dressing room, Kate was on her like scotch on rocks.

"It's obvious I made the right decision."

"As if you ever had a doubt," Jordan shouted over her shoulder.

"I thought maybe we could be friends or, at the very least, be civil with each other."

Jordan stormed through the dressing-room door with Kate still in pursuit. Kate positioned herself in the doorway, arms folded expectantly, ignoring William off to the side removing his stage makeup.

"You dump me and then expect everything to be all warm and fuzzy between us?" Jordan yelled, almost in tears.

"I just figured—"

"Look, I'll be professional with you if I need to be in the future, but friends? Forget it. Check back with me in about fifty years on that one."

"Perfect," Kate said. "Maybe you'll have had a chance to grow up by then." Even Kate winced at that one.

Jordan gasped. She grabbed William's wig and hurled it, Styrofoam head and all, at Kate.

"Uh, hello?" he spat.

"I can't believe your audacity." Jordan exploded. "You broke up with me, and now you're going ballistic when you see I might actually be getting on with my life? That's beyond twisted." She turned away from them, but Kate saw her shoulders moving in rhythm with her tears.

"Jordan," Kate said softly. She glanced at her shoes, shamed by Jordan's accusation and the devastation on her face. How could she have allowed it to escalate to this point? This wasn't a Kate anyone would recognize. What had misfired inside her to make her lose it like that?

"This isn't Madison Square Garden," William griped as he jammed his arms into a dress shirt. "Why don't you take it outside, talk this over like reasonable people, and then kiss and make up."

"Reasonable?" Jordan snorted. "Make up? Have you met this woman?"

"Just once, but from what you've told me—"

"Not happening," she shouted and turned her back to Kate.

"I'm sorry, William," Kate said. She motioned toward Jordan but thought better of it. "Jordan, I'm sorry. I don't know what..." she stammered. "I just..."

Jordan sniffled quietly, refusing to turn around.

Kate glanced at William as she backed out of the dressing room, beyond embarrassed. "Terrific show, William, really." She picked up his wig off the gritty floor, brushed it off, and tossed it to him on her way out. "I'm sorry for the intrusion."

❖

At the bar, Kate was finishing her third glass of Jim Beam Honey on the rocks when Didi found her.

"Thank God, you're still here," Didi said. The relief on her face shifted rapidly to near panic. "What are you doing?"

"Getting drunk," she said, twirling her finger at the bartender for another.

"No, no, you can't do that," Didi said as she reached for the glass.

Kate wrenched her arm away in time to down the last sip. "Yes, I can." She was starting to slur her words. "I've made a complete asshole out of myself in front of Jordan, et al, tonight, and now I'd like to stand here and get obliterated, if you don't mind."

"I do mind."

"Then take me home," Kate said. "I'm determined to get loaded somewhere."

"No. Let's get back to our table, and you can get loaded when it's time to go home." Didi tried to pry her away from the bar, but she wouldn't budge.

"I have one more drink coming, and then I'll close my tab," Kate said.

"No. The awards presentation is starting now." Didi finally shook Kate's foothold loose and led her to their table. "Then Jordan is going on."

"Who cares about those lame awards? And after what I did to Jordan, she probably won't even perform now."

"Kate, what has gotten into you tonight? What did you do to Jordan?"

"I made her cry." Kate's eyes began to well up.

"What? Ugh. Never mind. We'll talk about her later. Oh, Jesus, don't you start crying now."

"What are you so tweaked out about?" Kate said.

"You'll find out soon enough." Didi lowered her into a chair at the table. "We need some coffee here," she beckoned to a passing waiter. "Stat."

Shelley Summers sauntered out onstage again with the microphone in one hand and a fruit-garnished cocktail in the other. The spotlight hit her as she approached the stand.

"Ladies and gentlemen, bois and queens, may I have your attention, please? Before we get that hot lesbo, Jordan Squire, up here—" She stopped for the roar of cheers. "Calm down, girls. Don't get your labia in a twist. She'll be out here in a minute. But first, Marney Sellers, the director of the New Haven chapter of True Colors, would like an opportunity to say a few words to us this evening. Marney?"

Marney, a sleek butch in a sharp royal-blue tux, came out onstage to another round of applause.

"Oooh, listen to them," Shelley said to Marney. "They must be all drunk and nasty now."

"Thank you, Shelley," Marney said. "I hope they're not too drunk. We still have a lot of show left tonight."

"Let me know when she's done babbling." Kate threw her arms on the table and buried her face in them.

Viv hoisted her up by the back of her hair. "Kate, pull yourself together."

Marney continued her speech. "I just wanted to take a moment to acknowledge all of the volunteers who've made this event the huge success it is every year. I'd especially like to thank Jordan Squire, who took time out of her busy schedule to perform for us tonight." She paused to clap along with the electrified crowd.

"But before we get her out here, I'd like to extend special thanks on behalf of all of the LGBTQ organizations in Connecticut to a special volunteer who's gone above and beyond the ordinary call of volunteerism with her extraordinary efforts at organizing and fund-raising over the last decade. We have a brand-new program for at-risk trans youth thanks to her fund-raising endeavors and the charity bingo tournament she organized here last summer. So, without further ado, I'd like to present the Exceptional Volunteer award to a woman of enormous compassion, class, and integrity, New Haven attorney Kate Randall."

The crowd cheered as Marney scanned the audience for Kate.

"What did she just say?" Kate slurred her words, hoping her drunken stupor had dulled her hearing.

Didi looked at Viv. "I'm thinking keeping this a surprise wasn't our best collaborative decision."

"How were we supposed to know she was gonna pick tonight to lose her shit?"

"True," Didi said. "Go ahead, Kate. Go get your award."

Kate ambled over to Marney, her footsteps slow and exaggerated as she attempted to cross the stage with grace while her head was spinning. She stepped in front of the microphone, and it squealed with feedback at the close proximity of her face.

"Thank you," she said, methodically calculating her words. "Thank you so much for this award—this heavy award," she said, bobbling the glass triangle. "I'm honored to be honored by such an honorable organization, the um…the uh…Well, it's an important organization that does important work."

She squelched a burp and continued, fired up by the outburst of applause by an audience seemingly eager to see if Kate would still be standing by end of her speech. She raised her fist in solidarity, then grabbed at the mic stand to steady her balance.

"You know," she said, slurring her words. "It's nice to know that we can still receive awards for doing stuff even when in our own personal lives we sometimes may not always make the most honorable decisions for ourselves. Christ, it's hot in here. Is anyone else roasting like a pig on a spit?" Still mumbling about the heat, she worked her way out of her light blazer and threw it across the stage. The crowd of ladies shouted their approval at Kate's tanned and sculpted upper arms. "I mean just because a person reaches a certain echelon of success doesn't mean they're no longer entitled to make mistakes…"

At that point, Didi appeared onstage and grabbed the award from Kate. "Kate would again like to thank True Colors and the members of the academy for acknowledging her charity work with this prestigious award. And the bartenders, who clearly know how to make a stiff one."

Didi led Kate offstage amid vociferous applause and sat her down in front of a cup of black coffee. "Drink this, and then we're leaving."

"No. We should leave now," Viv said, nodding toward the stage. She and Maia stood and gathered Kate's cell phone and clutch purse.

Kate stood, too. "I don't want this coffee. I want water."

"Okay. We'll get you one on the way out," Viv said. "Now let's go."

"And miss tonight's main attraction?" Kate said, trying to steady herself.

"Honey, you were the main attraction," Viv drawled. "Now let's split."

"Ladies and gentlemen," Marney shouted. "Jordan Squire."

Jordan bounded out onstage, and the audience exploded with applause. "Thanks, everybody. Hope you're having a great time so far, and congrats to the great Kate Randall on her award." She strummed a few chords on her guitar as the crowd again vocalized their gratitude.

Kate slunk into her chair with a hand over her eyes and guzzled water from someone's glass like she'd just been rescued from a desert island.

"As some of you may know," Jordan said, "I'm a die-hard fan of Carly Simon, so I thought I'd open my set with a song that means a lot to me personally."

Kate perked up from the throes of an early onset hangover. Was Jordan about to dedicate their song to her? Her heart fluttered wildly as she anticipated the first notes of "Nobody Does It Better," her smile stretching to the ends of her face.

Instead, she got the opening chords of "You're So Vain" and an unabashed glare in her direction from Jordan. When she belted the line about thinking this song is about you, Kate could bear no more. She dashed into the ladies' room and purged everything from the ghastly evening. When she opened the stall door, Didi, Viv, and Maia were lined up against the counter like a tribunal.

"Well, if it isn't the A-team," Kate said as she headed to the sink to rinse her mouth and splash her face with cold water.

"Shall I bring the car around now?" Viv asked.

"Why don't you just throw a tablecloth over my head and usher me out the service entrance?"

"That won't be necessary," Didi said. "You didn't make that big of a fool out of yourself."

"That's funny," Kate said as she followed them out. "Even though I seemed to have given it my best shot?"

The silence in Viv's town car haunted Kate even more than the vivid flashbacks of her antics earlier in the evening. She felt the weight of three sets of eyes repeatedly glancing at her, but after witnessing her transformation from Attorney Jekyll into Madam Hyde, they were understandably tentative.

Kate pressed her forehead against the window and continued to torment herself with self-reflection.

"Obviously, your compulsion to accost Jordan and her companion tonight means something," Didi finally said.

Kate studied her for a moment. "You don't say," she deadpanned, then returned her forehead to the window.

"Want to talk about it?" Viv said.

"Talk about what? How I acted like a sociopath toward Jordan and accepted an award while a drunken mess in front of a room packed full of people who used to respect me? Yes, let's talk about that."

"We're gonna let that go. You're too vulnerable right now." Didi slapped Kate's thigh in sympathy.

Kate glared at her. "The one time you actually have a reason to debase and humiliate me, and you pass on it?"

"It's no fun kicking a sister when she's down," Viv said.

"After the way I behaved tonight, I deserve everything you got."

"You deserve patience and understanding," Maia said, reaching over Viv and taking her hand. "Everyone's fallen victim to love's powerful charms. It makes people do crazy things sometimes."

Kate recalled the series of impassioned dramas between Viv and Maia that had finally culminated in a domestic charge and restraining order. "Thank you, Maia," she said, squeezing her hand. "That means a lot coming from you."

Didi fluffed out the sides of her hair. "Look, all I was suggesting is that you only acted that way because you're still in love with Jordan."

"I'm not *in love* with her." She faced Didi only long enough to stab her with an evil glare. "But apparently, I still have some unresolved feelings for her."

"I don't understand what you're doing," Didi said. "You fell in love with her, yet you were bent on destroying the relationship. You got rid of her faster than the mob gets rid of witnesses."

"I didn't get rid of her." Kate turned back to the passing city. "Look, I made a decision I thought was best under the circumstances."

"What circumstances? You were two were crazy about each other."

"Didi, how many times do I have to say this? She's got so much yet to experience, so many epiphanies before she can be the person I'd need her to be. More importantly, she needs to be free to pursue her music career."

"Kate, nobody's ever the person you need them to be." Didi covertly tilted her head toward Viv and Maia. "I thought we're at the stage in life where we no longer waste time sweating the small stuff."

"This is hardly what I'd call the small stuff. If all we were looking for is a good time, then it wouldn't be a big deal."

Didi sighed in frustration. "I completely disagree with you, but

I'm on your side no matter what. I only brought this up again because you wouldn't have reacted this way if you weren't truly, deeply in love with Jordan. But go ahead. Keep living in denial."

"It doesn't seem like Jordan's hers to get rid of anymore," Viv said.

Kate and Didi both looked at her.

She sucked her teeth. "What? Looks like she might be back on that young chick, the ex. And not for nothing. Didn't y'all catch that song dedication?" She chuckled absently. "Ouch."

"We don't know that was meant for Kate," Didi said.

Viv looked her up and down. "We don't?"

"Yeah, we do," Kate said, and her head fell back against the seat.

CHAPTER NINETEEN

Raging Bull

In the week after her public meltdown, Kate kept a low profile. No happy hours in trendy New Haven wine bars or restaurants lest someone from the fund-raiser recognize her and request an encore performance. But a more pressing issue troubled her: Jordan. Time was not easing her longing for her and what they shared. She was becoming obsessed, taunting herself with grotesque visions of Jordan reuniting with her weaselly ex or jetting off to some private exotic island owned by a bloated music mogul to elope with Alexandra. She was losing precious peace of mind and countless hours of her life hunting for evidence of either all over social media.

To prevent a liquor-induced text she would most certainly regret, she opted for a bit of retail therapy after an unanswered text to Didi. A few laps around the mall facilitated moving China Panda's combo number four through her digestive tract. As a reward for her workout, she stopped at the Froyo stand and indulged in some self-care: a healthy serving of Greek vanilla—loaded down with Health chips, M&M's, and gummy bears. She sat spooning it in, rolling her eyes at happy, love-struck teens strolling by hand in hand, then smiled with sinister thoughts of them drowning themselves in their awful music when the loves of their lives dumped them a week later for the new kid.

Before backing out of the parking space, she checked her phone again and grew concerned that Didi still hadn't answered. Rather than going home to an evening of cyber-sulking, she drove by Didi's condo.

After Kate rang the bell three times, Didi finally cracked open the door. "What are you doing here?"

Kate made a face at that question, then indicated Didi's worn T-shirt and cotton gym shorts. "Did I wake you up or something?"

"No. I just wasn't expecting company."

"You would've if you checked your phone."

"Sorry. I left it upstairs charging."

They stared at each other like alley cats ready to brawl in a turf war.

"Not that you're dressed for it," Kate said, eyeing her with suspicion, "but do you have someone in there?"

"What are you, writing a book?"

"Didi, cut the crap. I could really use a friend right now."

Didi exhaled and ran a hand through her disheveled hair. "There seems to be a lot of that going around tonight."

"What are you talking about? Someone really is here?"

Didi mouthed the word "Jordan."

"She's here?" Pictures on the wall rattled from the seismic volume of Kate's voice.

"Oh, my Christ, shut up," Didi said in an angry whisper. "Go home, and I'll call you when she leaves."

"Why should I go home? You're my friend."

Kate nudged the door open and walked into the living room. The sight of Jordan looking incredibly sexy with her arms splayed across the back of the couch and her long legs crossed triggered a swell of irrational jealousy.

"Good evening, Jordan. Moving on to yet another conquest?"

"Huh?" Jordan jumped up, seeming lost for words.

"Kate." Didi admonished her with a nervous look.

Kate glared at Didi like a bull facing a matador. "Let me guess. This isn't what it looks like."

Didi said, "I don't know what it looks like to you, but—"

"You don't? Well here, let me spell it out for you." She began counting off on her fingers. "You don't answer my texts, you tried to get rid of me the second I got here, and your hair looks like you've been testing wind tunnels for the Air Force. How big a fool do you think I am?"

Didi self-consciously smoothed down the back of her hair. "In my defense, it's unusually humid for October."

Jordan inserted herself into the debate. "I'd like to answer your question: you're a giant one if you think I'm here fucking your best friend."

"Come on, Jordan. You told me how much you love older women. And what better way to get back at me?"

Jordan's mouth dropped open. "You are so full of yourself. I'd never be so petty and vindictive that I'd waste my time trying to get back at you."

"Oh, right. I guess you'd have to have genuinely loved me to be bothered."

"Are you kidding me?" Jordan shouted. "You didn't care how I felt about you when we were together. Why do you care now?"

Didi slid between them. "Kate, calm down. There's nothing going—"

"And you." Kate pointed her finger in Didi's face. "You expect me to believe this is innocent after all the lewd remarks you made about Jordan when I was with her?"

"She what?" Jordan's eyes darted between them.

Didi's face ignited in a blush, but she somehow managed a casual rebuttal. "The one or two observations I may have made were clearly taken way out of context."

"How can you take 'I'd love to jump her bones' out of context," Kate exclaimed.

Jordan gasped.

Didi casually brushed her hand across her forehead. "Let's not get into this now, okay, Kate?" She then wheeled around on her and mouthed the words *shut the fuck up* in a blaze of fury.

"What's the matter?" Kate said as though cross-examining a witness she knew was perjuring herself. "You don't think Jordan would get a kick out of hearing about your mental note to check out her ass?"

"Didi?" Jordan groaned.

Didi bit her lip and closed her eyes in apparent humiliation.

Jordan recoiled in disgust. "I feel so dirty."

"Jordan, it was a joke," Didi pleaded with a cheesy smile. "A crass, tasteless joke but nonetheless one intended in only the most whimsical of spirit."

"Thanks a lot, Didi. I thought you were my friend." Jordan stormed toward the door.

"I am," she said with a helpless shrug. She whirled around to Kate, who was basking in the chaos she'd unleashed.

Jordan yanked open the door. "This is just too bizarre for me. And I used to live with a drag queen."

After Jordan slammed the door, Didi stood silently, her back to Kate, seemingly to regain her composure.

"Well, it looks like I may have misjudged the situation," Kate finally said, her tone syrupy with artificial innocence.

Didi scoffed. "I didn't think it was possible, but you've actually sunk to an all-new low. Another esteemed honor for your awards mantel."

"C'mon, Dee. You had to know that seeing Jordan in your living room might set me off, especially with the mood I was in. You're my friend. What were you doing fraternizing with the enemy?"

"She showed up looking like an orphan dumped on my doorstep. What was I supposed to do?"

"What did she want?"

"What do you think she wanted? She wanted someone to talk to who could understand what she's feeling. She actually asked me what she did wrong to make you break up with her."

"What did you tell her?"

"The truth," Didi said. "That she didn't do anything wrong. That she was the kind of girlfriend anyone in her right mind would consider herself lucky to have. That you're the one with the issues—not that that was any shocking revelation."

"How nice of you to throw me under the bus like that."

Didi groaned in frustration. "You know something? You've regressed into a complete adolescent since the summer. And don't blame this on Jordan. She's behaved more like an adult than both of us. What is up with you? Is this some perimenopause eve-of-destruction thing?"

"I don't know," Kate said, plopping into a chair. "I'm sorry. I shouldn't have gone off on you like that."

"No, really?" She dropped into the chair across from Kate. "You know, the only crime I'm guilty of here is having an overabundance of empathy for my friends." A pensive pause. "And maybe not knowing when to keep my mouth shut sometimes."

"Sometimes?"

Didi growled and threw the lid of her melted pint of Ben & Jerry's ice cream at her. "You're such an asshole. Don't you know I'd never make a play for your ex, no matter how much I may have drooled over her? I have way too much respect for you and our friendship."

"Yes, I know that," Kate said, collapsing back into the cushions. "I'm sorry. I really think I'm starting to unravel."

"*Starting?* Oh, honey, you don't have any thread left on your spool. Once you were a sensible, dignified professional. Now you're trolling social media, picking fights at drag shows, and flying into jealous rages. What are you going to do for an encore, pierce a nipple?"

Kate grabbed a throw pillow and hugged it to her chest. "What's happening to me? How did everything go so wrong so fast?"

"You mean a smart cookie like you can't figure that out?"

"What's that supposed to mean?" Kate fired back.

"You know, all I wanted tonight was to watch *Whatever Happened to Baby Jane* and devour a few pints of ice cream. But no, that was too much to ask. Instead, I had to spend it in the roles of therapist and referee. Now I have to sit here and pretend to be sympathetic while you feel sorry for yourself and whine about your imperfect life. By the way, you're not the only one in the throes of your own personal Greek tragedy. I'm miserable, too, but does anyone care about that?"

"Oh, that's right. How are you doing? Has Rhea tried to contact you?"

"Forget it. One catastrophe at a time. Let me tell you something, Kate. Nobody's life is perfect, but yours was as close as it gets—that is until you had to go all manic and trash everything." She leapt out of the chair. "Are you really so insecure that you'd sabotage a great relationship?"

Kate jumped up and got in her face. "Boy, the view must be spectacular up there on that soapbox. It wouldn't kill you to show a little compassion right now, especially since this free-fall I took into a love affair I wasn't prepared to handle never would have happened without your interference."

"Yeah, it's all my fault," Didi shouted back. "Wait. Let's cue the violins. She's just a younger woman, for Christ's sake, not an alien from another planet. You don't want compassion. You want me to feed into your narcissistic pity spiral. Poor, lovelorn Kate. When will the winds of happiness ever blow her way? Well, I'm not doing it. I'm through holding your stupid hand."

"Get out of my face," Kate said, staring Didi down.

"You get out of mine," Didi said. "In fact, just get out of my house."

"Fine." Kate marched to the door and down the front steps of Didi's unit. Stopping at her car door as her tears overcame her, she canopied her eyes with a hand and cried, free and hard.

"Kate," Didi called from the porch after a few minutes. "I didn't mean to kick you out. Come back inside."

"I don't blame you. Even I can't stand myself right now. I'll just go home and have a pity party in solitude. The cat listens but doesn't yell at me."

Didi chuckled. "You're kidding yourself if you think the cat's listening."

Kate chuckled, too.

"Look, I feel like having a pity party, too," Didi said. "I have a couple of bottles of white chilling in the fridge. Don't let me feel like an alcoholic drinking alone—which I will if you leave."

"How could I call myself a friend if I allowed that?" Kate shuffled back up the sidewalk and into Didi's condo.

She suddenly grabbed Didi and hugged her, resting her chin on her shoulder.

After a moment, Didi gently pushed her back. "C'mon. Let's go in the kitchen. I bought a nice brie that'll go great with the pinot."

"Thanks. Look. I'm sorry I've been such a beast lately," Kate said as she sat on a stool at the counter. "But how do you think you'd react if the love of your life walked out on you after seventeen years? How long would it take you to trust falling in love again?"

Didi joined her with two glasses and the bottle. "Did you hear what you just said?"

"About being dumped after seventeen years?"

"You called Lydia the love of your life. Since when? You guys had your run, but since then you've been living the dream of the successful, independent single woman."

"I *was* living it," Kate said.

"Until Jordan swept in and knocked down all your defenses. This isn't about Lydia at all. You're clinging to that bad experience, using it as a shield against what you felt with Jordan."

"This thing with her is so intense—she's so intense. How is she so sure of what she wants at thirty?" Kate sighed, yielding to her emotional exhaustion. "I don't ever recall feeling for Lydia what I feel for her. If losing Lydia could destroy me, what could losing Jordan do somewhere down the road? I'm just not equipped to take that chance again."

"You're not the same person you were when you were with Lydia," Didi said. "You were young and unsure of yourself—an anxious mess with panic disorder. You're none of those things today—especially young." A smirk capered across Didi's face.

Kate allowed a slight grin. "I used to think I was so sure of myself." She shook her head in an attempt to clear the commotion in her mind. "I just prefer my life the way it was before I met Jordan. I was focused and in control, and I liked how that felt."

"Kate, I know this goes against all that's holy to you, but no one is ever truly in control of anything. Some of us are just better at managing the illusion of it. You couldn't stop Lydia from leaving, and you can't will away your feelings for Jordan because they're inconvenient."

Kate needed a healthy sip of wine to wash down that acrid dose of reality.

"Whether you're ready for this or not, it's here," Didi said. "I can tell you what I'd do, but we all live our own experiences and form our own perspectives. I'm your best friend, and I get you well enough to know this whole self-preservation through avoidance bit isn't serving you anymore. Jordan's revived you, and deep down, you don't want to lose her."

Kate exhaled heavily. "I already have."

"Well, I might've found out for sure if you hadn't stormed my condo like the DEA at a suspected meth lab. I was trying to figure out if she was scheming to get you back or just needed someone to talk with to help her get over you."

"It was probably the latter."

"You can always call and ask her."

"Uh, yeah," Kate said, dragging out her words. "I'll be sure to give that some thought."

Didi grinned slyly. "No, you won't." She topped off their wineglasses and motioned for Kate to follow her to the living room.

"I said I'd give it some thought." Kate kicked off her shoes and threw her feet on the coffee table.

Didi followed Kate's lead. "I'll tell you one thing. I'm pretty certain that after that shit show tonight, you've finally cured me of my penchant for meddling."

"Ah, so something positive came out of this after all."

Kate raised her glass, and Didi tapped hers against it.

CHAPTER TWENTY

Close Encounter of the Awkward Kind

When Kate received the text notification that her court case had been moved down on the docket until Friday, she indulged in the breezy autumn afternoon with an iced coffee on the green—alone. After the scene with Jordan and the one with Didi that almost compromised a thirty-year friendship, she'd kept to herself as much as possible, thinking and overthinking until the Ambien kicked in each night. All the while her mother's words, "You should think about her," streamed across her mind like skywriting. As much as it pained her to admit it, her mother had a point. If Jordan had shown up on Didi's doorstep seeking closure, who was Kate to stand in the way of that?

When she got back to the reception area, Didi wasn't at her desk. She called out to her. No answer. She walked into her office to a startled Jordan standing at the round conference table clutching her iPad.

"Jordan," she said, frozen in the doorway.

"Kate." Jordan stared for a moment as though Kate might be a mirage. "Uh, Didi called me to help her with the site."

"Oh, okay." She dropped off her briefcase on her desk and stood there. "Where is she?"

"She just left to pick up some sandwiches down the street. She said you'd be in court most of the afternoon."

"I was supposed to be, until the clerk moved my case."

"If you'd rather, I can come back another—"

"No, no, that's silly. You're already here."

With a curt smile, Jordan sat back down and continued working, offering no indication whatsoever that she was open to peace talks.

Kate tried not to look disappointed; considering their last encounter, she should've known better than to hope for a warmer reception if they'd ever run into each other again.

She pulled her laptop out of her valise, waiting for Jordan to look up. No dice.

"I'll just be outside, so I don't disturb you."

"No. It's your office," Jordan said, barely acknowledging her. "Besides, I'm almost done. Fifteen more minutes, and I'll be out of here."

"Okay." Kate sat behind her desk and fired up her laptop, stealing glances in Jordan's direction. She was brilliant at the cold shoulder. Kate tried to focus as she scanned a research website on legal precedents, but the silence drifted over and chilled her like a damp fog. Research at this point was futile as long as Jordan was in the room.

She stood up and groaned as she stretched her arms out in front of her. What the gesture lacked in subtlety, it made up for in effectiveness as Jordan finally glanced up.

"Do you have a minute?" Kate said.

"Sure."

"Jordan, I owe you an apology," she said across the room, behind her desk. "I don't know what I was thinking at Didi's the other night. Displaced aggression never used to be my style."

"For a novice, you're exceptionally good at it." Jordan reclined in her chair, appearing to relish the upper hand Kate had served her.

"Lesson learned," Kate said clumsily. "Again, I'm truly sorry."

"Thanks," Jordan said. "I appreciate that." She offered a lukewarm smile and returned to her iPad.

Kate's lips parted as she attempted to scrape together the right phrase that might begin to clear the wreckage of their relationship. Kate hated how cold Jordan was toward her and hated even more the idea of hard feelings. What was needed at that moment was a profound sentiment that could neutralize the tension between them.

"So, how've you been?" *Brilliant, Kate. Right on target.*

Jordan looked up again, this time clearly contemplating if Kate was serious. Or sane. "Uh, I'm fine, thanks for asking."

"Jordan, this may be hard to believe, but I never meant for it to turn out this way."

"I bet. Most people toss their garbage to the curb and never expect to see it again. But, sucky for you, I keep turning up like spam in your inbox."

"Please don't leave here believing I felt that way about you. It was never because of you. I really cared…" She stopped herself with a sigh, wary of what might've dribbled out next.

Jordan stood and folded her arms across her chest. "What would you like me to walk out of here believing, Kate? Every time we see each other, it just gets more confusing. I mean, the *It's not yous* and the *I never wanted it to end this ways* add a nice touch, but they don't mean anything."

"Jordan, I'm trying to apologize for hurting you."

"Thanks, but I don't care that you never meant to hurt me. Maybe I will someday, but right now, knowing that doesn't change anything." Jordan began to gather up her things.

"Please. You don't have to leave."

"Yeah, I do," she said, heading for the door. "I wasn't looking for a relationship either, Kate, but I fell in love with you. It didn't matter how young or old you were or how scary it felt falling. I just wanted to be with you. I don't get how you could walk away from that if you truly loved me. That was probably the issue all along."

Kate followed her into the reception area. "Jordan, wait. Let me…"

"I can't." Jordan finished both of their sentences with a shake of her head and stormed to the door, slamming it on her way out.

Kate flinched from the bang. "Dammit," she bellowed and dropped onto the couch.

A few minutes later, Didi returned to the office. "What are you doing here?" She put the bag of sandwiches and chips on her desk as her eyes scanned the room.

"I work here, remember?"

"You were supposed to be in court." She lowered her voice and pointed toward Kate's office. "Is Jordan in there?"

Kate shook her head.

"Then that was her I spotted down the street. I thought another hot girl like her was roaming the city."

"You couldn't have handled your website questions over the phone?" Kate said, then became animated. "Or at least warned a sista she was coming in?"

"In light of your past performances, I thought I'd take my chances getting her in and out before you got back. Figures this had to be the day you get moved." She joined Kate on the couch. "So what happened? You didn't go postal on her again, did you?"

"No. In fact, I apologized. Quite sincerely, I might add."

"How'd she take it?"

"Wasn't having it. She's still hurt and pissed. She might not have come right out and told me to suck it, but trust me, the sentiment was there."

"Well, I'm proud of you," Didi said as she pulled a veggie wrap from her bag.

"For what?" Kate shook off Didi's offer of the extra sandwich.

"For apologizing to her and keeping calm in the situation. It must've been difficult since, well, you know, because you're still in love with her and all."

"Just eat your stupid sandwich," Kate said and headed back into her office.

"Life sucks sometimes, doesn't it?" Didi said.

"Are we still going to the Yankee game tonight?" Kate tapped her watch. "Or should we just head over to group therapy?"

"We have to get the 4:07 train. Viv is meeting us at the stadium at 6:45."

"She's still coming, huh? She must've bought off the person sitting in the seat next to us so Maia could come." Kate giggled to herself.

"No. Maia isn't coming," Didi said casually. "It's just us."

"Oh, no. Did they break up?"

Didi huffed. "No, Kate, they didn't. You know how hard Viv is trying to get it right this time. I'm convinced she's finally grown up. She's getting married. You should be less sarcastic and more supportive with her."

"Well," Kate said, hiding her shame with a creepy, genial tone. "Thank you for the new butthole I wasn't aware I needed. Would you care to run home and get ready for the game after you finish your lunch?"

"Yes, I would. Thank you," Didi replied with a victorious smile. "Thank you very much."

❖

As Kate watched the Yankee stadium grounds crew drag rakes across the infield from two rows behind the first-base dugout, she entertained Didi's earlier suggestion that Viv had finally grown up and was an actual participant in a healthy, adult relationship. Talk about the slings and arrows of outrageous fortune. At the moment, she hated herself for privately begrudging Viv. During all the years she'd remained single after Lydia, at least she could celebrate the feather in her cap of being dysfunction-free, while Viv and Didi scrambled around the dating field like toddlers at their first T-ball game. Viv knew what she wanted and was doing the work to earn the prize. How petty of Kate to wish it was her instead.

She examined the perfect amber of her draft beer, then sipped it hoping to find her Zen place before Didi and Viv returned for the start of the game. Her first ALCS game. She should've been jumping out of her skin. Rather, she had wanted to climb out of her skin, if only to assume a different identity, one that hadn't been acquainted with the pain of loving and losing Jordan. Although breaking up was a logical decision, weeks later, her heart was still playing for the opposing team.

"Dinner is served," Viv announced as she and Didi climbed over Kate with bags of sushi delivery.

"It's about time," Kate said. After standing for the pledge of allegiance, they tore into the bags and balanced the containers on their laps.

Didi leaned across Viv to address Kate. "While we were waiting for the Kumiyama delivery guy, Viv was wondering why you've come down with such a tragic case of resting bitch face. I wanted your approval before I told her." She shoved a salmon-avocado roll into her mouth. "Notice how much better I'm getting at keeping my mouth shut?"

"Yes. I've noticed. Now try it while you're eating." Kate flicked away an errant grain of rice that landed on her leg as Didi was talking.

"So can I tell her?" Didi asked.

Kate turned directly to Viv, seated between them. "It's Didi's fault."

"Yeah, right," Didi snapped. "I do my job consulting with our website designer, and because her court case gets postponed, I'm the villain."

"Simmer down, bitches," Viv said. "This ain't the *Newlywed*

Game." She licked soy sauce off her fingers. "Kate, you can't be coming down on my girl Didi because you're miserable over Jordan. Remember, you left her, not the other way around. Either you go and win back that sexy mama you tossed aside, or you gotta own your actions and move on."

Kate bent forward and addressed Didi. "Is this really happening? She's the wise one now?"

"After what I've witnessed from you lately, she's got my vote." Didi sat back in her seat and resumed eating.

Kate closed her eyes as a conflation of anger, angst, and generalized disgust boiled within. She gulped her beer and picked through her container of sushi, unmoved as the surrounding crowd shot up around her like time-lapse footage of growing grass blades when the Yankees scored their first run.

"How's Rhea," Viv asked Didi after the crowd settled down.

Kate whipped her head toward Didi, who suddenly looked as though a line drive was screaming toward her face.

"Rhea? She's history, isn't she?" Kate asked.

Viv and Didi glanced helplessly at each other.

"What is going on today?" Kate said in disbelief. "Did we all get off at a subway stop in the twilight zone?"

"This is exactly why I didn't tell you, Kate," Didi spat. "The mother superior at my junior high school would've been less judgmental about the news."

"You're seeing her again?"

Didi puffed up her chest and nodded with confidence.

"So now you're willfully involved with a married, bisexual woman?" Kate said. "Please tell me this is some sort of social experiment that you fully anticipate will turn out badly, because no way in hell will I know how to console you when she destroys your hope of ever finding romantic happiness. Even Freud couldn't."

When the Yankees scored again, the delirious fans rose around all three of them, who sat eerily resembling the three "no evil" monkeys.

When the crowd settled again, Kate patted Didi's knee. "Thank you. Just…thank you."

"For what?" Didi said.

Kate only tapped her leg again with deepening appreciation.

Viv studied Kate's demeanor for a moment, then translated. "She's expressing her gratitude to you for outdoing her in the dumbass-life-decision department."

"How do you know?" Kate and Didi asked in unison.

Viv smiled with pride. "Maia and I learned about picking up on our partner's nonverbal cues in therapy this week."

"Who knew you were such a good student," Kate said.

"If Dr. Feldman was here now, she'd take one look at your tense, wound-up ass and ask when you're going to admit to yourself that you want Jordan back."

"Never," Kate said. "Yes, I miss her like crazy, but I think it's safe to say she's no longer a fan."

Didi glared at her. "She's not that fond of me anymore either, thanks to you."

"I told you I was sorry for that."

"Ugh. Listen to us," Didi said with a sigh. "We're best friends. We're supposed to be each other's support system, not wrecking crew."

"Didi's right." Kate grabbed their hands. "I've been the worst offender lately. Viv, I owe you an apology for constantly ridiculing your decision to go back with Maia and showing absolutely no faith in you in your effort to become a better person."

Viv regarded Kate as though she'd shown up wearing a pair of mom jeans. "How long have you felt that way about me?"

"And, Didi," Kate went on. "I'm sorry for judging you about seeing Rhea. You're a grown woman who's smart and experienced enough to make your own decisions, and as your oldest and dearest friend, it's my role, no, my obligation to stand by you."

Didi clutched Kate's hand. "Aww, Kate. I think I'm gonna cry. This signals such profound personal growth in you. Do you really mean it?"

"No. I think you're bordering on incoherent for getting involved with Rhea again, but I love you, both of you." She grabbed Viv's hand again. "And I'll always be there for you no matter what. Even if it kills me."

Didi glared at her. "You keep on apologizing like that, and it just might."

"Aww, let's give her a pass, Didi," Viv said. "It's not every day that a stubborn, crotchety know-it-all like Kate has this kind of epiphany." She draped her arms around them. "It's a momentous occasion that she's realized what a douche she's been to us and wants to apologize for it. We forgive you, Katie."

"We're having a real moment here, girls," Didi added. "We're all experiencing epiphanies in our lives together. Think about it. I'm living my renaissance as a recovering straight woman. Viv, you've got a second chance to make things right with Maia. And, Kate, you've actually proved you're not too bitter and twisted to at least take another crack at relationships, even if they do fail miserably.

"Life, love, it's all a journey, man, a crazy ride on a mystical carousel. Who said we only get to go around once?"

Kate smiled at her friends and lifted her beer. "Here's to twice around."

Three drinks met in the middle, and on the next run scored by the Yankees, everyone stood and shouted in exuberance.

Despite the Yankees' win and a much-needed female-bonding session with Didi and Viv, Kate lay balled up in bed recapping the earlier part of the day when she'd run into Jordan. As the lights from the television dilated and constricted her pupils in fits, the vision of Jordan's face, cold and tight with disappointment, flickered whenever she closed her eyes. Just as the image of her face when Kate had broken up with her had begun to lose its edge, Jordan appeared to hone it back to a razor-sharp point.

She flipped over on her other side as the digital clock blipped to one thirty. Before Didi commandeered her personal life, she'd never experienced sleepless nights or agonizing confrontations with mortally wounded ex-lovers. She observed one thirty only during daylight, and confrontations arose only within the structured confines of courthouses and conference rooms.

She flopped back to her original position and stroked Ruby's tail as the cat slept beside her. She pulled Jordan's New England Patriots T-shirt out from under her pillow and balled it against her face, consuming the fading remnants of her scent.

Jordan wasn't the only woman in New Haven County nursing a broken heart. She could sleep in something else tonight.

CHAPTER TWENTY-ONE

The Epiphany

K ate returned to the office from court after five o'clock, so Didi was already gone for the day. As she settled in at her desk, she noticed a sticky note on her flip calendar with Didi's chicken-scratch handwriting.

"What the hell does this say?" she said out loud. She slipped on her reading glasses and held the paper farther away. "Check Jordan's page." Kate sighed and then mumbled, "Sure. Let me twist the knife in my heart and carve it out while I'm at it."

She fired up her laptop, itching with curiosity. What could be there that Didi wanted her to see? Probably pictures posted of Jordan and Alexandra, the new functional May-December couple, in various gross, narcissistic poses. A little backhand-to-the-face tough love to help Kate stop mooning over her and move on with her life. *Thanks, Didi.*

She clicked on Jordan's Facebook page, braced for the worst. The most recent post was a YouTube video of Jordan performing a song titled "Jaded." Kate gulped down air as she stared at the frozen image of Jordan and her guitar, petrified to click Play. Dear Lord, was this song about her? Of course, it was—a parody of her written as the ultimate revenge by a scorned ex-lover. It already had over two hundred views. Her heart pounded wildly as she recalled her embarrassment during Jordan's passive-aggressive rendition of "You're So Vain" at the fund-raiser. Imagine what havoc would ensue when everyone she knew recognized her in the song? No wonder Didi had left her a note. She hadn't wanted to bear witness to Kate's thorough humiliation.

After she stretched her arms and cracked her knuckles, she summoned the courage to press Play.

The song began with a few measures of mellow chords. Hmm, this isn't so bad, Kate thought as she watched the video that looked professionally produced.

She's a woman of dimensions, fearless and bold,
With a world of stories that haven't been told.
She believes in the fight, even if she'll fail,
Reads self-preservation like the Holy Grail.
Her passion for love, it hasn't faded,
She's got the soul of a true romantic.
Such a shame she's jaded...

When the song ended, Kate stared at the computer screen trying to process it all. She couldn't believe Jordan wrote such a beautiful song, and even more unbelievable was that it was about her.

Suddenly, tears streamed down. She was madly in love with Jordan, no matter how hard she fought to convince herself they were wrong for each other. She missed her desperately, regardless of their age difference and future aspirations. What sense did it make to stay away from her? To keep her heart protected from sadness? It was too late. Jordan already owned it.

She called Jordan's cell with no idea what she'd say when she answered. She just knew she needed to hear her voice, to finally admit to her that she'd made a foolish mistake letting her go. After several rings, when the call went into voice mail, Kate touched End.

On second thought, a face-to-face was the way to go. No great love story ever ended with a voice mail.

❖

As Kate approached Jordan's apartment door, the unflappable resolve that had propelled her there abandoned her for a fluttering heart and rubbery limbs. Bounding down the hallway clutching a bouquet of roses determined to win back her love felt a little more 1950s movie musical than she would've liked, but if she really was serious about making the second act of her life a success, a new, innovative attitude was in order.

She cleared her throat and knocked with authority on the door. Her heart pounded in her ears as the sound of approaching footsteps across the wood floor grew louder.

"It's you." William actually sneered at her. "If you're looking to tear out someone else's heart, sorry. That's already been done to mine."

"William, where is Jordan? I need to talk to her."

"She's not here."

"Where is she?"

"I don't know." He shrugged with attitude. "Probably out buying packing boxes."

"Packing boxes? Why does she need those?"

"Why do you think?" he said, gesticulating wildly. "She's flying the coop."

"What do you mean?" Kate demanded. "Where's she going? Back to Boston?"

He threw a hand on his hip. "Not quite, your wickedness. She's headed out to the City of Angels."

"Los Angeles?" Kate ran a hand through her hair as she considered her options. "How could she just go? Her business, her clients are all around here."

"Like she'd have a problem reestablishing herself anywhere. I'm the one who should be devastated. I finally get my life-long BFF back within reasonable visiting distance, and then you come along and ruin everything."

A wave of dread crashed over her. "Is she going out there to be with Alexandra?"

"Maybe. Maybe not," he said with a look of spite. "They make a handsome couple, and Alexandra doesn't seem quite as anal about age as someone I know."

"When will she be back? Text her and ask her where she is."

"Why should I? You broke her heart, you evil temptress."

"If you don't tell me where she went, how can I go unbreak her heart?" Kate said reasonably, her patience running on fumes.

"Ooh, Toni Braxton. I love her," he squealed.

She grabbed him by his crisp oxford shirt and yanked him up to her nose. "Look, I've never been the kind of person who resorts to physical violence," she said through a clenched jaw, "but you're making me rethink my position."

He flinched. "Not the face, not the face."

She released her grip and smoothed out the fist wrinkles on his shirt. "Now let's try this again like rational adults."

"You are so butch." He fished out his cell phone from the man purse slung across his torso and began thumbing a text to Jordan. "I want it noted on the record that I'm doing this for you under duress."

"Duly noted," she said. "Ask her to meet you for a drink somewhere."

He glared at her peevishly and swung his phone away from her when she lurked over his shoulder trying to read Jordan's response. "She's at some company in the Branford industrial park."

"Perfect. Ask her to meet you at Nellie's in an hour."

"Ooh. I've heard that place is great."

"William, focus. Make sure she goes there and doesn't know we spoke. Got it?"

He retreated slightly. "Got it."

Kate cradled the wilting flowers in her arm as she headed to her car. She considered the chance she was taking and prepared for the possibility of rejection. Even if it was too late, even if she and Alexandra were exploring their options, she couldn't let Jordan move away without first hearing her out.

❖

Speeding down the interstate in her BMW toward the restaurant, Kate rehearsed what she'd say. If she'd had the time, she could've composed a stellar closing argument that was sure to dazzle Jordan right back into her arms, but seeing that she had less than forty minutes, a few carefully chosen notes on a cocktail napkin would have to suffice.

With the key points jotted down, Kate neared the bottom of a glass of chardonnay. She checked the time on her phone as her knee bobbed on the barstool like it needed an exorcism. It was after six thirty. Jordan should've been there by now. William must've filled her in after Kate had finished manhandling him. Well-played, William, well-played.

She caught the bartender's attention and pointed to her empty wine glass as she called Didi's cell.

"How'd you like the song?" Didi asked without saying hello first.

"I'm still speechless. Where are you?"

"Just leaving Kohl's."

"I'm down the street at Nellie's," Kate said, her elbow digging into the wilting roses as she pressed her face against her fist. "I need someone to drink with."

"Save me a seat." Didi ended the call.

With an order of dinner salads and a fried calamari app, Kate and Didi moved on to something stronger than wine. Didi licked a few grains of salt off her margarita glass, took a sip, and exhaled.

"I don't get it. The summer started off so promising."

Kate shrugged. "Yet it ended just as I'd predicted—horribly."

"And you're proud of that?"

"No," Kate said. "But I've always been the realist in this friendship. And when you think about it, the warning signs were there. We just chose to ignore them. It's that damn Frank Sinatra 'Summer Wind' curse. We saw our relationships through rose-colored sunglasses."

"I don't regret one moment of it," Didi said. "I had a good time with Rhea...until I learned she lied to me. And that she's married. To a man. That kinda let the wind out of my sails."

"Maybe she'll drive that stupid Mini Cooper off a bridge, so you can at least find a little solace in that." Kate smirked before sipping her drink.

"That's not nice," Didi said, trying not to smile. "I'm staying friends with her. Despite her shortcomings, she's a quality human being."

"Lying and cheating are shortcomings? That's rather generous of you."

"Shame on you. Yes, Rhea was dishonest in her approach, but we've talked about that, and she's apologized several times. I can empathize with her. I came out late in life, too. It was difficult for her. Her snooty friends weren't very supportive, but luckily her husband is. She's not cheating if he knows. But I've made it clear I can't share anyone I have feelings for, and she's cool with it, so why not?"

Kate smiled like a proud big sister. "You impress me."

"I do? How?"

"In one summer, you've managed to graduate from a needy, menopausal adolescent, entirely bankrupt of self-confidence and lucid judgment, to a woman of towering strength and wisdom. You've become me."

Didi laughed as they raised their forks and touched calamari rings in celebration.

"What can I say?" Didi said. "I surround myself with quality people. So, what are you going to do about Jordan?"

"What can I do? I've played my last hand. I told William to get her here. I'm sure he informed her why, and the fact that she hasn't shown up tells me she's over anything I have to say. Besides, I have a feeling that nasty Kris Kardashian knockoff already has her on the hook."

"That's ridiculous. Maybe he never even told her." Didi grabbed her phone. "Let me text her."

"No, don't. I'm sure he relayed the message, and I'm even surer she doesn't care anymore. She was so hurt. I'll bet she can't wait to get on that plane and fly three thousand miles away from me."

Didi grew animated. "Find out when she's leaving and meet her at the airport, beg her not to go. How romantic would that be?"

"Not nearly as romantic as it was all the times it was done in a hundred different rom-com films throughout time. I'm going to send her a long text before she leaves and explain everything I was feeling— in case she never comes back. I do much better writing it all down first."

"Yes, you are the sovereign of the succinctly worded closing argument," Didi said. "But that's the dullest, most unimaginative attempt at winning someone back I've ever heard. It won't work."

Kate sighed and borrowed from Jordan's philosophy that everything did indeed happen for a reason. If nothing else, it was convenient. "If it doesn't work, then it's not meant to be. Maybe it's all part of the universe's plan. She needs to be free now to pursue her music." She looked away as her eyes welled with tears. "I should start accepting that."

"This is pathetic, watching you surrender like this."

Kate had to look away. If she tried to defend herself, she would've broken down right there in the restaurant.

While Didi was in the ladies' room, she tried to regroup from the burden of sadness and defeat suddenly bearing down on her. Was she surrendering? Jordan refused to meet her there, and she couldn't blame her. Jordan had worked so hard trying to build something meaningful between them while Kate fought it and minimized it at every turn. A good woman would only take so much of that before cutting her losses and moving on, especially when a glamorous city like Los Angeles and an opportunity of a lifetime came calling.

Didi returned to the table reading her phone. "Jordan's flight is at 8:20 out of Bradley tomorrow morning."

"How do you know?"

"I texted her in the bathroom, wishing her well on her journey, and just casually asked when she was departing for her new adventure."

Kate rolled her eyes. "Not too obvious."

"It worked, didn't it? Look, I'm not suggesting you go there and pull some heroic Nora Ephron movie stunt. But instead of sending her a text, give her your closing argument in person. I know you, Kate. In the long run, you'll feel much better for having done it the right way."

Kate sat back in her chair and sighed as a cautious grin tickled her lip. "And if I don't go?"

Didi grinned back. "That glimmer in your eye tells me there're no *if*s about it." She raised her glass to Kate and polished off the rest of her drink.

The next morning, Didi pulled into the temporary parking lot at Bradley International Airport acting as though she were transporting the secretary of state to the most important political negotiation of the twenty-first century.

"Ready, Counselor?"

Kate downed the last of her coffee and poured a mouthful of Tic Tacs into her hand. "This sounded much more like a genius plan last night when we were buzzed."

"Every idea sounds like a genius plan when you're buzzed. You're doing the right thing, Kate. Even if Jordan shouts out to the entire terminal that you have a bomb strapped to your Spanx, at least you've tied up the loose ends that would've left you a wretched old woman haunted by regret."

"You have quite a way with words," Kate said, crunching the Tic Tacs. "But you're right. She deserves better than a text."

"Atta girl."

Once in the terminal, Kate marched with purpose toward the

security area, with Didi and damp armpits her constant companions. Come what may, she would pour her heart out to Jordan so she'd know, beyond a doubt, that what they'd shared meant as much to Kate as it did to her.

They arrived at security and watched as airport employees checked passenger IDs and boarding passes.

"We don't have boarding passes," Kate said, staring straight ahead at the crowd of sleepy, shoeless people loading their belongings onto the conveyor belt.

"No, we don't," Didi said, also staring ahead.

Kate, still staring, "Why didn't we think of this sooner?"

Didi, still staring, "They never think of these things in the movies."

Kate finally turned and shot Didi the filthiest glare. She then consulted her phone. "She's gotta be in line at the gate already. Her plane leaves in twenty minutes."

"Don't move. I'll be right back." Didi jetted off toward the baggage-check area.

Kate shook out her hands as she tried to calm down and not look suspicious to the security personnel glancing at her from their posts. Suddenly, an announcement came over the PA system.

"Jordan Squire, please report to passenger security check. Jordan Squire to passenger security."

Didi strolled back to Kate wearing a satisfied grin.

"How did you…"

"Don't ask," Didi said. "I'm going to be ashamed of myself for a long time for what I'll have to do for convincing that woman to page her." She arched her eyebrows lasciviously. "I'm just gonna pop over to the ladies' room."

Kate smiled as she watched Didi head down the hall toward the restrooms. After a moment of musing on how much she treasured their friendship, she turned around and saw Jordan eyeing her from the other side of the body-scan booth. She pointed to a less-congested area, where they met and stared into each other's eyes.

But Jordan's look of fond surprise soon faded. "What are you doing here, Kate?"

"I…I heard you were leaving and wanted to say good-bye."

"Why?"

Kate squirmed slightly at the sting of Jordan's stern eyes boring into hers. "I don't want you to hate me. I may be asking too much, but if you happen to be flying out of here for good, I want you to leave knowing that I truly loved you. I still love you with all my heart."

Jordan folded her arms and looked away. "Is this supposed to be making me feel better or you?"

"I was hoping it would make us both feel better. Is it working?"

Jordan shook her head.

"Yeah. It's not for me either."

"Kate, I could never hate you, but I also know I can't be friends with you, if that's what you're looking for. If coming here is some twelve-step thing, then you've made your amends."

"Twelve-step? I'm not an alcoholic," she said, then muttered, "not yet anyway." Back to the matter at hand. "No, listen. I'm here because, well, what if I said I wanted more than a friendship with you? That I…"

A muffled voice came over the PA system. "Last call for general boarding for American Airlines Flight 624 to Los Angeles."

"That's me," Jordan said, suddenly seeming less confident about her departure.

"I know." Kate looked up from the floor and marveled at Jordan's reserve. "Jordan…"

"What?"

Despite the pooling in Jordan's eyes, she stared back at Kate stoic, unwavering. Under the watchful eye of an armed guard, Kate reached her hand over the security fence and held it out for a moment until Jordan clasped her fingers in Kate's. Tears rolled down both their faces as they held each other's hand until the guard approached and asked Kate to step back and away from the security area unless she had a boarding pass.

"I have to go," Jordan said. She wheeled around and hurried off to her gate.

Kate watched her until she disappeared around the corner toward the terminal. She looked down and pressed her fingers into her eyes until kaleidoscopic shapes flickered behind her lids. She didn't have nearly enough will left to stop the deluge. As if she hadn't attracted enough attention to herself milling near a restricted area, there she stood, all alone, sobbing in the middle of the airport.

"Dare I hope those are tears of joy?" Didi said. When she placed her hand on Kate's shoulder, Kate clamped her arms around her neck and sobbed into her jacket.

"Oh, Kate." Didi held her as she cried.

CHAPTER TWENTY-TWO

Encore! Encore!

Kate stared at the naked tree branches on the snow-dusted lawn of the Wilmington estate. As her breath fogged the cold window, she was oblivious to the clamoring of Viv's mother, two sisters-in-law, a close cousin, and Didi as they created a cacophony of cackling and screeching behind her.

Vivienne's wedding day.

Talk about hell freezing over. After what she'd gone through with Viv when she and Maia had broken up earlier in the year, Kate had never imagined she'd ever see them together now, so happy and functional and ready to embrace the dream of happily-ever-after. Kate, too, had come so far from when that serendipitous chain of events had led Jordan to her back in June. Jordan had taught her how to see life from a new perspective, how to love again—most importantly, how to want to love again and be swept away in its irresistible tide. It had been refreshing, exhilarating, and terrifying. Yet, there she was, alone again, staring out at the blankness, feeling as gray as the December sky.

She hadn't felt Didi sidle up to her.

"Kate," she whispered. "You need to get your head in the game. Viv is stressing out that you're not peeing yourself with unbridled joy on her big day, and I'm too busy crafting my plan to seduce Mrs. Wilmington to babysit you."

"You're right," Kate said as she turned to face the lively living room. "I have to shake off this…Wait, what did you say you're crafting?"

"Shhh." Didi turned away toward the window. "Mrs. Wilmington was a supermodel in the late sixties. You know she used to get all freaky at those wild LSD parties they had back then. All I have to do is get her tipsy enough to wear down her inhibitions, and then, boom, I'm sharing the master-bedroom suite in this palace with her tonight."

Kate stared at her. "I'd love to experience your unfiltered audacity for just one hour."

Viv approached with a look of concern, throwing her arms around each of them. "Girl," she said to Kate. "I know the new Viv is supposed to be less self-centered and more sensitive to the wants and needs of my loved ones, but you can't be trippin' like this on my wedding day. I need my girls, *both* of my girls, to be on point today, the most important day of my life. So, snap the fuck out of it, and let's start having ourselves a time." She kissed Kate's face hard enough for her no-smudge lipstick to leave a scarlet imprint on her cheek.

Kate smiled. "You're not being selfish to want that, Viv. You have every right to have the wedding of your dreams."

"I'm so proud of you for finally coming to your senses," Didi said. "I've never seen you so content."

"I have my two best friends, and I'm about to marry the love of my life," Viv said. "What more do I need to be happy?" She wrenched them both closer for a group hug. "I love you bitches."

"Aww, we love you, too," Didi said.

Kate joined the squealing as they squished her face between theirs, but the emotion fueling the expression resurrected her longing for Jordan.

Later, at the reception held at Vivienne's father's country club, Kate pulled Didi aside during the cocktail hour to make one final plea for her to come to her senses in the way that Viv had. Realizing who wasn't right for us was as crucial a growth step as realizing who was.

"Really?" Kate said before sipping from her pomegranate martini. "Rhea was the best you could come up with for a wedding date?"

"Kate, you know I hate going to weddings stag. It's like being at a wake with club music."

"Hello? We've could've been each other's date."

"Thanks, but in the likely event I get drunk and horny, it would be best that I make inappropriate overtures at a friend with whom I don't have quite so much history."

"Truer words," Kate said.

"Besides, not everyone needs to erase their exes from their lives like they never existed. Jordan is a genuine soul, and anyone would be lucky to call her a friend."

"I agree," Kate said sullenly. "I didn't erase her. It just worked out that way."

Rhea approached with drinks and handed one to Didi. "Kate, can I talk to you for a minute?"

"Sure."

Rhea led her off to the side. "I just wanted to apologize to you."

"For what?"

"This past year has been unexpectedly crazy for me, and I did some things I'm not proud of as I was attempting to sort it all out. Flirting with your girlfriend last summer was one of them."

"Jordan and I aren't together anymore, but I appreciate the gesture. Didi, however, is still my best friend, so I am concerned about her getting hurt. She fell for you, and I just hope you're being straight with her now—if you'll pardon the expression."

"I am, completely," Rhea said. "Didi's been amazing. She's helped me so much to understand myself and the implications of the decisions I'll make from here on out. She listens to me and knows exactly what it's like to experience such a profound revelation at this stage in our lives. I'll forever be in her debt."

Profound revelation. Yes, Kate was also familiar with what it was like to face one of those at a certain age. She wanted to believe that hers would help her evolve into a better person despite how she still felt about losing Jordan. It wasn't like losing Lydia. After a year of therapy and introspection, she'd realized with Lydia that she should've thrown away a flower once vibrant with life, not left it languishing in a pot of poorly nourished soil. But with Jordan, she'd thrown away the flower while it was in full bloom.

"Heads up," Didi said as she accosted them. "They're coming."

As the cocktail-hour music faded, the DJ's voice boomed through the speakers, and the lights began twirling and twinkling.

"Ladies and gentlemen, I'd like to direct your attention to the front of the room so that you can join me in welcoming for the first time in public, partners for life, Vivienne and Maia Wilmington-Carter."

The guests roared and cheered their welcome as Viv and Maia walked through the doors like lesbian Cinderella and her Princess Charming, stunning in tailored, cream-colored Armani pantsuits and smiles that were like looking at the sun.

Kate and Didi stood side by side, as wowed as the rest of the guests.

Didi leaned toward Kate's ear as she applauded. "Ever wish you and Viv had had more than just a one-nighter?"

"Not until this very moment," Kate said and almost meant it.

"Did you ever wish you'd had a one-nighter with me?" Didi said, still clapping.

"Not for one second," Kate replied, still clapping.

"Good thing for you that you didn't 'cause I'm like a Lay's potato chip, baby."

"What's that? Greasy and bad for my digestion?"

They nudged each other and laughed as Viv and Maia made it to the floor. The DJ announced their first dance to Bruno Mars's "Just the Way You Are."

They were a vision, arms around each other swaying together like cattails in a summer breeze. Kate returned Didi's smile, refusing to let her wistful thoughts of Jordan diminish her enthusiasm for the next, wonderful adventure on the journey she'd been sharing with her friends for decades. At least one of them would know true, everlasting love.

As the song trailed toward its ending, the DJ broke in. "Now, before y'all sit down and start feasting on filet mignon and lobster, the brides would like one more dance. But they don't need me for this one. They have a very special guest to help them out. Let's show her a whole lot of love."

Jordan walked out of the shadows carrying a mic stand and acoustic guitar strapped over her shoulder.

"Ms. Jordan Squire," the DJ announced.

Before Kate had the chance to think, breathe, or blink, Jordan was at the mic lightly strumming the guitar strings. "This one's for my friends, Viv and Maia, and anyone else who's ever been lucky enough to have the best."

She began performing Carly Simon's "Nobody Does It Better" with the charisma of a Grammy Award–winning artist. Kate was mesmerized. Was it really Jordan or some digitally advanced hologram? She'd been missing her so much that the whole scene could've easily been a waking dream. But no, it was her—live, in real-time 3D, her voice imbuing the room with warmth and energy.

And if Kate hadn't been totally deluding herself, Jordan glanced directly at her on certain key lyrics.

Halfway through the song, Jordan invited everyone to join Viv and Maia. Didi pulled Rhea onto the dance floor, but Kate hung back, leaning against a support column, her eyes riveted to Jordan, her heart beating in rhythm with the melody.

After the song, and hugs and kisses from the brides, Jordan sauntered over to Kate, her eyes locked and loaded. The closer she came, the wider Kate's smile stretched.

"So," Jordan said as she stuffed her hands into her pockets. "Not sure if you still need a date for the reception, but it just so happens that I'm free now."

"Well, since I never changed my RSVP, you're still listed as my 'plus one.' Chicken, right?"

Jordan smirked. "Fish."

"Right." Kate could no longer fight the goofy smile teetering on the corners of her mouth. "You know, I feel pretty confident saying I was more excited by your performance here than the brides. You were phenomenal, as always."

"Thanks. You know, I'm certain I was more excited to perform for you than the brides. But don't tell them."

"Never," Kate said, shy as a schoolgirl. Then suddenly inspired by Viv's take-no-prisoners attitude, she looked into Jordan's eyes. "I'm so happy to see you."

Jordan replied with a smile and a tender kiss. Kate absorbed her in an embrace, her legs weak as her senses consumed every molecule of Jordan's being.

"I love you so much." Jordan's voice in her ear seemed to quench a lingering, insatiable thirst.

"I love you, too," Kate whispered.

Jordan faced her with eyes like shining portraits of love and devotion, an exhibition Kate had never seen before. "I can't move to

California, Kate. I can't pretend I don't need you or want you or love you with all my heart and soul."

"Jordan," she whispered, holding her close in complete surrender.

"Do you still want me?" Jordan whispered.

"More than ever." She brushed Jordan's hair aside, studying the face she thought she'd only ever see again in web videos.

"Then let's do this, Kate. Let's do it right this time."

"I want to so much, Jordan, but I don't want you to have to choose between me and your dream."

"Without you, it's not a dream. It's just a dazzling way to kill time. Nothing makes me happier than being with you."

Kate cupped Jordan's adorably vulnerable face in her palms and kissed her with more passion than a newly married couple could dream of knowing. "I don't want to be afraid to love you anymore. I'm crazy about you, Jordan. That's all that matters. This time I know it's true."

They embraced again, so close their hearts kept the same beat.

"Uh...I hate to interrupt," Didi said, "but the main event is happening over there."

Jordan tried to pull away, but Kate held her a moment longer—just to make sure she was real. Jordan giggled softly, and they kissed.

Didi cleared her throat.

"What are we waiting for?" Kate took Jordan's hand, and they followed Didi to the brides' table.

"By the way, Viv and Maia requested that this time you make your speech sober," Didi said.

Jordan chuckled. "I don't know. I thought her incoherent acceptance speech at the True Colors fund-raiser was rather enchanting. Just give her a mic stand to clutch, and she'll be fine."

Kate groaned. "Uh, no. If it's all the same to you folks, I'd rather not make the cut in a YouTube compilation video of wedding disasters."

"Then let's get this toast out of the way," Didi said. "I feel a drink coming on."

❖

After dinner and the customary cake-smearing, Viv and Maia joined the rest of the ladies at the brides' table and fed each other a taste of the French-vanilla wedding cake with forks instead of their fingers.

"So, what are you all doing next June?" Viv asked as she sipped her coffee.

Before Kate could answer the oddly random question, Jordan cut in with "Celebrating our year anniversary." She fed Kate a forkful of cake, then kissed the excess frosting from the corner of her mouth.

"With a trip to New York City and a drink at Moxy's?" Kate said with a smile.

Jordan beamed. "Sounds fabulous."

"I'll probably still be chasing this one," Rhea said.

Didi resisted the temptation. "You'll surely have run out of excuses to give your husband by then."

"No more excuses or lies," Rhea said. "He knows I'm with you tonight. As scary as it is, I'm following my heart on this one. It's been hard to look back since meeting you, Didi. I hope you know how much you mean to me."

Kate and Jordan exchanged glances with the brides.

"Thank you," Didi said, and pulled her in for a kiss on the cheek.

"I think I know who's gonna be diving for the bouquet," Viv said.

"She'll definitely have some competition," Maia said, looking at Jordan.

"Fine," Viv said. "So, it sounds like you'll all be free to attend the baby shower in June."

"Baby?" Didi exclaimed.

Maia smiled as wide as when she had said "I do" to Viv earlier in the evening.

The table erupted into screams and exaltations.

"We wouldn't miss it for the world," Kate said.

Everyone jumped up and showered the brides in additional hugs and kisses at the news. As Jordan and Rhea continued congratulating Viv and Maia, Didi led Kate aside.

"In case you weren't aware, I've returned to my roots of meddling in people's love lives, but only for one night."

"You're responsible for booking the special musical guest?"

Didi buffed her nails on her chest. "Duh."

Kate threw her arm around her and led her toward the bar. "You're going to be gloating about this for years to come, aren't you?"

"Decades," Didi said.

After the bartender handed them two cosmos, they turned to the table where their friends and lovers were immersed in raucous celebration and clinked their glasses together.

"Here's to meddling friends and summer flings," Kate said with a grin.

About the Author

Jean Copeland is a writer and English/language arts teacher at an alternative high school in Connecticut. Taking a chance on a second career in her thirties, Jean graduated summa cum laude from Southern Connecticut State University with a BS in English education and an MS in English/creative writing. She has published numerous short fiction and essays online and in print anthologies. In addition to the thrill of watching her students discover their talents in creative writing and poetry, she enjoys the escape of writing, summer decompression by the shore, and good wine and conversation with friends. Organ donation and shelter animal adoption are causes dear to her heart.

Books Available From Bold Strokes Books

Beauty and the Boss by Ali Vali. Ellis Renois is at the top of the fashion world, but she never expects her summer assistant Charlotte Hamner to tear her heart and her business apart like sharp scissors through cheap material. (978-162639-919-8)

Fury's Choice by Brey Willows. When gods walk amongst humans, can two women find a balance between love and faith? (978-162639-869-6)

Lessons in Desire by MJ Williamz. Can a summer love stand a four-month hiatus and still burn hot? (978-163555-019-1)

Lightning Chasers by Cass Sellars. For Sydney and Parker, being a couple was never what they had planned. Now they have to fight corruption, murder, and enemies hiding in plain sight just to hold on to each other. Lightning Series, Book Two. (978-162639-965-5)

Summer Fling by Jean Copeland. Still jaded from a breakup years earlier, Kate struggles to trust falling in love again when a summer fling with sexy young singer Jordan rocks her off her feet. (978-162639-981-5)

Take Me There by Julie Cannon. Adrienne and Sloan know it would be career suicide to mix business with pleasure, however tempting it is. But what's the harm? They're both consenting adults. Who would know? (978-162639-917-4)

Unchained Memories by Dena Blake. Can a woman give herself completely when she's left a piece of herself behind? (978-162639-993-8)

Walking Through Shadows by Sheri Lewis Wohl. All Molly wanted to do was go backpacking...in her own century. (978-162639-968-6)

A Lamentation of Swans by Valerie Bronwen. Ariel Montgomery returns to Sea Oats to try to save her broken marriage but soon finds herself also fighting to save her own life and catch a murderer. (978-1-62639-828-3)

Freedom to Love by Ronica Black. What happens when the woman who spent her life worrying about caring for her family finally finds the freedom to love without borders? (978-1-63555-001-6)

House of Fate by Barbara Ann Wright. Two women must throw off the lives they've known as a guardian and an assassin and save two rival houses before their secrets tear the galaxy apart. (978-1-62639-780-4)

Planning for Love by Erin Dutton. Could true love be the one thing that wedding coordinator Faith McKenna didn't plan for? (978-1-62639-954-9)

Sidebar by Carsen Taite. Judge Camille Avery and her clerk, attorney West Fallon, agree on little except their mutual attraction, but can their relationship and their careers survive a headline-grabbing case? (978-1-62639-752-1)

Sweet Boy and Wild One by T. L. Hayes. When Rachel Cole meets soulful singer Bobby Layton at an open mic, she is immediately in thrall. What she soon discovers will rock her world in ways she never imagined. (978-1-62639-963-1)

To Be Determined by Mardi Alexander and Laurie Eichler. Charlie Dickerson escapes her life in the US to rescue Australian wildlife with Pip Atkins, but can they save each other? (978-1-62639-946-4)

True Colors by Yolanda Wallace. Blogger Robby Rawlins plans to use First Daughter Taylor Crenshaw to get ahead, but she never planned on falling in love with her in the process. (978-1-62639-927-3)

Heart Stop by Radclyffe. Two women, one with a damaged body, the other a damaged spirit, challenge each other to dare to live again. (978-1-62639-899-3)

Undercover Affairs by Julie Blair. Searching for stolen documents crucial to U.S. security, CIA agent Rett Spenser confronts lies, deceit, and unexpected romance as she investigates art gallery owner Shannon Kent. (978-1-62639-905-1)